Get away from here, the cold voice advised. Put some distance between you and this scene of death.

He thought hard, chewing at his sleeve.

All his short life he had been used to doing what he was told. To be forced to make a decision for himself was a unique experience.

Which perhaps excused its being such a poor one.

Without another glance at his dead master, he stood up, silently rolling his few possessions into a compact bundle and stuffed it inside his cloak and, with the box on the chain still held tight in his hand, tiptoed out of the shelter.

He stepped cautiously and lightly along the path until he was a good distance away from the small knot of buildings ⟨...⟩ up his robe and ran.

Also by Alys Clare

Fortune like the Moon
Ashes of the Elements
The Tavern in the Morning
The Chatter of the Maidens

About the author

Alys Clare lives in Tonbridge. *The Faithful Dead* is the
fifth in the series of medieval mysteries set in and around
the Weald of Kent. She can be reached at her website,
www.alysclare.com

ALYS CLARE

The Faithful Dead

NEW ENGLISH LIBRARY
Hodder & Stoughton

Copyright © 2002 by Alys Clare

First published in Great Britain in 2002 by Hodder and Stoughton
First published in paperback in 2003 by Hodder and Stoughton
A division of Hodder Headline

The right of Alys Clare to be identified as the Author
of the Work has been asserted by her in accordance with the
Copyright, Designs and Patents Act 1988.

A New English Library paperback

4

A CIP catalogue record for this title is available
from the British Library

ISBN 0 340 79330 9

Typeset in Plantin Light by Palimpsest Book Production Limited,
Polmont, Stirlingshire

Printed and bound in Great Britain by
Mackays of Chatham plc, Chatham, Kent

Hodder and Stoughton
A division of Hodder Headline
338 Euston Road
London NW1 3BH

For Geoffrey

Primo pro nummata vini
ex hac bibunt libertini;
semel bibunt pro captivis,
post hec bibunt ter pro vivis,
quater pro Christianis cunctis,
quinquies pro fidelibus defunctis.

It's first to the wine seller
That the dissolutes raise their mugs;
They have one drink for the prisoners,
Three for the living folk,
Four for all Christendom,
Five for the faithful dead.

Carmina Burana:
cantiones profanae

(Author's translation)

Thames
London
Acquin
Mense
Rhine
Worms
Wertzberg
Metz
July 1147: Louis joins with
Emperor Conrad of Germany
Nuremberg
Paris
7 June 1147:
At a service in St Denis, Louis
entrusts his realm to Abbot Suger;
the Pope hands him the oriflamme
Ratisbon
Vezelay
Easter Day, 31 March 1146:
Bernard of Clairvaux preaches the
Second Crusade; Louis VII of France
and Queen Eleanor take the Cross
Loire
Seine
Rhone
Dordogne

N
W E
S

Douro

Guadalquivir

——————— outward journey of the Second Crusade
- - - - - - - homeward journey of Geoffroi d'Acquin

A Map of Outremer and Europe

Vienna

The Crusaders follow the route of the River Danube

Belgrade

Danube

Niš

Sofia

Constantinople
The Crusaders arrive on 3 October 1147. Louis crosses the Bosphorus on 26 October: there is a solar eclipse

Nicaea

Pergamus

Smyrna

Ephesus The Crusaders arrive for Christmas 1147

Laodicea

Attalia

Antioch
The Crusaders arrive on 19 March 1148

Damascus
The Crusaders attack, 24 July 1148

Acre

Jerusalem
The Crusaders arrive in May 1148

Nile

The Family Tree of the d'Acquins
of Acquin, in the River Aa Valley of Northern France

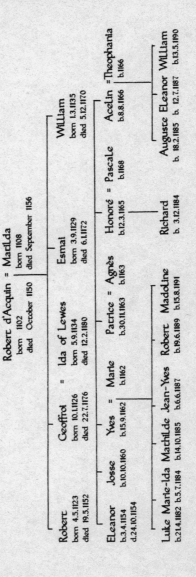

Robert d'Acquin = Matilda
born 1102   born 1108
died October 1150   died September 1156

Robert
born 4.5.1123
died 19.5.1152

Geoffroi = Ida of Lewes
born 10.1.1126   born 5.9.1134
died 22.7.1176   died 12.2.1180

Esmai
born 3.9.1129
died 6.1.1172

William
born 1.3.1135
died 5.12.1170

Josse
b.10.10.1160

Yves = Marie
b.15.9.1162   b.1162

Eleanor
b.3.4.1154
d.24.10.1154

Patrice = Agnès
b.30.11.1163   b.1163

Honoré = Pascale
b.12.3.1165   b.1168

Acelin = Theophania
b.8.8.1166   b.1166

Luke
b.21.4.1182

Marie-Ida
b.5.7.1184

Mathilde
b.14.10.1185

Jean-Yves
b.6.6.1187

Robert
b.19.6.1189

Maddline
b.15.8.1191

Richard
b. 3.12.1184

Auguste
b. 18.2.1185

Eleanor
b. 12.7.1187

William
b.13.5.1190

The old man's loud breathing was keeping the boy awake.

It was now some hours since they had lain down in the draughty shelter. The supper provided by the monks had been adequate, but hardly what you would call tasty. Still, over the past weeks, the boy had become accustomed to going to bed on an empty stomach, so to have it filled – even with watery, bland soup without the savour of salt, and a big hunk of rough bread – was better than usual.

No, he reflected, turning on his side and edging further away from the old man. No, I have no complaints on *that* score.

But how he wished the snoring, rasping breaths would stop and let him get some *sleep*!

Flinging himself on to his back, he wondered idly – not for the first time – if it would be a kindness to hold a folded cloth over the old fellow's face and put him out of his misery. Raising himself up on one elbow, he stared down at his master. In the light of the one dull lamp illuminating the sleeping area, the face showed up deathly pale and glistening with sweat. As the boy watched, another brief coughing fit rattled the old man's thin frame. It was not enough to wake him, though. Not that time.

Ah, but he'd been a good master, the boy reflected,

lying down again. Tough – he'd driven his servant hard, accepted no excuses for slackness or laziness – but fair. Aye, there had always been appreciation for a job well done. And, the boy reminded himself, grinning faintly into the darkness, the master had promised him a silver coin if he made sure the two of them got safe home again.

A silver coin!

He lay for several very happy moments while he contemplated what use he might make of a silver coin.

Ah, but home was such a long way away, he thought, dismay clouding his pleasant reverie. Once admitted, depression seemed to flood through him; he suddenly found himself feeling unaccountably miserable.

One silver coin? It was as if another's voice spoke inside his head, a cold, faintly jeering voice that was strangely insistent. Just one coin? After all you've done for him? Why, the help and support you've given him during the trials and hardships of this journey alone are surely worth more than that! One coin, my lad, is nothing more than an insult.

The boy felt the skin on the back of his neck stir, as if someone had run a rough hand against the natural direction of the fine hair that grew there. And from a different – better – part of his mind came the urgent message: don't listen! Close your ears! Do not pay heed to the Evil One!

For a few heartbeats, he felt sick with terror. Then he thought, no, I am allowing my imagination to run away with me. Here I am lying in the pilgrims' shelter of one of the holiest spots in England, not fifty paces from Our Lady's Shrine and her blessed, healing spring! Come on, you fool, this is the last place that the – that any harm is going to come to you!

He made himself relax. The old man's breathing was getting rougher, more painful, and now there seemed to be a little pause between each laborious outward breath and the next drawing in, as if, even in his sleep, the old man was trying to decide whether further effort was worth the pain that it cost him.

The boy looked at him again. He's no pauper, he reflected, for all that he's dressed like one. No, he's got wealth all right, aye, and rich possessions and all. He has his reasons for pretending to be a poor pilgrim, and I reckon I know what they are. He's—

With an abrupt snort, the old man launched into a violent fit of coughing, chest heaving, spasms shaking his whole body. From another part of the sleeping area the boy heard a faint protest, cut short as a different voice – a woman's – muttered, 'For pity's sake, Jack! He's not doing it just to annoy you, the poor soul can't help himself!'

The boy watched as the old man spat into a filthy, stained piece of cloth, then, muttering to himself, settled down again. Soon the painful breathing resumed.

The old man's movements had disturbed his cloak, in which he had wrapped himself, and the thin blanket that the monks had provided. The night air was chilly – it was late August, but a storm earlier in the day had left a nip in the air – and the boy reached out his hand and gently rearranged the covers. There, that was better; the cloak was quite thick, it'd give some warmth to his chest, and—

In the midst of his careful attentions, the boy suddenly caught the glint of metal. The lamplight was reflecting off something tucked inside the old man's clothes, something which, formerly hidden, had slipped out and into view during the coughing fit.

The cold voice was back inside the boy's head. It said, go on! Have a good look! You won't do any harm; you're only going to have a peep, aren't you?

The boy watched as, almost without his volition, his hand stretched out towards the old man's frail body. Stretched out – further – a little bit further – until the grasping fingers closed on the object. It felt cool to the touch, and the metal of which it was made was smooth . . . and, in shape, a square, a rectangle . . . a little box?

He pulled. But the object was attached to something, perhaps caught up in the old man's clothes, and at first would not come.

It's on a chain round his neck! the boy realised suddenly, with a brief, violent surge of fury that quite surprised him. I can't get at it, he's got it too securely fastened.

No, he hasn't, the cold voice said. Try again.

The boy did as he was told. The chain came free of whatever had been obstructing it, and he held the object up to the light.

It *was* a box; he could see tiny hinges where the lid met the base and, on the opposite side, a latch and a fastening. The workmanship was exquisite; even the boy, well travelled as he was, had seen nothing like it. Such detail! And so minute! And the way in which the faint light made the metal glow – as if it were lit from within – surely suggested that it was precious. Could it be – was it possible that it was – silver?

For quite a long time, he lay and stared at it, the shock of finding such an object hidden away in the dirty, threadbare garments of his master so great that it seemed to bring all thoughts to a standstill.

But the amazed reaction was short-lived.

Where did the old man get it? the boy began to wonder. And what's he thinking of, carrying it with him on a journey such as we've just endured, when the least worrying possibility was that he'd lose it, and the most alarming that someone would have spotted it and killed him for it? Why, it was foolhardy to take the risk! Not only for him, but for me, too! No murdering thief stealing from the master would have left the servant alive to bear witness, that's for sure!

His rage against his master was briefly so great that it blanked out everything else. For a short while he forgot where he was, what he was doing there, the very night around him.

When, in due course, he came back to himself, he realised that something was different.

The light had changed, for one thing. Was that what it was? The moon had risen, and was bathing the clearing outside the shelter in chilly silver.

The boy frowned in concentration. No, there was something else . . .

Then he knew.

The noise, that annoying, sleep-interrupting noise, had stopped. The old man was no longer breathing.

Still clasping the box on its chain, the boy stared dispassionately down at his master. Should he call one of the monks? The old fellow could only just have stopped breathing. They could send for that big bossy nun who was in charge of the infirmary. She might be able to help. She could give the master some medicine, get those lungs working again.

Couldn't she?

But the cold voice in his head said, no. Too late for that. Your master is dead.

'Dead,' the boy repeated in a soft whisper.

Nobody knows about *this*, he thought, tightening his fist around the metal box in his hand. It was heavy, he noticed; he shook it to see if it would rattle, which would imply there was something inside it, but it made no sound. And he *had* been promised a silver coin, which he surely would not be getting now that his master was dead.

For who was there to give it?

Another thought struck him, a dreadful thought that made him shake with fear. They'll say I did it! They'll say I finished him off! They'll say I should have taken better care of him, fetched someone when he had that awful coughing fit earlier!

Wanting to moan but afraid to wake the other people in the shelter, the boy stuffed his ragged cuff into his mouth.

Get away from here, the cold voice advised. Put some distance between you and this scene of death. The monks and the nuns don't know who you are or where you come from, do they? To them you're just a servant, nameless, unimportant. They'll never find you. They probably won't even bother to look for you. Run, now, while you've got the chance. Morning is far off; you can be miles away by the time they find out the old man's dead.

He thought hard, chewing at his sleeve. It was good advice. Wasn't it?

All his short life he had been used to doing what he was told. To be forced to make a decision for himself was a unique experience.

Which, perhaps, excused its being such a poor one.

Without another glance at his dead master, he stood up, silently rolled his few possessions into a compact bundle and stuffed it inside his cloak and, with the box on the chain still held tight in his hand, tiptoed out of the shelter.

He stepped cautiously and lightly along the path until he was a good distance away from the small knot of buildings in the Vale. Then he hitched up his robe and ran.

PART ONE

England, Autumn 1192

I

Josse d'Acquin stood with his manservant, Will, looking gloomily out over the meadow which, last night, had contained the household cow and her calf.

The meadow was now empty, and there was a gap in the ragged hedge large enough for a cow and a calf to have squeezed through.

Will was muttering under his breath. The general tone of voice suggested he was a little disgruntled.

Josse patted his arm. 'Don't blame yourself, Will,' he began, 'we both knew the boundary was weak just there and—'

'I weren't blaming myself,' Will replied, with an uncharacteristic display of spirit; Will, devoted and hard-working, usually tended to take the responsibility for everything that went wrong at New Winnowlands on his own narrow shoulders. 'I was saying, it's too much. There's only so many hours in the day and, for the life of me, I can't be in two places at once.'

Greatly surprised, Josse turned to look at him. 'I agree, Will,' he said gently. 'But what am I to do? Whenever I have suggested that we take on more hands, you say you can manage. You say that you and Ella prefer to look after me on your own.' Ella was Will's wife, or perhaps his woman; Josse had no idea whether or not they were wed and certainly had never enquired. Ella worked as hard as Will and, although chronically shy, could turn her hand to any task within the house and quite a few outside it.

'That we do, sir, that we do.' Will was frowning, chewing his lip; clearly he had something on his mind.

'Then I repeat: what am I to do?'

Will stood silent for some time, as if pondering over the relative merits of speaking out or keeping his thoughts to himself. Eventually – he was still glaring out over the empty meadow – he decided to unburden himself.

'See, sir, it's like this,' he began, a hand rubbing at the small of his back. 'Me and Ella, we don't like taking orders from anyone, leastways, saving old Sir Alard, who could be tricky, God rest him, when an east wind put him in an ill humour. And yourself, a' course, Sir Josse, and you're not a demanding man. What we – I mean, it's not as if we've ever been under the charge of others, and we're probably too set in our ways to learn.' He looked up hopefully at Josse to see if the significance of his little speech had been understood.

Josse, still in the dark, said, 'I'm sorry, Will. What are you saying?'

Will sighed. 'We wouldn't take to it, sir. If that's what you decide to do – and it's for you to say, I do see that – then me and Ella might . . . we might . . .' Whatever depressing image he was imagining was clearly moving him; his eyes blinked rapidly a couple of times and he swallowed hard, making the prominent Adam's apple in his thin throat bob up and down. 'And we're settled here, settled and secure, and we're that fond of our little place,' he muttered, voice breaking.

Suddenly Josse understood. And hastened to correct his poor suffering manservant's misapprehension.

'Will, I would never put someone in over you, or over Ella,' he said, forcing all the sincerity he could muster into his voice. 'Why on earth should I want to do so? The pair of you have looked after me well these two years or more, and I have never had cause for complaint. I must assure you that I have no desire to change the arrangement – I do not intend to risk upsetting the applecart, not when it rolls along so smoothly!' He tried to lighten the mood with a laugh, but Will did not join in.

'And there's my back,' Will went on, as if he had not heard. 'I've a pain down here' – he was still rubbing – 'like some little imp's got in there with a red-hot pitchfork.' He raised mournful eyes to Josse. 'Maybe I'm getting too old, sir.'

When troop morale was as low as this, Josse reflected, remembering his soldiering days, the best thing to do was to organise a distraction. Take the men's minds off feeling sorry for themselves.

'Come, Will,' he said bracingly. 'First we'll round up that cow – she can't have gone far – then you must get Ella to put a warm poultice on your bad back. I can mend the gap in the hedge – a couple of hurdles should do it.' Will shot him a dubious look. 'Then I suggest that you cast around for a likely young lad to come and give you a hand here. Not just at the busy times such as sowing and harvest' – he hoped he sounded more authoritative than he felt, being still far more a soldier than a farmer – 'but on a

regular basis. There must be someone, some son of one of
my tenants growing out of childhood and with energy to
spare.' He waved a vague hand, as if suitable youths were
lining up in the courtyard in front of the manor house,
eager and alert, just dying to come and work under Will.

Will sniffed, managing to put a lot of expression into
the brief sound. He said shortly, 'Maybe.'

I do not know enough about the people who live on
my land, Josse reflected. And, since the manor is but
a small one, I have no excuse. I inherited my tenants
from old Sir Alard, I take their rents and a portion of all
that they produce and, presumably, Will organises their
labours when they fulfil their commitments to me as their
landlord.

He stood deep in thought but, try as he might, he could
not bring to mind the face, features or demeanour of any
of the peasants who lived, worked and, eventually, would
die on his manor.

It was a sobering realisation. And one which, he felt,
reflected badly on him. What would his friend the Abbess
Helewise say? She, he was quite sure, knew every one of
her Hawkenlye nuns, aye, and the monks too; their names,
what work they did, their strengths and weaknesses, their
likes and dislikes. What would the Abbess say to a man
who knew absolutely nothing about the people on whom
his very existence depended?

Making up his mind, Josse clapped a hand across Will's
shoulder. 'We will do this task together,' he announced.
'Tomorrow we shall ride out all around the manor, and
you shall tell me all that you can of the people who inhabit
it. We shall try to find you a young apprentice. It is time,

Will.' He gave his manservant another bracing slap. 'It is time.'

Wrenching his startled face away from his rapt contemplation of his master with what seemed like quite an effort, Will said, with a slight but quite definite shake of his head, 'I'll go and find that cow.'

The next day, however, brought its own problems, and Josse's fine resolve had to be put aside.

He was finishing an early midday meal – Ella had produced a dish of bream with a piquant, mustard-flavoured sauce, and it had crossed his mind to wonder if the mustard had been left over from Will's poultice – when there came the sound of horses from outside on the road.

Many horses; from the commotion, perhaps as many as twelve or fifteen, even twenty . . .

A single horseman passing Josse's gates was a common enough occurrence. A hunting party of four or five was rarer. A group of fifteen or more was so rare as to be all but unheard of.

Pushing himself away from the table and wiping his chin on his sleeve, Josse flew across the hall, out of the door, leapt down the steps and ran across the courtyard. Despite his natural optimism, a small part of his brain was thinking, this is highly unusual. And the unusual tends to mean trouble . . .

He maintained the presence of mind to slow his pace to a steady, casual walk before he came into the sight of whoever was outside; it would hardly be the right image for the lord of the manor to appear at a gallop, red-faced and flustered.

He was very glad of his foresight. For, as he approached the gates and stepped outside on to the rough track, he came face to face with a large group of men dressed to a degree of finery that could only mean one thing: that they were courtiers. To a man they were well mounted, their horses groomed to a shine and expensively caparisoned.

Before he could utter the formal words of greeting and welcome – before he had time to wonder what such a party was doing out there in the depths of the quiet countryside – a man in a tunic of crimson velvet kicked his mount forward. As he swept off his cap – he had stuck a cockade of pheasant's feathers in it for decoration – he cried, 'Have I the pleasure of addressing Sir Josse d'Acquin, lord of New Winnowlands in the county of Kent?'

'Aye, sir, you have.' Josse made a perfunctory bow. 'May I know who has sought me out?'

The man laughed merrily, and others around him joined in. 'I am William d'Arbret, sir knight, but it is not I but another who seeks you.'

With another dramatic flourish of his hat – this time the feathers caught against the brow of a nearby horse, who snorted and, but for his rider's quick reactions and good horsemanship, would have bucked – he swept his arm up in a wide arc. As he did so, he reined his horse backwards and out of the way to reveal, in the midst of the group behind him, a strongly built man with dark auburn hair that curled thickly around his elaborately decorated black cap. He was in his mid-twenties, he sat a magnificent chestnut gelding with graceful ease and, as his blue eyes fell on Josse, an expression of amusement crossed his handsome face, as if he were about to burst into laughter at some private joke.

Still recognisable, after not far short of twenty years, was someone Josse had last seen when he was a lad of seven.

Despite what he had heard in the intervening years to suggest that the witty little lad he had liked so well had gone to the bad, Josse had always tried to reserve his judgement. It had not been easy; he himself had had occasion to refer to the man as a calculating bastard, although he had known full well that the latter epithet was inaccurate.

But now, coming face to face with him again after all that time, it was the most natural thing to fall to one knee in the dusty track, bow his head and say to Prince John, 'Sire, I bid you heartfelt welcome. My house is at your disposal, as am I, your servant.'

High above him on the chestnut horse, Prince John's amusement finally gained expression. His head still bowed, Josse heard that laugh he remembered so well – although now it was in the register of a man and not a little boy – and there was a rustle of costly fabric as John swung back his cloak and dismounted. Then Josse felt hands fall heavily on to his shoulders, he was hauled to his feet and Prince John was slapping him – hard – on the back.

Standing still to receive these attentions, Josse took in the Prince's stature, revealed more fully now that he had dismounted and was on his feet. Yes, he was broad and not overly tall, like his late elder brother, Geoffrey, whom he also resembled in his features and his colouring. He clearly had extravagant tastes; his garments were beautifully cut and of the most expensive cloth, and the wide bands of embroidery at the neck and cuffs of his over-gown shone like spring flowers with the dew on them. He wore a considerable amount of gold jewellery. There was, Josse observed, a particularly *clean* look about him, as if he changed his linen frequently and enjoyed the refreshing comforts of a regular bath.

As if aware of Josse's discreet scrutiny, the Prince gave him a final, even harder, slap across the shoulders. Then, moving round so that the two of them stood face to face, the bright, intelligent eyes looked up into Josse's and Prince John said, 'I like what I see, old friend. How say you?'

Sharp as ever, Josse thought, dropping his eyes. The man was fulfilling the promise of the child. 'It is a rare pleasure to meet again someone whom I remember so well,' he murmured, still staring at the ground; Prince John, he noticed, wore boots of soft leather, in a chestnut shade that almost exactly matched his horse. Mind working rapidly as he tried to recall just what foodstuffs and drink Ella might have stored away in her larder, he said cautiously, 'Will the company take refreshments with me, Sire?'

The laugh came again. 'No, Josse, the company will not,' Prince John said. 'We rest with old Sir Henry of Newenden, and he rushes forward to proffer food every time we so much as drop our backsides for an instant on the nearest bench. The silly old fool has stuffed us to bursting.' He glanced over his shoulder at the courtiers, raising an ironic eyebrow. 'He has a pretty young wife, however.'

The courtiers tittered at the witticism; recalling another rumour about John, Josse wondered if Sir Henry's pretty young wife had been enticed into the Prince's bed and decided that she probably had.

Straightening up – his neck was beginning to ache

from standing in such an unnatural position – Josse said tentatively, 'Then what service may—'

'Ah, yes,' John interrupted, 'to business, yes. William!'

The man with the pheasant feather cockade slipped from his horse, swept off his hat and came to stand, head bowed, by his Prince. John made a gesture as if he were flicking away a persistent fly, which seemed to have more meaning for William d'Arbret than it had for Josse, for he reached inside his tunic and drew out a roll of parchment, handing it to Prince John. The Prince took it without a word.

He studied it for a moment. 'New Winnowlands,' he murmured. Josse had a dread feeling that he knew what was coming. 'New Winnowlands . . . ah, yes!' The blue eyes looked up from the parchment. 'Formerly the dower house of Winnowlands proper, awarded to Sir Josse d'Acquin by my brother Richard in recognition of services rendered, and—'

It was not in any way wise to interrupt a prince, but Josse couldn't help himself. 'It was a gift, Sire!' he protested.

There was a distressing sense of familiarity about the exchange. Back in February, Josse had received a demand for rent on his gift of a house which, he surmised, had come from John. For John was in need of money, involved as he was in preparing for the increasingly likely possibility that he would become King.

Richard was still in Outremer, and news was in short supply. What there was of it was not good: it seemed almost certain now that the Crusade which had set off with such courage and optimism back in the summer of 1190 would turn out to be a dismal failure. Even now, crusaders were beginning to return to their homelands, bearing on their lips tales of defeat instead of songs of glory.

And there was no news whatsoever of Richard.

Glancing now at the King's younger brother – clever, scheming, ruthless – Josse had to admit that, although precipitate, John's actions were at least understandable. If Richard were indeed lost – God forbid it! – then John would probably be king. The true heir to the throne might well be Arthur of Brittany, Richard and John's nephew, but would the English barons accept an alien child in place of a Prince already known to them?

The word was that they would not.

In which case, was it not prudent of John to prepare himself by enlisting support and raising funds?

Prudent, perhaps. But Josse did not intend to assist in the fundraising by parting with money that he did not in truth owe.

Dropping his eyes once more, he repeated, trying to keep the truculence out of his tone, 'My manor was a gift, Sire.' A sudden and very welcome thought struck him: hadn't he ridden all the way to Amesbury Abbey, back in that icy, snowy February, to plead his case with John and Richard's mother, Queen Eleanor? And hadn't she written out, in her own fair hand, words confirming that Josse's manor was a gift? 'I have proof,' Josse went on urgently, 'proof in the form of an assurance from the Queen your mother herself that—'

But John, appearing abruptly to tire of the business, had rolled up the parchment and was waving it carelessly at William d'Arbret, who rushed forward to retrieve it.

'Ah, yes,' John said. 'A gift. Of course.' And the heavy

lids descended over the bright eyes as John gave a bored yawn.

Josse, not entirely convinced by this show of indifference, stood waiting to see what would happen next.

Prince John made as if to re-mount his chestnut gelding. Then, as if a thought had just occurred to him, he said, 'But now, I recall, there was another matter!' The languid pose now gone as quickly as it had come, the Prince turned, head moving from side to side as he searched among the group of courtiers, and called out, 'Magister! Where are you?'

The horsemen shifted to make room as a man slowly moved forward from the rear of the group. As his horse drew level with the Prince's, he swung down from the saddle and stood beside John, head bent as he awaited instructions.

Josse stared at him. He was perhaps in his fifties – sixties? – although it was curiously hard to tell. He was tall, thin, very pale, and with a long beard the colour of milk that seemed to blend and merge with his white skin. As Josse watched, Prince John muttered something to him, and the tall man bent so as to speak his quiet reply into John's ear.

Then they both turned to face Josse.

'The Magister reminds me that we are also come on another matter,' Prince John said, glancing across at his tall companion as he spoke. 'We seek a stranger to these parts, one Galbertius Sidonius, and we request of you, Josse d'Acquin, whether you have news of him.'

'I?' Josse was amazed. 'But you see where and in what manner I live, Sire, deep in the country and far from any centre of civilisation where I might hear tell of any strangers. Galbertius—?

'Galbertius Sidonius.' It was the pale man who spoke. His voice, low-pitched and melodious, was pleasant to listen to, with an almost hypnotic quality.

'No.' Josse shook his head. 'The name means nothing to me. I am sorry that I cannot help.'

'No stranger has come here recently seeking you out?' Prince John persisted. There was a fierce glint in his eyes that put Josse on his guard; this matter, whatever it might be, seemed to be very important.

It occurred to him suddenly – and somehow he knew he was right – that the feeble attempt to extract rent from him had been but an excuse, a superficial and not very convincing reason for the visit, considering that the matter had been settled beyond all dispute back in February. Which, given the way in which John had so abruptly backed down, he already seemed to have known.

His real purpose all along had been to seek news of this Galbertius Sidonius.

'Sir Josse!' Prince John's tone had risen towards anger. 'We ask again: have you recently had a visit from a stranger?'

Josse put on his most winning expression; when a Plantagenet was about to lose his temper, it was wise to placate him rapidly. And as a boy John had, when provoked, been known to chew the rushes on the floor and set light to the furniture.

'Sire, I have received no stranger these many months and years,' he said, smiling, 'save only yourself and your courtiers.' He concluded his remark with another bow.

When he rose up again – the silence was becoming uncomfortable – it was to see that the Prince looked calm once more. Almost calm, anyway. With a final intense stare at Josse, he gave a curt nod and turned away, once more going to mount his horse.

Up in the saddle, preparing to leave, he called out, 'Be sure and send word, Josse d'Acquin, if you hear anything. Galbertius Sidonius. Remember.'

With that he set spurs to his horse and hastened away, the courtiers, taken by surprise at this sudden departure, bumping and slipping in the saddle as their mounts surged forward in pursuit of the Prince.

Watching the group quickly fade from sight away under the trees that lined the road, Josse wondered just who Galbertius Sidonius might be.

And why Prince John, the likely next King of England, so badly wanted to find him.

2

The mood at Hawkenlye Abbey was far removed from its usual serenity.

It was a warm autumn day. Bright sunshine lit the ambers and oranges of dying leaves in the nearby Wealden Forest, making a pleasing contrast to the deep blue of the cloudless sky. And someone had just discovered a decomposing body.

They – or, more accurately, she, for the discovery had been made by the young daughter of a family of pilgrims visiting the Holy Water shrine in the Vale – had been drawn to the corpse by the smell. The girl was as well used to smells as any peasant child, living as she did so close to the rest of her family and to their animals. She probably would not even have noticed the stench of a festering midden, of a pile of cow dung, of ripe human sweat, of pigs in the sty.

But even a peasant child rarely came across the particularly sweet and disgustingly pungent odour of rotting human flesh.

Full of a six-year-old's curiosity, the girl had literally followed her nose, pushing her way deep into a tract of thick bracken beside the path, hardly noticing the scratchy, brownish fronds as she brushed them aside. The smell had grown alarmingly so that, beginning to retch, she had been on the point of turning round and running for the safety of the group of little huts where the monks allowed visitors to the Vale to put up. Where, indeed, her mother was just beginning to wonder what had become of her youngest child.

But just then the girl had trodden on something. Something that squished horribly under her bare foot and emitted such a wave of stench that the girl's piercing scream was abruptly cut off as she vomited up her scanty breakfast.

It was now noon. The child, now almost recovered from her horror, was actually beginning to enjoy all the attention.

She had been comforted, and her face – and, more crucially, her foot – had been bathed and cleansed. The infirmarer, large, kind and motherly, had attended to the girl herself. When repeated sponging with warm water had failed to rid the small, narrow foot of the clinging odour of dead meat, the infirmarer – her name was Sister Euphemia – had sent for an old nun with whiskers on her chin and very penetrating eyes. She – *her* name was Sister Tiphaine, and they said she was the herbalist – had brought a little pot of some sort of paste that smelt like summer flowers. She spread the paste on the stinky foot and mixed it with water, so that it frothed to a foam that at last got rid of the smell.

The child, with the suppleness of being six, kept sitting on the ground and bringing her foot up close to her nose. She didn't think she had ever smelt anything so lovely as the herbalist's flowery paste.

Watching the little girl now, hands tucked away inside the opposite sleeves of her black habit, was Abbess Helewise.

'She is over the shock, do you think?' she quietly asked Sister Euphemia.

'Aye, I reckon so,' the infirmarer replied. 'The resilience of youth, you know, Abbess.'

Helewise glanced away up the track that led alongside the pond and, ultimately, out of the Vale. It was beside this track that the body had lain.

Earlier, two of the lay brothers had performed the ghastly duty of shovelling the rotting body on to a hurdle and bringing it out of the bracken. It now lay a short distance further down the track – where its penetrating odour could not drift back to disturb the living – still on its hurdle and covered by a piece of sacking.

'We must look at the body, Sister,' the Abbess said firmly to the infirmarer. 'If there is any means by which we may identify that poor soul, we must find it. We cannot rest easy if we merely do as we wish to do and bundle him – her – into a hasty grave and try to forget him. Her.'

'A man, they say, Abbess.' The infirmarer kept her voice low.

'A man? How so?'

'Young Augustus went with Brother Saul to bring out the remains. And he—'

'Yes.' Helewise remembered all about young Augustus's talents. He had been her valued and trusted companion on a mission that she had had to make earlier in the year, and she knew from personal experience that he possessed the knowledge to tell the gender of a dead body. In the course of that mission, the puzzle presented to the young lay brother had been a burned skeleton. He had explained, with a modest and reassuring confidence, how the shape of the pelvis and the quality of the bones themselves – sturdy and robust for a man, lighter and finer for a woman – usually gave away a dead person's sex.

Now, if Augustus had declared a putrid corpse to be male, then the Abbess was prepared to believe that he was right.

'A man, then,' she repeated, in the same low voice. 'Did they discover anything else? His age, perhaps, or any article of clothing or personal possession to reveal who he was?'

Sister Euphemia hesitated. Then said: 'He was mother-naked, Abbess. And nothing was found near him, although Brother Saul and Augustus are still searching through the bracken.'

Yes, so they were. Helewise could see one of them – Saul, she thought – as he stood up and, head raised, took a breath of the purer air above the thick bracken. Poor Saul. Poor Augustus. What a terrible task. She could only hope that, with the body now removed, the smell was decreasing in intensity.

'They do think he was a young man,' Sister Euphemia ventured, her eyes, like Helewise's, on the distant figure of Saul, who, as they watched, bent down to resume his search and disappeared from view. 'They have asked me to look at him, to see if I agree.' She sounded less than enthusiastic.

'How will you be able to tell?' Perhaps, Helewise

thought, the poor infirmarer's professional curiosity would engage her and make the task slightly less repellent.

'Oh – a youngster will show none of the bent and deformed bones that give to the ageing such pain,' Sister Euphemia said. 'The teeth, too, will be in better condition, with less wear and fewer gaps.'

'Mm, I see,' Helewise said encouragingly. 'Anything else that you will look for?'

Sister Euphemia turned to her, faint amusement in her eyes. 'I thank you for your kind interest, Abbess, but I am sure you do not really want to know.' She cut off Helewise's half-hearted protest with a smile and a gesture of her hand. 'I think, with your permission, that it is time I stopped putting off the moment and went to study that poor fellow lying by the track down there. Then, as soon as it can be arranged, we can say our prayers for his soul and put him in the ground.'

Helewise, as eager for that ultimate step as her infirmarer, merely nodded and said, 'Yes, Sister Euphemia. Thank you.'

In the wake of Prince John's departure, it had occurred to Josse that the one place in the area where they *might* have heard of a stranger by the name of Galbertius Sidonius was Hawkenlye Abbey.

The Abbey, with its healing spring of Holy Water dedicated to the Virgin Mary, drew folk from near and far. The miracle of the cure of the fever-ridden French merchants who had first discovered the spring was now widely known; even the very poor would try to scrape together the funds for what was often a long journey, in the hope of curing injury and sicknesses of both body and mind in themselves or their loved ones.

Aye. Strangers a-plenty, at Hawkenlye. Maybe this Galbertius himself had visited – might even be there right now – and, provided he had revealed his identity, Josse could find out who and what he was simply by travelling the half-day's journey over to the Abbey.

So it was that he rose one morning, dressed, and summoned Ella to prepare a quick breakfast and Will to prepare Horace, his horse.

Then, in the golden sun of a fine autumn day, he rode off to Hawkenlye.

The porteress, Sister Ursel, was standing in the road outside the Abbey gates when Josse rode up. Shading her eyes against the bright noon light, she was peering down the track, almost as if she were waiting for someone.

For him?

Her greeting – 'Ah, Sir Josse, *there* you are, now! How glad I am to see you!' seemed to underline this impression, if not to confirm it.

'I am expected?' he asked, slipping down from Horace's back and returning the porteress's welcoming smile.

'Expected?' She seemed to think about it. 'Nay. But she will be highly relieved to see you, none the more for that.'

She. The Abbess? He wondered what might be the source of her relief at his presence. And whether, indeed, it would prove to be justified.

Leading Horace across to the stables – where, as both he and the horse knew from long experience, Sister Martha would care for the animal with a particular devotion that reflected the esteem in which she held its master – he said to Sister Ursel, 'Any service that I may perform for the Abbess is for her to command of me, naturally. But—?' He left the query hanging in the air, hoping the porteress would enlighten him.

She didn't. Instead, turning to go back inside her little lodge by the gates, she said, 'The Abbess is down in the Vale.'

A short time later, he was on his way to find her.

The main gates through which he had entered the Abbey lay to the east of the imposing Abbey church. Its great west door, with the magnificent tympanum of the Last Judgement above it, faced a second entrance, from which a path led down to the Vale. Here, a small and simple chapel had been built over the Holy Water spring. Beside it was a short range of wooden-framed, wattle-and-daub buildings where the monks who tended the spring and cared for the pilgrims were housed. There was also basic accommodation – clean, even if none too comfortable – for those pilgrims who lived too far away to make the journey to Hawkenlye and back in a day.

Old Brother Firmin was the most senior of the professed monks. Deeply spiritual, with a pure and sincere faith in the blessed Holy Water that he distributed with such love to the needy, he was inclined to keep his thoughts in Heaven and his hands in his sleeves. Although he had never admitted as much, the general view was that he considered practical work to be the realm of women – in this case, the nuns – while the monks devoted themselves to matters of the spirit.

The Abbess Helewise, however, had other ideas.

She maintained a gentle but firm pressure on the old monk, ensuring, as far as she was able, that he and his monks did their fair share of manual labour. Some of Brother Firmin's monks were co-operative, some were not.

The Abbess's great ally in the Vale, however, was her beloved Brother Saul. He was not one of the fully professed but a lay brother; he was also probably the most dependable, capable and handy man that the Abbess had ever known.

It was Brother Saul who Josse first noticed now, as he hastened down the path to the Vale. Saul was standing up to the waist in bracken and, as Josse raised an arm and prepared to call out, Saul seemed to take a deep breath, as if he were about to plunge into water, and disappeared beneath the thick, rusting fronds of the bracken. Turning his head to look down at the small clutch of buildings under the chestnut trees by the shrine, Josse saw two figures dressed in black, white wimples and coifs bright in the sunshine. One was round and stocky, the other taller, with broad shoulders. Despite the enveloping folds of their habits, it was clear that both were, even without the give-away white linen, female.

Breaking into a run, he went to join them.

'Sir Josse!' the Abbess exclaimed in surprise.

'My lady Abbess,' he said, giving her the formal bow reserved for a first greeting of the day, or after an absence.

'Right glad we are to see *you*,' Sister Euphemia said, grasping his hand in both of hers.

'What has happened?' he demanded. 'How may I aid you?'

'A body has been discovered,' the Abbess said. 'Badly decomposed, naked, nothing known save that it is that of a man, probably quite a young man.'

Against all reason – for why should it be, and, anyway, how would they know? – Josse almost asked, is it that of Galbertius Sidonius?

He restrained himself. Instead he said, 'I saw Brother Saul, deep in the bracken over there. He is, I imagine, searching for anything that might help identification?'

'He is,' the Abbess said.

'What would you like me to do?' Josse asked. 'Go to help Saul, or . . . ?'

'Brother Saul has young Augustus to help him,' the Abbess said. 'More people in the bracken might be more of a hindrance than a help, do you not think?'

'Aye. And I have big feet, with which I might tread some important find into the ground.'

'I am sure you would not,' the Abbess countered. 'But, Sir Josse, an unpleasant duty awaits Sister Euphemia.' She glanced at the infirmarer, whose face was impassive. 'She is just now about to look at the corpse, where it – he – lies yonder by the path. Will you – may I ask you to go with her?'

'You may, and I will,' he assured her. 'But whether I can aid the good Sister in her study of the body, I cannot say.'

'I'd be glad of your company either way, Sir Josse,' Sister Euphemia said bluntly. 'Poor soul's been dead a while, and his flesh is putrid and maggot-infested.'

'Ah.'

A brief flash of humour crossed Sister Euphemia's broad face. 'Not had your dinner yet?' she asked quietly.

'No.'

'All the better. Nothing for you to lose.'

With that encouraging remark, she bowed to the Abbess and led the way off along the track.

Josse was glad of those few preparatory remarks. Had he not expected the horror that lay beneath the sacking, he might well have disgraced himself. As it was, he took a deep breath as Sister Euphemia bent down to throw back the cover and, as the poor, purplish-black body was revealed, managed to retain his composure.

Only just.

Sister Euphemia stood for a moment, head bent, over the corpse. Then she said, 'Excuse me, sir, for what I am about to do, and I apologise. But it is necessary. I will be as swift as I can, then we will leave you in peace.'

Josse had assumed, at first, that she was addressing him. But he realised, as she closed her eyes in prayer, that her apology had been to the dead man.

Opening her eyes again, she picked up a short stick from the undergrowth, trimmed it with quick, strong hands to the required length, then, kneeling down, poked it in among the liquefying flesh and the maggots around what had been the man's thighs.

'Look here at the long bones, Sir Josse,' she said. 'Tidily rounded, no more growing to be done, I'd say. Means we're looking at a man, not a boy. In his twenties, at a guess.' The probing stick moved on down the length of the right femur. 'Here's the knee joint. Lower end of the upper bone, upper end of the lower one. See? Smooth, solid, no signs of wear. This man could have knelt all day in a puddle in a rock without much discomfort.'

'Mm.' Josse wasn't sure he could yet trust himself to speak. Besides, talking involved opening the mouth and, just then, he preferred to keep his shut.

Sister Euphemia adjusted her position and now, with another muttered apology, she gently pushed her stick into the mouth of the corpse.

'Quite good teeth,' she observed. 'One missing here' – she pointed with the end of the stick – 'but there's no hole in the jaw bone such as you see when a man's lost a tooth through infection. No. I'd say this fellow had been in a fight, and some other man's fist put paid to this tooth.'

Leaning away as far as possible without making it obvious, Josse said, barely opening his mouth, 'You would say, Sister, that the state of the teeth would confirm your estimated age? A man in his twenties?'

'I would, Sir Josse.' She glanced briefly at him. 'And there's no need to talk like you've a toothache yourself. Breathe as deep as you like, you'll not catch anything worse than a bad smell from *this* poor man.'

That the body could be the victim of some dread and fatal disease had not so far crossed Josse's mind. With an involuntary start backwards, he said, 'Are you quite certain, Sister?'

'As certain as I can be,' she said gruffly. Her left hand, he noticed, had slipped round beneath the corpse's shoulders. 'Not unless he was already sick when someone slid this into his heart.'

There was a brief movement in the body – a sort of lurch – as, with some difficulty, she pulled on some hidden object. Then she held up what she had discovered.

It was a knife. It was short – handle and blade together were probably little longer than Josse's extended hand – and the blade was narrow, with a slight upward curve at the tip.

Josse swallowed. 'It was still in him?'

'Aye. It was pushed in deep. It didn't even fall out when Saul and Augustus carried him out of the bracken.' She ran a thumb lightly along the curve of the tip. 'Probably designed to hold tight,' she muttered.

'And it would have penetrated his heart?'

'Aye.' She was staring down at the blade. 'Aye. It's thin enough to have gone clean between the ribs . . .' The stick was busy again as she probed. 'I can't see any notching on the bones. This man's killer knew exactly what he was about.'

A professional assassin, Josse thought.

And precisely why, he wondered, should that make Prince John spring instantly to mind?

'. . . because I don't reckon there's much more to be gained from studying him,' Sister Euphemia was saying.

'I'm sorry, Sister, what was that?'

She gave him a considering look. 'Thoughts far away, Sir Josse?' Before he could answer – although there was really no need, since her assumption was quite right – she went on, 'I was just saying, we can take him up to the Abbey now and prepare him for burial. The Abbess is eager to pray for him. Poor chap's lain out here long enough with nobody interceding with the Good Lord on his behalf.' She gave the body a tender look. 'But then I'm sure the Lord won't hold it against him, since it was hardly his own fault.'

Something she had said caught Josse's attention. After agreeing with her sentiments – his own view of God was of a stern but just figure, something like an awesomely authoritative but fair commanding officer – he said, 'Sister, have you any idea how long he might have been down here?'

She said instantly, 'He was put here when the blowflies were still active – they laid their eggs in him. Also, the flesh wouldn't rot as badly as this in a hurry, not out here in the fresh air. He's been partially eaten – foxes, I'd guess – but they're around all year.' She paused, considering. 'I'd say he was slain about five, maybe six weeks ago. We're now in late September . . . I'd guess mid to late August.'

Her guess, he thought, was the best he could hope for. Observant and experienced woman that she was, it was good enough for him.

She had stood up to talk to him but now, bending down again, she was tucking the sacking neatly around the dead man, with all the tenderness of a mother settling her child for a chilly night. When she had finished, she again bent her head and closed her eyes, and her lips moved silently as she prayed. This time, Josse joined in.

When, a little time later, they had both finished, they turned away and, without speaking, walked back along the track and up the path to the Abbey, to inform the Abbess that the burial could now go ahead.

Late in the evening, Josse went soft-footed along the

cloister to the little room in which the Abbess conducted the business of the Abbey. He had been told she had gone there; she had not come to the refectory for supper but had remained on her knees in the church, beside the corpse in its hurriedly made coffin. Now one of the monks had relieved her, and she had retired to her private room.

The dead man was to be committed to the ground the next day.

The door to the Abbess's room was slightly ajar, and a faint light shone out from within. Josse tapped on the door and she said, 'Come in, Sir Josse.'

He did so. 'How did you know it was me?'

She smiled briefly. 'None of my nuns or monks wears spurs that jingle as they walk.'

'And there was I trying to be so quiet and not disturb you,' he murmured.

She smiled again, then nodded towards the small wooden stool she kept for visitors. Accepting her invitation to be seated, he pulled it out from its place by the wall and settled himself.

'You bury him tomorrow,' Josse said.

'Yes. We cannot delay, Sir Josse, for all that we do not know who it is we bury.'

'I know,' he said. 'Besides, it seems there is nothing further to be learned from his body.'

'That is what I understand. No reason, then, to deny him Christian burial.'

'Mm.' Josse was frowning. 'Brother Saul and young Augustus found no clue?'

'No. And, knowing them both as I do, I feel that I may conclude that this means there is no clue to be found.'

'I agree.' Besides, he thought – although he did not say so to the Abbess – this murder appeared to be the work of a man who knew exactly what he was doing. Who stripped his victim of his garments and his belongings and who could surely only have made the blunder of leaving his knife behind because there was no alternative. Perhaps it was too soundly stuck in his victim's body. Perhaps he was disturbed.

As if the Abbess read his thoughts, she said, 'There is the knife.'

'Aye.'

'Sister Euphemia has it still,' she went on quietly. 'It is dirty and stained – she says with the poor dead man's blood – and she has undertaken to clean it thoroughly before we examine it.' She shot a look at Josse. 'Before *you* examine it, if you will.'

'I?'

'You know arms, Sir Josse,' she said gently. 'More than any soul, man or woman, in this community.'

He had been rather afraid that was what she meant. 'My lady, I—' He began again. 'It is a time since I was a man of war and, even then, no expert on weaponry.' Her watchful eyes held disappointment. 'But I shall do my best, nevertheless.' He tried to look confident.

'Your best,' said the Abbess, 'is all that anyone may ask of you. And now' – she got to her feet as she spoke and, instantly, he did too – 'I think it is time that I joined my sisters and retired.'

He stood back as she preceded him out of the room, and closed the door after them. They walked in silence across the cloister and, as she turned to the right to go around the church towards the dormitory, he went left towards the rear gate and the path down to the Vale. He had slept down there with the lay brothers before and Brother Saul, he knew, had prepared a place for him tonight.

'Goodnight, Sir Josse,' came the Abbess's soft voice out of the darkness. 'May God bless your sleep.'

On such a night, with the memory of a skilled assassin's ruthless work fresh in his mind, the blessing was very welcome.

3

The burial rites for the dead man took up a large proportion of the morning.

Father Gilbert, the priest of the community, was in sombre mood, and he spoke at length of the sinful state of a world in which a man could lie dead and unclaimed – unnoticed, was the silent accusation – for weeks. Watching the Abbess, on her knees at the front of the church, Josse felt a stab of sympathy. She will take the blame on those shoulders of hers, he thought, and she will embark on some private and surely unnecessary penance until she finds it in her heart to forgive herself for something that wasn't her fault.

How could he help?

Trying to ignore the effects on his own knees of the hard, cold floor of the church – his joints, he was quite sure, were no longer smooth and unworn like those of the dead man – he put Father Gilbert's stern voice out of his mind and concentrated on the problem in hand. Then, remembering where he was, he sent up a swift prayer of apology for having ignored such an obvious opportunity, and humbly asked God to help him help the Abbess.

The answer came – at least, an answer of sorts – as they rose to walk with the coffin out to the burial ground.

I must find out who he was, Josse told himself, staring at the coffin. And, with the good Lord's help, who killed him. I will set off down to the Vale as soon as this business is over, and find out everything I can about visitors to the Holy Water shrine over the past couple of months.

That, it seemed to him, was the best starting point.

The fact that it might also be a great help in proceeding with his own little puzzle – who was Galbertius Sidonius, and why was Prince John searching for him? – was something that Josse tried not to dwell on.

It was not difficult to encourage the monks and the lay brothers down in the Vale to talk; it was, in fact difficult to make them stop.

Although violent death was, sadly, no rarer an occurrence in the sacred environs of the Vale than anywhere else in late twelfth-century England, it was still sufficiently exceptional to get the monks all squawking and clucking away like hens round a split grain sack. Josse wasted quite a lot of time on the likes of Brother Micah, who claimed to have heard a saturnine figure dressed all in black creeping about the Vale ('And just how did you know he was dressed in black if you only heard him?' Brother Erse, the carpenter, astutely asked him), and Brother Adrian, who said anybody who went around naked was an affront and just asking for trouble. This time it was Brother Saul who quashed him, quietly telling him that it was far more likely that the murderer had stripped his victim after having killed him, so as to help disguise the dead man's identity.

After some time, Josse was able to corner Brother Saul, Brother Erse and young Brother Augustus. Leaving the

other monks to their thrilled gossiping, he indicated with
a nod of his head that he would like a quiet word, and
the three brothers followed him off along the path to
the pond.

He studied them as they walked.

Brother Saul he knew well; his opinion of the lay brother
accorded with that of the Abbess. Brother Augustus he had
met but briefly; the lad had borrowed Josse's horse in order
to act as one half of Abbess Helewise's escort on a trip she
had made earlier in the year, and Josse had been impressed
with the young man's sense and quiet confidence. He was
the son of travelling folk, and had heard the Lord's call
when his sick mother had been cured by Hawkenlye's
Holy Waters.

Brother Erse, now, Josse hardly knew at all. The carpenter was a silent man, broad-built with strong, well-shaped
hands. His workmanship had been pointed out to Josse,
who was impressed with the craft of a man who could turn
his hand to the practical and the beautiful with equal flair
and competence. The community, he thought, was lucky
to have Brother Erse. And, just now, hadn't he spoken with
the voice of cool logic in the face of Brother Micah's wild
and woolly speculation?

Yes. These three, Josse decided, were the best of the
bunch.

'The Abbess is troubled,' he began when, some distance
out of earshot of the community of monks, they stopped.
'I know we'll all do what we can to help, and it seems to me
that, as for myself, I can best serve her by trying to find out
the dead man's identity and have a try at discovering who
killed him.' The three brothers nodded their agreement.

'So, first of all, I need you to tell me about everyone who has been here over, shall we say, the last two months? Say, since the start of August.'

It was a tall order. He knew it, even before it was confirmed by the men's dubious expressions. Then Brother Saul spoke.

'We keep records of numbers all right, Sir Josse,' he said. 'We have to do that, since everything we order and use has to be accounted for.'

'Aye.' Josse was aware of it. Once he had taken a peek at the endless books of accounts that the Abbess used to keep, before she had been persuaded that that was one particular duty which could safely be delegated to another nun whose scholarly qualifications were, if anything, even better than those of the Abbess.

'But,' Saul was saying, 'as to who everyone is, well, that's a problem. We don't always ask, you see, sir, not when folks come in dire need of help. Asking a man to tell us his name and where he comes from doesn't always seem the most important thing, when he's come seeking the cure for his son crippled in the legs, his wife in the throes of a fever, or his mother wrong in her head.'

'I do see, Saul,' Josse said gently. 'But of those whom you do know about, will you tell me what you can?'

'Aye, and gladly.' Saul sounded relieved. 'Shall I start, brothers, and you put in when I forget?' He looked intently at Erse and Augustus, face anxious. They both nodded their agreement.

It was surprising, in fact, just how much the three of them did remember, between them, of the comings and

goings of the past two months. Their different recollections had a similarity about them: sometimes it was a
well-to-do merchant and his wife seeking a cure for her
barrenness, sometimes it was some worthy of the town
with a sick baby, sometimes it was a nobleman who could
not rid himself of a troublesome bellyache.

But, in the main, it was the lowly, ordinary folk of
England who came. Peasants who gathered up their few
precious possessions in a pack and set off on the long road
to Hawkenlye, not knowing how long they would be away
from home and not trusting that they would find their
goods untouched on their eventual return. They usually
came on foot so that, as Saul remarked ruefully, often the
first duty of the loving brothers in the Vale was to bed them
down and feed them up to counter their exhaustion.

None of the brothers remembered a young man on his
own who might have arrived some time in early August.

'Folks rarely come all by themselves,' Brother Erse said.
'Well, stands to reason. Who would travel the roads and
byways alone when they could have company? Safer, that
way. Somebody to watch your back.'

'Aye, you're right, Brother Erse,' Josse agreed glumly.

Perhaps noticing the defeatist tone in his voice and
wishing to offer some encouragement, Augustus said suddenly, 'There was that old feller who died. Remember,
Saul? He was thin, dressed poorly, and he had a nasty
cough. Died in his sleep one night, and then in the
morning—'

'In the morning, his young servant had gone!' Brother
Saul interrupted. 'Oh, well remembered, Gus! Why did we
not think of him before?' But, as quickly as it had come, the

happy smile left his face. Looking aghast, he said, 'Oh, no. Not the young man in the bracken?'

Josse, trying to follow the rapid exchange, said, 'What old man was this? And what's this about the servant?'

Brother Saul turned to him. 'I am sorry, Sir Josse. Let me explain. An old man came to us in . . . yes, in August. Round about the middle of August. There had been a hot spell followed by a storm, and he had a bad chest, which was greatly troubled by the sudden drop in temperature and the damp after the storm. We made him as comfortable as we could and he was due to take the waters in the morning, but he died in the night.'

'And was that an expected death?' Josse asked.

'Expected . . . ? Oh, yes indeed. Sister Euphemia had attended him on his arrival, and she spoke to me in private afterwards and said she was gravely worried about him. Sir Josse, I think we can be fairly sure that there were no suspicious circumstances concerning *that* death.'

'But what of the young servant?'

Saul's face clouded again. 'He vanished. He was there when we retired for the night – indeed, we remarked on the care with which he tended his master – but when we woke and found the old man dead, the boy had gone.'

The four of them stood silently, nobody, apparently, wanting to voice the conclusion to which they had all leapt. Finally Josse said, 'Brother Saul, Brother Augustus, the two of you saw both the living young man and the dead body. Yes?' They both nodded. 'Then can you say whether or not the two were one and the same?'

Saul spoke first, and that only after some moments' thought. 'It is possible, aye, Sir Josse. But in the absence

of a recognisable face . . .' He did not finish. Which,
Josse thought, was understandable; the face of the corpse,
bloated, half-eaten, a mass of purplish flesh and bare white
bone where the skull showed through, had not been a sight
to dwell on.

'Augustus?' he said gently, turning to the boy.

'I cannot be sure, either,' Augustus said. 'All that I would
venture is that it is not impossible that the dead man was
the old man's servant.'

'Very well.' Josse nodded. There was no point in pursuing the matter; Saul and Augustus had done their best.
Instead he now asked, 'I suppose neither the old man nor
the servant gave you their name?'

As one, the three men shook their heads.

Then Brother Erse said, 'They were foreign. Leastways,
the lad was.'

'Foreign?' Josse spun round to face him.

'Aye. He was dark-complexioned. Skin was sort of . . .'
He paused, clearly thinking. 'Sort of oak-coloured. If you
know what I mean. And he had black hair.'

'But many people have dark colouring without being
foreign,' Josse observed. 'Are you sure, Brother Erse?'

'I'm sure,' the carpenter insisted. 'He spoke funny.'

'Ah.' Would that be Brother Erse's interpretation of
someone speaking English when it was not their mother
tongue? It was quite likely; Hawkenlye's fame had grown
to the extent that people from other countries did now
make the long trip. 'And the old man? Did he appear to
be foreign too?'

'Couldn't say,' Erse said. 'He wore a hood mostly, and
he didn't so much as speak but cough.'

'I see.' Was the information helpful in any way, Josse wondered? Were they right in concluding that the dead youth was the old man's servant? But why was he murdered? And, indeed, why had he fled on the night his master died? Or was the whole thing completely irrelevant and serving only to distract them from the true victim and nature of the crime? Either way, it seemed they could go no further now. Josse was about to thank them and release them to return to their duties when Brother Saul spoke up.

'I was wrong just now,' he muttered. 'I've been thinking, and it wasn't right, what I said to Brother Adrian.'

'I'm sure he didn't take it amiss,' Josse reassured him, 'and, Saul, you spoke quite kindly.'

Saul flashed him a brief smile. 'No, that's not what I mean, thank you all the same, Sir Josse. No. I said to him that the poor dead soul was naked because his murderer had stripped him after he'd killed him. But that can't be right, else how did the knife end up still in the body? I mean, if you stick a knife in someone and then take off his jerkin or his tunic, the knife would be pulled out as the garment was removed. Wouldn't it?'

'Aye, in all probability it would,' Josse said slowly. An unpleasant picture was forming in his mind. 'Is it possible, then, that the killer made the victim strip before he killed him?'

Brother Erse made a sound of disgust. But Augustus said, 'That sounds unlikely, since the man was stabbed from behind.'

Josse tried to picture it. Indeed, it did seem unlikely, especially for a professional assassin, to make a man strip and then stand behind him to slip a knife between his ribs. To be stabbed in the back surely suggested an element of surprise – the dark figure creeping up behind his victim, soft-footed, silent. But then why had the victim been naked?

Saul said, 'Perhaps the assailant struck him down first and stunned him, then stripped him, then stabbed him?'

'Hmm.' I did not check his head for injury, Josse reprimanded himself. And, now that he is buried, it is too late.

Then he thought, *I* did not. But I am willing to bet that somebody else did.

He told the others what he was thinking. Then, thanking them for their time and their help, he hurried away to find Sister Euphemia.

'I was just coming to look for you, sir knight,' she said.

He had found her in the little curtained-off section of the long infirmary where she kept a bowl and a pitcher of water; she was washing something black and sticky from her hands, and he did not like to ask what it was. Noticing his quick glance, she said, 'A patient with a suppurating sore on her hip, poor soul. She suffers much, yet does not complain. I have given her some of Sister Tiphaine's strongest sleeping draught, in order that she may rest awhile. Now then—' briskly she dried her hands on a spotless linen cloth and rolled down her wide sleeves – 'you first. What did you come to see me about?'

He told her of the murder scene which he and the three brothers had just conjured up, of the difficulty of how a knife could have been left in a man whose clothes had been removed after death, and of the possible solution that the victim had been knocked on the head and rendered unconscious first.

Before he had finished, she was shaking her head. 'No, there was no injury to the skull, nor to the neck,' she said firmly.

'You are absolutely certain?'

'That I am. Of course, it's possible to fell a man without its leaving a dent in the skull.'

'Aye,' he sighed. He seemed to be getting nowhere.

Observing his face, she gave him a swift dig in the ribs. 'Cheer up, Sir Josse. Did I not just say that I was about to come looking for you?'

'Aye. What—?'

'I have been studying that knife.' She lowered her voice, beckoning him further into the little recess. Then she reached under the table on which the bowl and pitcher stood and pulled out a small bundle of cloth. She laid it on the table and unwrapped the cloth.

The knife lay on the scrap of linen. Clean now, Josse noticed the sheen on the thin blade – no doubt razor-sharp – and the faint carved design on the short, stubby handle.

But he did not study the knife for long; there was something else in the bundle.

He picked it up.

It was a piece of cloth, almost circular in shape, with a clean slit in the middle. Its outer edges were frayed, as if it had been torn.

Sister Euphemia said softly in his ear, 'When I cleaned the blood and the dirt from the knife, I found this piece of cloth around the point where blade meets handle. It was so soaked in blood that it had stuck tight to the knife.'

'And it was ripped from the dead man's garment when the murderer stripped the body?' Josse whispered. 'Is it possible, Sister?'

She took the small piece of cloth from him. 'It is possible, I reckon,' she replied. 'The knife was stuck fast in the body, and it could be that the garment gave way before the blade. The fabric is soft and fine – I think it is wool, perhaps from an undershirt.' She glanced up at Josse. 'A costly undershirt, mind – not many of the folks who go to the Holy Shrine would wear such a garment.'

Josse was picturing a well-dressed man, the sort who could afford a fine wool undershirt. In his mind's eye he saw the man's tunic, heavy, costly, perhaps padded and lined, open at the sides and held together at the waist by a decorative belt.

Aye. It was possible that a clever assailant, familiar with the dress of men of means, would know how to slide the knife inside the tunic and stab the man through his shirt.

Thoughtfully he wrapped both knife and wool fragment up in the cloth. He said, 'Sister Euphemia, I am truly grateful, as ever, for your all-seeing eyes and your delicate, skilful, capable hands.'

Again, she dug him in the ribs, rather more forcibly this time. 'Go on with you,' she said. 'You old flatterer!'

He returned her grin. 'May I keep this?' He held up the bundle.

'Of course.' Nudging him out of the way, she stepped past him and back out into the infirmary. Looking at him over her shoulder, she said softly, 'Good luck with your enquiries, Sir Josse. I will pray for you.'

Then she was off, walking quickly but quietly up the long room to where, at the far end, an elderly woman lay tossing and turning. The woman with the ulcerated hip? It was possible. Whoever she was, her chances of getting better had just gone up quite considerably, now that the infirmarer of Hawkenlye Abbey was fighting on her side.

4

<hr />

Helewise had returned to the Abbey church after the formalities concerning the interment of the dead man had finally been concluded. She had taken Father Gilbert's reprimand to heart. He was *right*, she thought desperately; what sort of an example does it set for an abbey, of all places, to be so lacking in vigilance that a visitor can be murdered and lie dead and unattended for *weeks*?

People come to us for help and for loving care, she told herself mercilessly, and it is our entire life's purpose here to succour the needy and, when all else comes to naught and God calls, to comfort the dying and pray for the dead. Oh, how I have failed! That poor young man, stabbed and thrown aside, and there he has lain ever since, ignored, unburied, nobody to offer up the shortest, smallest prayer on his behalf!

On her knees, she dropped her face on to her clasped hands and wept.

So wrapped up was she in her guilt and her misery that she did not hear the great door of the church open and quietly close, nor the soft whisper of steps as someone crossed the floor on light feet and knelt down by her side.

But then the slim figure beside her whispered, 'Abbess

Helewise, it is not right that you suffer alone for something that is the fault of all of us. Will you permit me to pray with you?'

Raising her face, brushing away the tears with a hasty gesture, Helewise saw Sister Caliste at her side.

Caliste. The little foster child of a woodland family, she had entered Hawkenlye as one of the youngest ever postulants. Now – and not without a trauma or two of her own along the way – she was a professed nun, a loving, optimistic, blithe soul who nursed even the contagious sick with devotion and courage, putting their wants and needs above her own. Just as her master, Christ, would have wished.

Of all of Hawkenlye, Caliste was the one person with whom Helewise could bear to share her torment.

As she nodded and the two of them closed their eyes in silent prayer, Helewise wondered tentatively if this – Sister Caliste's unexpected, unasked but totally welcome presence – was a small sign that God might be seeing His way to forgiving her.

Back in the privacy of her little room that evening – she had foregone supper, just as she had foregone the midday meal – she heard, once again, the jingle of spurs and the heavy tread of Josse's boots as he came along the cloister.

She called out 'Come in' before he had even knocked on the door.

He advanced into her room, stopped on the far side of the wide table that she used as a desk, and stared down at her. There was compassion in his face; she hoped fervently that he could not detect she had been weeping.

It was possible, though, that he did. For, in a situation where the most natural thing would have been to speak of the day's events, instead he said, 'Fine lad, that Augustus. And I like the carpenter, Brother Erse, as well. Augustus's background I already know, but what of Brother Erse? How did he come to Hawkenlye?'

Dear Josse, she thought as she told him briefly of Brother Erse's circumstances. Of the childhood sweetheart he had wed when both were fifteen, of the child born to them, of the plague that had swept through the village and taken away so many of the young and the weak. Including Erse's wife and baby. Desperate, wishing only to join them in death, Erse had been succoured by an exceptional parish priest and, finally, had come to understand that the Lord had a plan for everyone. Erse's road had been a particularly tough one, but, finding solace in Christ, he had presented himself at Hawkenlye in his capacity as a carpenter and, in time, taken his vows as a monk.

Josse was nodding sagely as she told the tale. When she finished, he said, 'It is to Hawkenlye's advantage that the latter role does not make him abandon the former.'

There was a short and, she thought, rather awkward silence. They had surely exhausted the subject of Brother Erse; would Josse now, she wondered, bring himself to say what he had come to say?

She waited. Josse stared down at his boots. So she said gently, 'Sir Josse, I have been, as I believe you perceive, in some distress over the day's events and, indeed, over what has led to them.' She paused and took a shaky breath; it was hard, she was discovering, to speak of her mental anguish and her guilt, even to as good a friend as Josse. She searched for the right words. Found them.

'I have been long at prayer,' she went on quietly. 'I have opened my heart and, I believe, I have been heard.' Looking up at him, suddenly she was smiling. 'I have been sent not one but two helpmeets,' she concluded. 'Is that not a sign of God's charity?'

'I – er—' He seemed confused as to whether or not modesty should make him disclaim the role of helpmeet; she could almost see him trying to work out if she had actually meant that he was one of the two she had mentioned.

Helping him out of his confusion, she said, 'Sir Josse, did you wish to speak to me? Have you anything to report?'

'Aye, I have,' he said, relief evident in his tone and in his face. 'As you know, the dead man was killed with a short-bladed knife which was left in the body. Sister Euphemia has cleaned it, and we have discovered a small piece of fine woollen cloth around the blade. We surmise that the victim was probably a man of wealth, since a poor man does not wear a fine woollen undershirt.'

'Stabbed when he wore but his shirt?' she asked.

'Possibly. Alternatively, stabbed through the gap where a padded tunic bellows out between shoulder and waist.'

'Yes. I see.' She tried not to picture the scene, but her imagination was off and running. She called back her flying thoughts. 'Does this advance our task of discovering the man's identity?'

He hesitated. Then said, 'Abbess Helewise, this is difficult to explain.'

'Do try.'

A brief smile crossed his face, there and gone in an

Alys Clare

instant. 'I have to confess to you that it was not in fact the dead man who brought me to Hawkenlye but another matter; some business recently come to my attention.'

'I see.' She suppressed a smile of her own; she had been so glad to see him arrive the previous day, when she was faced with the appalling discovery in the Vale, that she had not spared a thought for why he should so fortuitously have turned up just when she needed him. Later, she had been more than willing to ascribe his presence to divine intervention.

It seemed there was a more prosaic reason.

'Do go on,' she invited.

He was staring at his boots again, as if reluctant to speak.

'Sir Josse, what is the matter?' she asked gently. 'If you fear that I shall think the less of you for letting me believe you came merely to help us, when in fact you have a purpose of your own, then you mistake me entirely. For one thing, you encouraged no such illusion; I have scarcely given you a moment to speak of your own business. For another, do you not know that I – that is, that the Abbey thinks too highly of you to let such a thing affect us?'

He had raised his head and now his brown eyes were fixed on hers. He said simply, 'Thank you.' Then, after a moment, went on: 'I had a visitor. Several visitors, in fact; Prince John and a party of courtiers.'

She was taken aback. 'You keep exalted company, Sir Josse,' she murmured.

'Oh, he hadn't come to see me!' he said quickly. 'That is – well, in a way he had. He came seeking information. About a man by the name of Galbertius Sidonius?' There was a slight question in his voice, as if he hoped she was about to say, ah yes, old Galbertius! I know him well!

If that were so, then he was in for a disappointment.

'I am sorry, but the name means nothing to me,' she said.

'I am not greatly surprised. Your good men down in the Vale told me that you rarely record the names and conditions of the pilgrims who take the Holy Water.'

'No. Occasionally names are volunteered, or we hear one person call another by his or her name. Otherwise . . .' She raised her hands, palm upwards. 'I am sorry,' she repeated. 'Is it important that you find this man?'

'Important?' He seemed to pause for thought. 'It ought not to be so,' he said after a moment. 'In truth, all that occurred was that the Prince asked if I knew of or had recently seen this man, this Galbertius Sidonius. I said no, and he said be sure to send word to him if I *did* come across the fellow.'

'But?' she prompted. Clearly, there had to be more.

Frowning, Josse said, 'He gave such a daft reason for the visit, you see, Abbess Helewise. Only when we had dealt with that – in a matter of moments – did he pretend to remember this other business. I am convinced – although I cannot explain it in any more detail than I have already given – that Prince John is in fact extremely eager to speak to this man.'

'And, aware of the Prince's reputation,' – she refrained from saying anything more judgemental – 'you wish to find the man before he does?'

'Exactly!' Josse cried.

'Do you fear for his safety?' she asked quietly.

'I – to speak the truth, I do not know if I do or not. It's only that I feel involved, somehow. I mean, Abbess, why should Prince John come to seek me out, deep in the countryside and far away from court life, unless he had reason to think that I *did* know something of the man he seeks?'

She was nodding her understanding. 'And your involvement has aroused your curiosity?'

He grinned. 'Precisely.'

'Then – forgive me, but I am still not clear why you came to Hawkenlye.' Suddenly she thought she was. 'Unless it was because we have so many visitors that you conjectured Galbertius Sidonius might be among them?'

'Aye.'

'And all we can tell you is that we regret that we take no record of people's names,' she finished for him. 'Oh, Sir Josse, what a disappointment!'

He shrugged. 'It was worth a try.'

There was a brief silence. Then, as an alarming thought occurred to her, she said, 'You do not – oh, can it be that our dead man is the man you seek?'

His eyes met hers, and she saw the same suspicion in his anxious frown. 'I fear it may be so, aye. There is no logical reason for it – as you have just said, Hawkenlye receives many visitors, and Galbertius may not even have been one of them. And, even if he was, why should he be the one poor soul whose pilgrimage ended with a knife through the heart?'

'And yet?' She sensed there was something else.

'And yet I keep seeing that little circle of fine cloth,' he said. 'And I say to myself, this man was a man of quality, not a poor peasant. Which sort of man would be more likely to arouse the interest of a prince of England?'

'I see what you mean.' She chewed at her lip, thinking. 'All we know, other than that he wore a fine undershirt, is that the dead man was quite young. If you were to go to the Prince and ask what age is his Galbertius Sidonius and he replied that he is a middle-aged or an elderly man, then you would at the least know he does not now lie buried with the Hawkenlye dead.'

Josse grinned at her. 'That, dear Abbess Helewise, is exactly what I propose to do.'

When Josse was preparing to ride off in the morning, the Abbess came out to speak to him.

She stood at his stirrup, gazing earnestly up at him. Her eyelids were still a little swollen, he noticed, but she no longer looked as woebegone as she had done the previous day. He was glad; it had wrenched his heart to see her suffer so.

'Sir Josse, I have been thinking,' she said. 'I believe you are right to see a connection between yourself and this Galbertius Sidonius. For, unless the Pr—' She glanced around, noticed that both Sister Ursel and Sister Martha were in earshot and went on, 'Unless the visitor of whom you spoke expected to run his quarry to earth at New Winnowlands, would he not have come here searching for him? Like you, he would surely have reasoned that the Abbey was the largest target for visitors in this region, yet, instead of coming here, he went to seek you.'

Josse nodded slowly. Aye, she was right. And, in addition, New Winnowlands was hardly a renowned manor; few people seemed even to have heard of it. Prince John might have known of its existence right enough, but even he must have had to go to some trouble to find it.

To find Josse.

He bent down and said softly to the Abbess, 'My lady, as ever you think wisely.' He grinned at her and added, 'I wish you were coming with me. I could do with a clever brain.'

The Abbess returned his grin and said, equally quietly, 'Sir Josse, you already have one.' Then, as he wheeled Horace and prepared to put spurs to him and be off, she called, 'God speed. Come back to us soon.'

Which, he decided, meant: be sure and tell me what you find out, as soon as you possibly can.

'I will!' he called back. Then Horace, well fed and well rested, responded to his heels and, breaking into a smooth canter, hurried him away.

Josse knew the town of Newenden, having put up there some three years ago, before King Richard had given him New Winnowlands. Having ascertained the location of Sir Henry of Newenden's manor, he rode out to see if the Prince and his party still lodged there.

The manor house was grand, with moat, walled court-yard, generous accommodation for the family and, all around, well-tended fields. One or two reasonably prosperous-looking peasants touched their caps to Josse as he rode by, and a shepherd tending a large flock of sheep wished him good day.

Josse could see from a distance that the Prince's company were no longer with Sir Henry; as he rode towards the courtyard, the air of peace and calm was not suggestive of the presence of a royal visitor.

Turning Horace's head in through the gates – fortunately, standing open – he saw a groom working on the silvery coat of a grey mare. He called out, 'Halloa! Is the master at home?'

The groom turned, gave Josse an enquiring look and said, 'Who wants to know?'

'I am Sir Josse d'Acquin,' Josse said. 'I am from New Winnowlands, where, a few days ago, the Prince John and his company visited me. They were staying, so they told me, with Sir Henry of Newenden. I have business with the Prince' – how grand it sounded – 'and have come to seek him. But—' He waved a hand around the deserted courtyard. 'It seems I am too late.'

The groom, still looking slightly suspicious, said, 'Aye, they've been gone these two days since. My master Sir Henry rode with them.'

'Where have they gone?'

The groom gave him a pitying look, as if to say, do you reckon they'd have told me? But then, relenting, he said, 'Word is they were heading for London. Business with the Knights Templar, they do say.' He made a gesture with his right thumb, forefinger and middle finger, rubbing the digits together, and Josse decided that this meant the business in question was in all likelihood of a financial nature.

'London?' he repeated. It was an imprecise answer; did it mean Prince John now lodged at Westminster? Or with the Templars in their enclave on the north bank of the river? Or even out at Windsor?

The groom shrugged. 'London. It's all I know.' He went as if to return to the grey mare but, turning back, said, 'The old geezer's still here, if he's any use to you.' The contemptuous tone suggested that the old geezer, whoever he was, was not, nor ever could be, of any conceivable use to the young groom himself.

'Old geezer?'

'Aye. The one they all call Magister.'

The Magister! Josse remembered the man with the milk-white beard. 'Aye, I would speak with him,' he said firmly. Dismounting, he held out Horace's reins to the groom, who grudgingly took them. 'Direct me, if you will, to the Magister's presence.'

Inside the manor house, the standards of housekeeping and the luxurious nature of the furnishings were as Josse had expected from its prosperous, well-kept exterior. The groom had hailed a serving man, who led Josse across the great hall with considerably more civility than the groom had shown. Then, as they came to a stair concealed behind a tapestry – to prevent draughts? What a comfortable home this must be! – the serving man called up to a woman who was working above. She in turn showed Josse up the stair and into a sunny room where a figure sat up in a high bed, a velvet cap on his white hair and a blanket tucked up under his chin, his milky beard neatly combed and spread out on the soft wool.

It was the Magister, and he was clearly suffering from a very heavy cold.

'What a pleasant distraction,' he said in a voice thick with rheum, 'to have a visitor! Give the fire a poke, Sir

Josse d'Acquin, and throw on a handful of those herbs in the basket' – Josse did as he was bade and a sharp, clean smell filled the air – 'then pull up a stool and tell me why you have come.'

'I came seeking the Prince,' Josse said, settling himself on a wooden stool with a padded top, 'but I am told he has gone to London.'

'He has,' the Magister agreed. 'And why did you wish to see him?' The penetrating dark eyes were fixed on Josse's and he thought suddenly that it would be difficult to tell this man a lie. Fortunately, he wasn't about to.

'When you came to New Winnowlands, you sought news of a man, Galbertius Sidonius.'

Josse wasn't sure, but he thought a swift light shone in the depths of the Magister's dark eyes. 'Yes?' the older man said coolly. 'And do you bring such news?'

'I do not,' Josse admitted. 'But I visited the Abbey at Hawkenlye to see if this man had been there, it being such an attraction of the area.'

'And?'

'The nuns and monks of the Abbey were in the midst of a tragedy. A man's body had been discovered, victim of a brutal murder.'

'This man's identity?' The voice came sharply.

'Not known.'

There was a pause. Then the Magister said, 'How long had the body lain undiscovered?'

'Five, six weeks.'

'And so the man was unrecognisable.'

'Aye.'

Another pause, longer this time. The Magister's eyes

had become dull, as if his sight were turned inwards. Josse wondered if he was trying to decide what questions he could safely ask without giving away anything that he wanted to remain secret.

Eventually he said, 'Was this corpse that of an old man, did they think?'

'No. A man perhaps in his twenties, probably no older than that.'

The Magister said neutrally, 'I see.' What exactly he saw, clearly he was not going to reveal it to Josse.

Which meant that Josse was going to have to ask. 'This Galbertius Sidonius,' he said, with more aggression than he had intended. 'Was – is he a young man?'

The Magister's eyes turned towards him, staring at him for some time. Eventually he said, 'No.' There was a pause and, for a brief instant, an expression almost of wonder crossed the pale face. Then the Magister said softly, 'Not young. *Ancient.*'

Josse felt his heart sink. How he would have liked to return to the Abbess and tell her that the mystery was solved! But it had been a faint hope; all along, the likelihood had been that his mission would prove that the dead man was *not* Sidonius rather than that he was.

The Magister spoke again; there was, Josse had noticed, a faint accent: Welsh? He said, still regarding Josse with those dark eyes, 'You had reason to wish that your dead man was Galbertius Sidonius?'

'Eh? No, not really.' It was too difficult to explain about the Abbess, and wanting to help her by identifying the corpse, so he didn't try. In fact, he said nothing further.

But the Magister had not finished with him. 'You know

of this man, this Sidonius?' he probed. 'For all that you told my lord the Prince that you do not.'

'No!' Josse protested vehemently. 'Believe me, sir, I do not!'

A smile broke the pale, solemn face. 'I do believe you,' the Magister said. 'I know when a man lies to me, and you, I see, speak true.'

Staring hard at him – the levity in his voice as he had made the reply seemed to permit a certain relaxation in his approach – Josse thought that there was something familiar about the older man. He said, 'Forgive me, Magister, but have we met before? Were you perhaps at court when the King and his brothers were lads, in the time of King Henry, their father?'

'I was.'

'They call you Magister,' Josse pressed on, 'but may I know your name?'

'It is no secret,' the older man said mildly. 'My name is John Dee.'

John Dee . . .

The name, like the face, had a familiarity to it. Josse thought hard. Did he recall a man called Dee when he had attended the young princes? No. He did not believe he did. Brows descending in a frown of concentraton, he pushed his memory further back.

And, from nowhere, remembered Geoffroi, his father, telling tales beside the fire to his young sons. Of a man who read the future in the stars, who warned of events that were to come, who saw the wind with his deep, dark eyes and whom sailors – always a superstitious bunch – feared as a sorcerer.

Sorcerer. How the word had thrilled and scared the small boys crouched at their father's knee! How they had both yearned for him to go on and tell them more, and prayed that he would stop before he frightened them so much that they would not sleep!

The sorcerer's name had been John Dee.

'My father knew you!' Josse exclaimed. But no, that wasn't quite right; Geoffroi told stories not of someone he had met, but of a legendary figure from the past. A man who had advised kings and princes, yes, but many years ago. The courts to which the John Dee of Geoffroi d'Acquin's tales belonged had been those of the first William and, later, that of his ill-fated, short-reigning son, the second William, and his brother, Henry.

Kings who, or so it was whispered, kept at least one foot in the Old Religion . . .

This man who now lay in the bed before Josse was far too young to be one and the same as that figure from the fireside tales! But he was probably a descendant.

'I know of you, John Dee,' Josse said, reverence in his voice; it was not every day you met the kinsman of a magician. 'My father used to tell us tales of the John Dee who advised the first of the Norman kings, who, I would venture to conclude, was your ancestor?'

The Magister said nothing for a moment. Then, softly: 'John Dee was always there, and always will be.'

Ah, yes, Josse thought. It was as he had thought; the post of court sorcerer, or magician, or seer, or sage, or whatever they called it, must be an hereditary one. Passed always from father to son, as was their traditional family Christian name of John.

He sat back on his stool, regarding the man in the bed with pleasure. 'John Dee,' he said, awe in his voice. 'John Dee.'

Dee waited to see if he was going to add anything more challenging. When he did not, Dee said, 'I do remember your father. For all that he told tales not of my present doings but of events from the past' – there was a faint sparkle of humour in his eyes – 'I did not hold it against him. A good man, Geoffroi d'Acquin.' The humour vanished, to be replaced by a sharp, calculating look. 'He lives still?'

'No.' Josse shook his head. 'He died – oh, all of sixteen years ago, now. Back in '76.'

'Ah, yes.'

Staring at Dee, Josse had the strange sensation that he had known all along that Geoffroi was dead.

Why, then, ask?

As if to distract him from that vaguely disturbing thought, Dee was speaking, a hypnotic note in his voice that, against his will, instantly grabbed Josse's attention. 'Ah, what sorrow that was,' he murmured, 'for a man of but fifty summers to die, cut down, like the Corn King, with the harvest.'

'Aye,' Josse said softly, remembering. 'That he was. We—' But then his head shot up as, with a shiver down his back, he stared at Dee. 'How did *you* know?' he demanded. 'I never mentioned that he died in the summer!'

But Dee was speaking again, the soft, lulling note stronger now; Josse, knowing himself to be disturbed over something but unable, for the life of him, to remember what it was, had no choice but to be quiet and listen.

'His death was inscribed on the fabric of the past, present and future, as are those of us all,' Dee whispered. 'It is but as a book, to we who learn how to read it. Your father's time came, and he was taken.'

'Aye,' breathed Josse. He felt as if he were dreaming, yet, at the same time, still awake. Awake sufficiently, anyway, to be aware of the smell of the herbs on the fire. The soft, comfortable padding of the stool beneath his buttocks.

Dee's strange voice.

'Your father's death is the reason,' Dee continued. 'The reason why I tell you that the stranger must come to you.'

'Nobody has come!' Josse protested; the effort of speech was hard, and he felt as if he were pushing his words out through thick, muffling cloth.

Dee, appearing briefly surprised – was he not used to people answering him back when he held them in thrall? – made a smoothing, soothing gesture with his right hand. It wore, Josse noticed, a large, pale blue-green stone; in his head a distant voice said, *aquamarine. The Seer's stone.*

And the right hand, he recalled as if from nowhere, was the power hand . . .

Either the hand gesture or the ring – or both – worked on Josse as, presumably, Dee had intended. Mute, receptive, he sat waiting for what would happen next.

'I say again,' Dee murmured, 'the stranger will come to you. Possibly not he himself – the picture is unclear – but one who comes from him.'

'But—' It was no use; whatever skill or power Dee was using was now too strong for Josse to fight.

'He will come,' Dee said, waving his hand again. 'Only wait, and he will come.'

Josse felt his eyelids grow heavy. His head went down, chin tucked into his chest, and he saw darkness bloom before him. Then – he had no idea how long afterwards – he gave a sudden snort-like snore, and woke himself up.

He sat up straight, rubbed his eyes and stared at Dee, who was watching him with amused eyes.

'The herbs on my fire aid my breathing,' Dee said, in a matter-of-fact voice. 'But, to those unused to their smoke, they can induce sleep. I apologise, Sir Josse, for having caused you the embarrassment of nodding off when your intention was to cheer a sick man by your visit.'

Josse, horribly confused, said, 'Aye. No. Sorry, sir.' Standing up, he managed to knock the stool over, and he tripped up over one of its legs as he lunged for the door. 'Goodbye, Magister,' he added.

'Farewell, Josse d'Acquin! Go in safety!'

Dee's valediction was – there was no mistaking it – accompanied by rich, happy, slightly mocking laughter.

5

Josse was back at Hawkenlye long before the Abbess would have expected. As Sister Ursel brought her the news of his return, she was filled with a sense of foreboding; whatever he had found out, she thought, it could surely not have been the identity of the body in the new grave.

It was late – too late for an audience, for the nuns were retiring for the night – so Helewise sent word back to Josse that she was glad for his safe return, wished him sound sleep and a restful night, and that she would see him in the morning.

The fact that, all night, she burned with anxiety to know what he had found out was, she told herself firmly, another small penance for the sin of having neglected a dead body for six weeks.

She received Josse after Tierce. She had been awake for hours, but word came from the Vale that Josse slept on, and she ordered that he should not be disturbed. When, at last, he stood before her, she could tell from his face that his mission had not achieved the result they had both hoped for.

'The Prince had gone,' he told her, after carefully closing the door against eavesdroppers, 'but one of his party remained behind. He's sick in bed with a bad cold. He told me that Galbertius Sidonius is not a young man.'

'Oh. I see.' It was only when she knew for certain that the dead man had not just been tentatively identified that she realised how much she longed to give him a name. 'There is no doubt?'

'Absolutely none. The Magister — that's what they all call him, although his name is John Dee — is as sharp as they come. We can take his word for it, my lady.'

'Oh.' She could not think of anything else to say.

Josse stood before her, brows knotted in a ferocious frown of concentration. 'I wish I could have come back with something positive,' he muttered, 'instead of presenting us with another blank stone wall. I—'

He was interrupted by a soft tap-tapping on the door. Helewise, startled, said, 'come in!' and, as the door was slowly opened, the lined, old face of Brother Firmin appeared in the gap like a tortoise poking its head out of its shell.

'My lady Abbess,' the old monk said, making a low and very formal reverence.

'Brother Firmin,' she replied. She restrained her impatience as he went through his usual litany of opening remarks — was she well? what a fine day it was, thank the Good Lord; how gracious it was of her to spare him a moment of her precious time, and he would be brief, he promised her.

When he had finished, she said, forcing a smile, 'What can I do for you, Brother Firmin?'

'Eh? Oh, well, it's not really me so much as him.' He

jerked his head towards the half-open door. 'May I tell him to step into your presence, my lady Abbess?'

'Yes, please do.'

She did not have to wonder for long who 'him' might be; as soon as the old monk began to say, 'You can come in, Brother Augustus,' he was there before her table, and his bow was as deep and reverential as even Brother Firmin could have wished.

'Brother Augustus.' She could not keep the affection out of her voice. 'You wished to speak to me?'

'Aye. There's something I've thought of.' The young man shot a swift and apprehensive glance at Brother Firmin, who was watching him with a slightly accusing expression, as if he felt the youth should not be wasting his Abbess's time. 'I've been thinking, and—'

Helewise held up her hand and, instantly, Augustus fell silent. She turned to the old monk. 'Brother Firmin, I know that you love to pray in the Abbey church by yourself but that you rarely have the chance, so busy are you down in the Vale. But I believe there are few people within at present; would you care to take this opportunity for some private worship?'

The old man's eyes lit up, and she had a stab of self-reproof at her duplicity. 'May I really?' he whispered. She nodded. With another deep reverence, he was gone.

She turned back to Augustus, who was smiling his gratitude. 'Now, Brother Augustus,' she said. 'Will it be easier to tell just Sir Josse here and myself?'

'Aye, and thank you.' He shot Josse a friendly grin then, taking a deep breath, said, 'I woke early this morning, like you do when something's niggling at you. I lay there, trying to think of nothing in particular and let the thought come to me in its own time, and eventually it did.' He met her eyes and said, 'Sorry. I'm being as long-winded as my dear esteemed Brother Firmin. Oh! Sorry!' He blushed, apparently instantly ashamed of the mild criticism.

'It's all right, Augustus,' Helewise said. 'Please, go on.'

'It just came to me, all of a sudden, and I thought, why are we all thinking the dead man was killed in the Vale? Is it not possible that the murder was done somewhere else, the body stripped and all, and *then* the killer put him in the bracken? I mean, if it was at night, and the murderer didn't know the shrine and the shelter and that were there, he might have believed he was concealing the poor dead soul in a hiding place right out in the wilds, where he would *never* be found.'

'But surely everybody knows about Hawkenlye Abbey,' Josse said.

Augustus turned to him. 'Not strangers,' he said. 'Foreigners, like. Why should they?'

'We receive many foreign pilgrims, Augustus,' Helewise put in gently.

'Aye,' Josse agreed. 'Why, Augustus, don't you remember? Brother Erse was talking of someone who he claimed was a foreigner – who was it, now?' He made a circling movement with his hand, as if this would somehow magic the memory out of the air.

'He meant the young servant who came with the old man who died,' Augustus said. 'And yes, before either of you says it, I know. He was foreign, or at least according to Erse he was, and *he* knew about the Shrine and the Abbey.'

'But Augustus may still quite well be right,' Helewise put in. She could see the disappointment in the eager, intelligent young face. 'Just because one supposed foreigner knows of our existence, it would be supreme folly to assume that we are known to every single one.'

'That's what I was getting at, Abbess Helewise!' Augustus cried. 'I mean, maybe I shouldn't speak of it, not here in the Abbey, but' – his voice dropped to a whisper, as if he did not want to hurt God's feelings – 'not every foreigner is a *Christian*!'

'No indeed,' she agreed, 'and – Sir Josse? What ails you?' Josse's face had creased into such a scowl of concentration that it almost looked as if he were in pain.

'Nothing, nothing.' He waved a dismissive hand. 'It's just that I've just had one of those moments that young Augustus was describing, when you know there's something worrying at the back of your mind and you can't think what it is, or why it's important . . .' He trailed off, still frowning. 'Never mind. It'll come, in its own good time.'

'Try going through the names and ages of all your relations,' Augustus advised. 'That's what I did, and when I got to my mother's Auntie Meg's husband's mother, who claims to be a hundred, though nobody believes her, I remembered what I was trying to bring to mind.'

Josse chuckled and, reaching out, ruffled the boy's hair. 'Happen I don't have as many relatives as you, lad,' he said. Then, after a moment, 'I don't know, though.'

Helewise looked from one to the other, affected by their ease in one another's company. They were almost like father and son. It crossed her mind to wonder briefly why Josse had no family; no sensible, affectionate wife, and no son to follow in his footsteps.

Then she remembered something. Something she was trying very hard to forget. No, she told herself firmly. Do not dwell on Joanna de Courtenay, and of what may or may not have passed between her and Josse. You do not know for certain, and it is none of your business.

But, despite herself, she thought: February, it was, when Joanna was hiding out in the Forest. And now it is nearly October. If Sister Euphemia was right . . .

No.

Firmly putting the speculation from her, she turned her attention back to Josse and Augustus, who were laughing helplessly at something Josse had said about his sister-in-law's mother. Helewise cleared her throat and both men jumped; Josse, looking abashed, said quickly, 'Ah, but I should not make fun at her expense, she means well, I dare say, although—'

There was another tap on the door. Wondering if it might be Brother Firmin, cutting short his prayers for some reason of his own, again Helewise called out, 'Come in.'

It was not Brother Firmin but Sister Anne.

Round eyes alight with the fascinated interest of someone whose daily round did not include very much excitement or even variety – Sister Anne, none too bright but well-meaning, scrubbed pots in the refectory – the nun said, 'Ooh, Abbess Helewise, Sister Ursel sent me, she's busy attending to the man's horse and didn't want to leave him, not that there's anything amiss but—'

'Sister Anne?' Helewise prompted.

'Yes, sorry.' Sister Anne shot at Josse a glance that, in any other woman, might have been called flirtatious. Then: 'It's another man called d'Acquin, see. Just like Sir Josse here, only this one's a bit smaller and a bit younger and he says his name is Yves.'

The Abbess, to Josse's relief, took the startling announcement in her stride. She must have noticed his amazement – hardly surprising; he felt as if his jaw had dropped at least to his knees – and she said calmly, 'Sir Josse, what an honour for us to receive a visit from your brother! Let us go out straight away to greet him.'

He and Augustus stood back to let her precede them out of the room, Sister Anne bobbing along beside them like a rowing boat attending a sailing ship. Watching the Abbess's straight-backed figure gliding along just ahead of him enabled him to regain something of his composure so that, by the time they were approaching the little group at the gate – Sister Ursel, Sister Martha, Yves's bay and, naturally, Yves himself – Josse was ready – eager – to rush forward and take his brother in his arms.

'Yves, Yves!' he said against the warm and slightly sweaty skin of his brother's neck; he must have been riding hard, for the bay, too, was lathered. 'How good it is to see you!'

Straightening up and pulling away slightly, he held Yves by the shoulders and studied him. His brother's pleasant face was beaming his delight, which, Josse fervently hoped, suggested that, whatever had brought him to England to seek out his elder brother, it was nothing too terrible.

'Josse, you look good!' Yves was saying, slapping Josse on the arm. 'This English country life must suit you!'

'Aye, it does.'

'They told me at New Winnowlands where I might find you and, after they'd put me up for the night – she's a good cook, that serving woman of yours, isn't she? – they gave me directions and saw me on to the right road.' Another grin. 'Ah, dear God, but it's good to see you!'

Josse, suddenly remembering where they were, took a step back. 'Yves,' he said, 'a moment, please.' Turning to the Abbess, he said, 'Abbess Helewise, may I present to you my younger brother, Yves d'Acquin? Yves, this is Abbess Helewise of Hawkenlye Abbey.'

Yves bowed deeply. 'My lady Abbess, it is a great honour at last to greet the woman we at Acquin have heard so much about,' he said gravely. 'I am your servant.' He bowed again.

Josse, observing the Abbess, hoped that she would not find Yves's manner rather overcourtly; he does not know, he fretted, that she is a plain-speaking, down to earth woman, even if she *is* an abbess . . .

He need not have worried. The Abbess, smiling, was clearly unperturbed by Yves's display of Gallic charm; she was asking him the usual questions that one asked a new arrival, about his journey, were the family well and so forth, clearly at her ease.

That particular small concern out of the way, Josse thought, but why is he here?

The Abbess, bless her, must have read his mind. Turning to him, she said, 'Sir Josse, your brother will, I am sure, desire to speak to you in private. You may take him to my room, if you wish, and I will send refreshments.'

Josse looked at Yves, who nodded swiftly. 'Aye, then, Abbess Helewise,' Josse said, 'if you are sure we shall not put you out?'

'Not in the least,' she said smoothly, 'I am expected over in the infirmary.'

With a silent but steely look around at the various members of her community – Sister Martha, Sister Ursel, the wide-eyed Sister Anne and Brother Augustus – the Abbess dismissed them back to their duties.

And Josse took his brother's arm and led him across to the cloisters and along to the Abbess's room.

'Now then, what has brought you all the way across the Channel to see me?' Josse asked him as soon as the door was closed behind them. 'Is anyone sick? Is there trouble at Acquin?'

'No, everyone is well, thank the good Lord' – 'Amen,' Josse said fervently – 'and the estates run smoothly. We had an excellent harvest this year, Josse, we've got it all in now and we shall do well this winter, us and the animals, although we'll be putting plenty of meat down to salt come Martinmas to see us through the lean times, and—'

'Yves,' Josse reprimanded him. 'I may know very little of farming, but even I know about that.'

'Of course. I apologise, Josse, you must be keen to know my news.'

'Keen,' Josse murmured, 'is an understatement.'

Yves leaned forward – Josse had shown him to the Abbess's throne-like chair; it seemed, he thought ruefully, that he was forever destined to perch on the uncomfortable and insubstantial little stool – and said, 'Josse, we had a visitor.'

'A visitor?' Surely, not such a rare occurrence.

'Aye. He came looking for Father. He was dressed simply and he had but the one lad with him, yet there was something about him, some air that suggested he might not be the poor man he posed as. He said, "I come from far afield in search of one Geoffroi d'Acquin, and I have at last made my way here to Acquin." Well, we told him straight away that Father was dead – Mother, too, though he did not in fact ask after her – and then he said to me, "You are his heir." So then I said no, I was the second son, the eldest was Josse – you, that is – and the man said, "Where, then, is this Sir Josse?"'

'And you said I had a manor in England, aye?' Josse, impatient, wished Yves were not quite such a long-winded teller of tales.

'Aye, that I did. So then this fellow said, "To England I must go," and, even though we offered to put him up for a while – he didn't look too well and he had a nasty, hacking cough – he wouldn't hear of it. He kept saying, "I have already left it too late, I fear. I have missed Sir Geoffroi, and this I must bear as best I may." So Marie gave him some of her green liniment to rub on his chest – you know, that stuff that stings like the Devil's prongs and makes your eyes water? You once said you preferred the cough – and we gave the two of them, the man and his lad, a hearty meal and some good, red wine.'

'And then?'

'Then they left. Patrice and my Luke rode with them

some of the way and reported back that, when last seen, the old fellow and the boy were stepping out strongly on the road to Calais.'

Josse was thinking very hard. About an elderly man who had died in early August in Hawkenlye Vale. Who had had a bad cough, and been attended by a youth. A foreigner.

Abruptly he said to Yves, 'When was this? When did the old man arrive at Acquin?'

Yves shifted uncomfortably in his chair. 'You'll not like to hear this.'

'Go on.' Josse's tone was relentless.

'It was back in July. Round about the middle of the month, maybe later. Oh, I'm that sorry, Josse, I know full well I should have come to tell you sooner – after all, we had no idea what he wanted with you and, for all I know, he could have meant you harm. But, you see, we were just beginning on the harvest and then, early in August, we had a week of storms – terrible, they were, rain like you never saw – and it put us back. Then there was a deal of pumping-out to do – the Aa overflowed her banks here and there and some of our lower pastures were flooded, too, and we had to—'

'It's all right, Yves.' Josse got up and went to put a hand on his brother's shoulder. 'I understand. There are great demands made on the farmer, I am aware of that well enough, even if I don't fully know what they all are.'

'Please don't think that I am complaining,' Yves said earnestly. 'I love the life, love Acquin like my own life's blood. I'm only glad that—' He broke off abruptly, looking confused and slightly embarrassed.

'Glad that your elder brother decided he was a military

man and not a farmer?' Josse supplied, with a laugh. 'Yves, my dear brother, if you are glad, so am I, to have someone not only capable and willing but *eager* to take on Acquin and all its dependants and responsibilities.' He hesitated. He was reluctant to embarrass his brother further, but some things needed saying, and he did not get the chance very often.

'You do a fine job with our family estates,' he said quietly, after a pause to collect his thoughts. 'I do not come home near as often as I should, but, whenever I do, it is to find everything running smoothly and efficiently, a happy, healthy family in residence and, in our lands all around, what appears to me to be a contented and prosperous population of peasants.'

Yves, red in the face, muttered something about having a deal of help from Patrice, Honoré and Acelin, but Josse knew full well that the younger brothers were followers, Yves the leader.

After himself, that was.

And, as he had just said, he did not go home nearly as often as he should.

Changing the subject – which, he thought, would come as a relief to them both – Josse said, 'Did the old man say anything else? How he had come to know our father, for instance?'

Yves shook his head. 'No. We pressed him, well, as far as politeness allowed, but he would say nothing of his mission. He kept repeating, "I must keep faith with my friend. It is too late for him, so I must find his eldest son and present myself to him instead." He didn't seem like a threat really, Josse, in truth he didn't. If we'd felt that he was dangerous, we should not have told him where to find you.'

'I know that well enough, Yves. Do not punish yourself.' Josse walked across the room and back, thinking. Then: 'In any case, even if he did intend harm, it is too late.'

'Too late?'

'Aye. If your old man is the man I am thinking of, then he's dead. He came here. His cough must have got worse, for he wanted to take the healing Holy Waters administered by the Hawkenlye monks down in the Vale. Only he left it too late. During the night before he was due to take the cure, he died.'

Yves crossed himself. 'God rest his soul,' he said quietly.

'Amen.'

'He seemed a decent enough type,' Yves mused. 'And you have to admire an old man who takes a long journey to keep faith, whatever that meant, with a friend from the past.' He sighed.

Josse said cautiously, 'A long journey?'

'Yes. He'd come up from Lombardy. Or was it Liguria? Somewhere foreign, anyway.'

Foreign. There was that word again.

'I don't suppose,' Josse said, his heart thumping, 'that your old man supplied a name?'

'Oh, yes,' Yves said easily. 'Didn't I say? Well, he didn't actually supply it – he was rather cagey, if I remember rightly. But I overheard that lad of his one day – he was in a right bother, looked nervous and edgy, as if he'd done something bad and was waiting to feel the weight of his master's wrath. Anyway, he was muttering something about keeping out of the old man's way – at

least, that's what I thought – and he referred to him
by name.'

'And?' Josse fought to retain his patience.

'He was called Galbertius Sidonius. Strange name, isn't
it? See, I said he was foreign!'

They had, Josse thought, deprived the Abbess of her room
for long enough. Still stunned by Yves's revelation, Josse
led his brother across to the infirmary, where they found
the Abbess in conversation with the infirmarer, to whom
Josse presented his brother.

'We have much to talk about, my brother and I,' Josse
muttered to the Abbess. He told her about Yves's old man
and, more crucially, his identity, and the Abbess's eyes
widened.

'I see what you mean,' she murmured back. 'Will you
not make use of my room to untangle this maze, if
you can?'

'Thank you but no, my lady. We will find a quiet
corner in the accommodation down in the Vale where
we can talk all night, if we need to, without feeling that
we disturb you.'

'And where, with luck, you yourselves will not be disturbed,' she added shrewdly. 'You have told your brother
of your royal visitor?' She was whispering so softly now
that he could hardly make out the words. 'And of your
interview with John Dee?'

'No, not yet. But I shall.' He added grimly, 'I have the
strong sense that it will require every scrap of knowledge,
and more intelligence than I fear Yves and I possess, to
solve this mystery.'

She shook her head. 'Sir Josse, do not predict defeat before you have even begun!' she admonished him. 'I have faith in you, and I shall pray that God guides you towards illumination.' Briefly she pressed a hand on his arm, and he was grateful for her touch. 'Now, if you will excuse me, Sister Euphemia awaits.'

'Of course. Please.' He bowed and, catching Yves's eye, led him out of the infirmary.

Down in the Vale, he told Brother Saul what he required and Saul, after a moment's reflection, provided it. Soon Josse and Yves were settled in a draught-free corner, screened from curious eyes by a few sheep-hurdles, with adequate bedrolls to lie on and a small fire to cheer them. Since dusk was beginning to fall, it also provided them with some welcome light.

When Saul's quiet footsteps had faded, Josse told Yves of Prince John's visit to New Winnowlands, of the dead man found in the bracken, of his trip to see John Dee and everything else that he could think of that might have the remotest relevance.

When he had finished, Yves was silent for so long that Josse was beginning to think he had gone to sleep. But then he said, with a deep sigh, 'Josse, this is all very well.'

'What is?'

'This wealth of detail with which you have just assailed me.' Josse heard the smile in his brother's voice.

'But?' Josse was quite sure there would be a 'but'.

'But it's not the place to start,' Yves said firmly. 'This mystery begins, if we think about it logically and in sequence, with Galbertius Sidonius deciding he must come to see Father. I would guess, in retrospect, that Galbertius knew he was dying, and wanted to make his peace – what was his expression? Keep faith, yes – with Father before it was too late.'

'He and Father must have been friends, then, long ago,' Josse said. 'Do you recall the name, Yves?'

'No.'

'Neither do I. Not a very good or close friend, then, else surely he would have visited Acquin, got to know Father's wife and family.'

'You speak sense,' Yves agreed.

Sense it might be, Josse thought as the silence extended. But it serves our purpose not at all.

He said cautiously, 'Perhaps there is another way into this maze. Perhaps, Yves, we should look at it from Father's point of view. Could we not remind ourselves of his life – what he did, whom he knew, that sort of thing – and see whether any sudden shaft of light comes to aid us?'

'Would that help?' Yves sounded dubious.

'Well, it can't hurt.' Josse leaned on one elbow and looked across at Yves, on the other side of the little fire. He looked in that moment so like his father that Josse's heart gave a lurch; they had all loved Geoffroi dearly and Josse, for one, still missed him; the death of a beloved father left a hole that could never really be filled. 'Would it not be a rare treat,' he added slyly, after a moment, 'to lie here in the soft darkness and, with our memories and our love, conjure up our father?'

There was the faint sound of a sniff, then Yves said, somewhat shakily, 'Aye, Josse. It would.'

PART TWO

Outremer, Summer 1148

'God has instituted in our time holy wars, so that the order of knights and the crowd running in its wake may find a new way of gaining salvation.'

Guibert of Rogent

6

---◆◆◆---

Geoffroi d'Acquin, twenty-two years old, healthy and strong, sang lustily along with the other soldiers as they rode out of Antioch on the long road south to Jerusalem. Many of the soldiers were old campaigners, and were putting their own lewd words to the familiar tune; Geoffroi, who had picked these up months ago, sang them too, laughing as he did so with the sheer joy of being young, fit, mounted on a fine horse and riding to war.

Geoffroi knew, almost as soon as he knew anything, that he was going to be a soldier. His first sword had been a small bolt of wood; not very large but heavy enough to lay open his elder brother's head when Robert failed to duck out of the way in time. The three-year-old Geoffroi had received a beating – not a severe one, for his parents did not believe that the right way to discipline children was to thrash obedience into them – and, far more painfully, he had been deprived of both his little sword and his hobby horse for a whole week.

Geoffroi would say as he grew up that he had ridden before he walked, although this was a slight exaggeration; the riding in question had been sitting in front of his father on the great bay, Heracles, his shrill, ten-month-old voice screaming with a mixture of excitement and terror. By the time he was five, he was looking after his own pony (with the discreet help of a kindly groom) and was, as his mother used to remark, too fearless for his own good.

Geoffroi had always understood that it was Robert, his elder by three crucial years, who was the heir to the Acquin estates. His parents, Sir Robert and the lady Matilda, encouraged their second son in his military ambitions; Robert was more than capable of inheriting the responsibilities of the landlord's role, in due course, and it would be better to have his closest sibling and natural childhood rival out of the way when he did so. Besides, there were other children to stay at Acquin and augment its population; there was Esmai, three years Geoffroi's junior, and the youngest child, William. Born after a gap of six years, he was the baby of the family and its pet.

When Geoffroi was seven, he went away from the family home at Acquin to do his service as a page in the household of one of his father's oldest friends. Sir Girald, a vassal of Geoffrey Plantagenet of Anjou, was a tough master and, despite his affection for the boy, he showed him no leniency. Geoffroi learned his craft the hard way. In time, and still in Sir Girald's household, he became a squire; impatient, restless, Geoffroi waited for the chance to put all the skills that he had acquired over the last ten years into practice.

He did not have too long to wait. In 1145, when he was nineteen, he was sent with a detachment of Sir Girald's fighting men to join the retinue of the young Henry FitzEmpress. Henry, the son of Geoffrey Plantagenet and his wife, the Empress Matilda of England, was, through his mother's line, grandson of Henry I of England. His father had been invested the previous year with the ducal crown of Normandy by his overlord, Louis VII of France. Henry, although still but twelve years old, was already showing strong signs that he would follow in his father's ambitious and energetic footsteps – Geoffrey's acquisition of Normandy had been by conquest – and the excitement, daring and ambition of the Plantagenet court suited Geoffroi down to the ground.

He won his spurs in the autumn of 1145.

The timing was perfect.

For the past year, worrying news had been reaching Western Europe from the east. Fifty years ago, the First Crusade had succeeded in wresting the Holy Places of Outremer from the Turks; the four crusader states had then been established, the most important being the kingdom of Jerusalem. In the winter of 1144, however, the city of Edessa, capital of the first crusader state, fell to the Saracens under the command of Zengi, governor of Aleppo and Mosul. Although Zengi did not live to enjoy the fruits of his conquest for long – he died in the following September, assassinated, so they said, by a slave – he was succeeded by his son, Nureddin, whose reputation as a cruel fighter preceded him. A religious fanatic, he made it no secret that he would not rest until he had brought about a full Moslem reconquest of the Holy Land.

The crusader states, hard pressed, sent increasingly desperate pleas for help and, in December of 1145, the new Pope, Eugenius III, responded.

The Pope delegated the great Bernard of Clairvaux

to preach the new crusade. At Vézelay, over the Easter celebrations of 1146, his passionate address moved thousands; led by King Louis of France and his Queen, Eleanor of Aquitaine, men and women of all stations in life raced to follow their example and take the cross. Such was the demand that the supply of cloth crosses ran out and Bernard had to tear up part of his habit to make more.

Among the enthusiastic press of people, his face alight with a mixture of religious devotion (Bernard of Clairvaux was a charismatic speaker) and sheer high spirits, went the new knight, Sir Geoffroi d'Acquin.

Preparations for the great enterprise took a full year. While the King and Queen taxed their subjects until they squeaked and churches rushed to proffer their treasures, ordinary knights such as Geoffroi hurried home to see how many debts could be called in, and just how much could be sold or bartered, in order that they should set out fully equipped. A good horse, armour and weapons did not come cheap; that his family would have to tighten their belts and make sacrifices, Geoffroi well knew. However, knowing them as he did – as he *hoped* he did – he also knew that, in this most vital of the services that Christendom rendered unto God, they would do so willingly and give him their wholehearted support. They would also – he did not even have to ask – pray for him constantly.

The vast crusading army – royalty, lords and ladies, noblemen, knights, crossbowmen, foot soldiers, siege engineers, craftsmen, clerics, nurses, cooks, camp followers and general hangers-on, numbering some 100,000 people in all – finally set out from Paris in June 1147. They met up with the Emperor Conrad of Germany in the city of Metz, and the two armies then proceeded by separate routes eastwards and southwards. Geoffroi, marching with the French, travelled down through Bavaria to the Danube, which they followed through Hungary and Bulgaria.

By October they had reached Constantinople. After their long trek down across the continent, the armies were ready for a rest and might have stayed longer – despite the fact that their welcome was swiftly running out – had it not been for an eclipse of the sun in the fourth week of the month. Before the army's confidence and resolve could be undermined by the swiftly-spreading rumours that this was a bad omen and meant the crusade was doomed, Louis ordered that they strike camp and march on south.

The evil fortune that so many felt to have been predicted by the eclipse was not long in striking. A disobeyed order in the desolate, windswept hinterland of Turkey laid the great army open to attack; the Turks ambushed the crusaders in a narrow pass and slaughtered thousands. The shocked crusaders regrouped and made for the coast, where, after enduring terrible conditions, plague and near-starvation, those who were left finally took ship for the Holy Land.

The malign influence of the eclipse's curse had not yet finished with them. Storms and tempests beat down on the fleet of ships, many of which foundered; some of those who landed safely had spent almost a month at sea, for the relatively short and normally calm crossing from Anatolia to Antioch.

Geoffroi, recovering in a hastily-erected hospital tent from the combined effects of diarrhoea (the drinking water on board had been foul), severe dehydration (it had run out three days before they reached Antioch) and a cut on the temple (someone had dropped a barrel on him as the ship tied up), felt that the ten-month journey from the north had aged him ten years. At the least.

He recovered swiftly, however. After little more than a week, he felt totally well again. Moreover, like the rest of the gallant remainder of the army that had set out so jubilantly and optimistically from Paris all those months and miles ago, he was eager to press on. So many had died – by enemy action, accident, of sickness, injury, plague, and by drowning – and so many had simply run out of food and money and given up. You could not, Geoffroi thought charitably, blame a man for his failure of courage; the circumstances had, far too often, been so frightful that it was surely amazing that more had not become disheartened and fallen by the wayside.

He went to give thanks to God that he had not been one of them. Praying, his eyes on the tormented figure on the cross that stood on the altar before him, his heart was filled with love and pity. His Redeemer had suffered far more than any of the crusaders, Geoffroi reflected; surely they could bear their own small echo of his pain, in this great enterprise to secure the Holy Places. 'For Thee, dear Lord,' Geoffroi murmured, 'it is all for Thee.'

Closing his eyes and bowing his head, he prayed, with renewed fervour, that he be given the strength and the courage to do God's will.

The next day, the army left Antioch and set out south-wards for Jerusalem.

'They say that the King and Queen are at odds again.' The speaker was an English knight, rather older than

Geoffroi; tall, broad in the shoulder and thickset, his rich auburn hair shone in the hot spring sunshine of Outremer. 'Hardly to be wondered at, when she has been making eyes at her Uncle Raymond throughout these days we've been in Antioch.'

Geoffroi grinned. '*They say*, Herbert,' he said. 'Who have you been talking to? The washerwomen?'

Herbert of Lewes laughed. 'It is not only washerwomen who gossip,' he replied. Urging his horse closer, he dropped his voice and went on, 'She tires of him, they say. No wonder she made moon-eyes at Raymond; even if he is her uncle, he's strong and handsome, and a deal more virile, I'd guess, than your precious, pious Louis.' Belatedly remembering that he was addressing one of Louis's subjects, even if Geoffroi had become a friend, he added, 'Piety is, naturally, greatly to be prized, and I—'

'Enough, Herbert,' Geoffroi said good-naturedly. 'I have not taken offence, so there is no need to talk yourself into further difficulties.'

Apparently feeling himself forgiven, Herbert plunged on. 'She was woken at midnight, you know. They burst into her chamber, shooed out her maids and bundled her up in a blanket! Carried her out to a covered litter and hurried her away before Raymond knew aught about it!' Another rich chuckle. 'No fond farewells *there*, you can be sure!'

They rode on, Herbert keeping up a steady flow of chatter, most of it increasingly wild speculation about King Louis and his Queen. They no longer shared a bed. She wanted to divorce him, claiming they were really cousins and should never have married in the first place.

The King's preference for prayer over the pleasures of his marriage bed meant he could now no longer satisfy any woman, and especially not the alluring, hot-blooded Queen Eleanor. She was going to run away, back to Antioch, marry Raymond and rule beside him.

Geoffroi, the hot sun on his back and the stark, dramatic countryside of the coastal strip unfolding vividly before his enchanted eyes, stopped listening.

Herbert was a good sort, he reflected, but, by the blessed Holy Mother, how he did go on! They had met when both were being treated following the terrible voyage from Anatolia. The meagre food supplies – dry, starchy stuff and little of it – and the lack of water had combined to make Herbert very constipated, and the poor man had been suffering dreadfully from piles. Side by side in the hospital tent, Geoffroi's bowels turned to water and Herbert's to stone, they had – eventually, when they began to recover – seen the funny side of it. With nothing to do all day but moan and talk to each other, they had become friends. Herbert had even done Geoffroi the great honour of telling him all about his family back home in England, including (and in particular) his favourite, his beautiful daughter Ida: 'Hair the colour of autumn leaves, eyes like the midsummer sky, and a tiny little waist that you could encircle with your two hands'. Now, although they rode with different contingents, often they sought one another out.

'. . . it's likely, they're saying, that she'll keep her head down now.' Herbert, craning round to look into Geoffroi's face, said accusingly, 'You've not been listening to a word I've said!'

'Yes I have.' Geoffroi gave a guilty start. 'The Queen has eyes for her uncle and Louis no longer goes to her bed. And – er—'

Herbert gave him a friendly shove that almost unseated him. 'Go on with you! I'll warrant you were thinking of the fighting ahead, eh?'

'No, I—'

But Herbert was not to be robbed of the picture he was forming, of an eager young knight ablaze with ardour for the coming battles. As he set off on another favourite tack – the glory of the fight for God's Holy Places – Geoffroi went back to his calm contemplation of the scenery.

The march from Antioch to Jerusalem took over a month. As the army neared the Holy City, fatigue, illness, home-sickness and injury were all forgotten as a sort of collective ecstasy overcame the crusaders. When, at long last, they finally had their first sight of the walls of Jerusalem, still far off but shining in the bright light like a beacon to welcome them, many were totally overcome.

We are so close now, Geoffroi thought as, with his comrades, he knelt in prayer that night. Although not entirely certain what action he would see – Jerusalem was safely in Frankish hands, it seemed, and there would surely be no call to fight there – he knew that he *would* go into battle, sooner or later. His fingers found and stroked the crusader's cross sewn on to the shoulder of his tunic. Worn now, fraying a little at the edges despite his mother's tiny, careful stitches, he would wear it, he knew, until the vow he had made as he received it was fulfilled.

He recalled the words that had been spoken on that

unforgettable day. The crusaders, Bernard of Clairvaux had informed them, were uniquely fortunate in being given this opportunity for salvation. God was doing them the supreme favour of *pretending* to need their service to win back his Holy Kingdom whereas, in fact, his true motive was to allow the crusaders to fight for him so as to be able to bestow upon them remission of their sins and everlasting glory.

Geoffroi was not at all sure he had understood that line of reasoning at the time. He was even less sure now. But he told himself it didn't matter; God had called, he had answered, and now here he was, prepared to do whatever he was told, prepared to give his very life, if it were to be called for, to win back God's earthly realm. The fact that this supreme act of penance would, or so they promised, absolve him from all his sins – both those he was aware of committing and those he wasn't – was a sort of ongoing, perpetual reassurance. A comfort. No, he thought, struggling to put his profound emotion into words, more than that. A—

But at that moment the officiating priest raised his voice and literally cried out to heaven, and Geoffroi, swept along on the huge tide of emotion, had no more time for private thoughts.

After that night there was a long period of inactivity. The sense of anticlimax was great; as Herbert remarked, they had come all that way and suffered so much to see Jerusalem at last, only to find themselves camped in a field with nothing to occupy them, kicking their heels while endless councils and conferences decided what to do next.

There was discord among the leaders of the crusade, that

much was well known. Queen Eleanor's Uncle Raymond had declared he wanted no further part in the proceedings, which, Herbert observed, was hardly surprising, all things considered. And the Count of Tripoli, 'so they said', had been accused of trying to poison a fellow count and had gone off in a huff.

'You see, your King Louis,' Herbert pontificated, 'devout and pious soul that he is – and he *is*, we all know that! – isn't what you might call a political man. Is he, now?' Geoffroi, to whom these remarks were addressed, agreed that no, he wasn't.

'See,' Herbert went on, 'there's so much happening under the surface, as you might say, that a straight-thinking, simple-minded, God-fearing man like Louis just doesn't comprehend. Which is all to his credit!' he added hurriedly, in case Geoffroi might be taking offence. 'See, there's so much intrigue and political manoeuvring going on and, besides, many of our precious leaders seem more interested in what they're going to get out of the whole business than what they may or may not be called upon to do for God. And – listen to this! – some of these Outremer Franks, these very people whose appeal for help we've come all this way to answer, don't seem to want us here! We're interfering, so they say, and poking our noses in where we're not wanted.' Indignation soared through him and he said furiously, 'Imagine that!'

'What are we going to do?' Geoffroi asked.

'Do?' Herbert repeated. Then, with a shrug, 'I don't know, lad. Wait for our orders, same as always, and then obey them.'

*   *   *

The orders, when at last they came, seemed at first incomprehensible. The vast crusading army, which had come so far at such great cost, was to attack Damascus.

'But I thought Damascus was a friend, not a foe!' Geoffroi said when the ever-reliable Herbert brought the news.

'Friend or foe, that's what we're to do,' Herbert repeated. Then he fell into an uncharacteristic silence.

'But you don't make war on your allies, not—' Geoffroi began, eventually frightened into making some comment.

Herbert glowered at him. 'Not for us to question our orders, lad,' he said starkly. Then, relenting slightly, 'I reckon it's those Templars that are behind this. They've been in secret conference with the Emperor Conrad, or so I've heard, and this – this assault on Damascus – is the result. It'll be strategy, you mark my words. Strategy.' The last word was almost spat out.

Geoffroi, not understanding, hoping for the best and praying for the courage to face what he must face, had no answer.

The next day, they marched off to attack the Turkish emirate of Damascus.

7

The short-lived and ill-conceived assault on Damascus was a fiasco.

Not that Geoffroi and his fellow knights could know that as, in late July, they approached the city and prepared for battle. Taking communion that morning, after humbly confessing his sins, Geoffroi had prayed for the success of the engagement.

Then, in an action which swiftly turned from an ordered attack into a rout, he rode into battle.

Beside the crusading army rode contingents of Frankish settlers but, even with this welcome addition to their numbers, the task seemed daunting. Unable to gain entry to the fiercely defended city, the army laid siege.

Stalemate.

Rumours began to circulate.

Someone within the city – maybe even the Emir – had bribed the Jerusalem lords to give up and retreat. Reinforcements had been sent for, and a vast Muslim army was even now heading for Damascus, intent on slaughtering every Christian they laid hands on. Nureddin himself was on his way, his fanatical eyes alight at the thought of heaps of Christian dead. The Frankish settlers were planning to abandon their newly arrived comrades and, even worse, turn them over to the Turks. Or the Muslims. Or both.

Morale plummeted.

On the fourth day, the siege was lifted and the Christian army was ordered to retreat.

Then all hell broke loose.

Fighting for his life, with no clear idea of what his orders were or, even, of what was the most sensible thing to do, Geoffroi copied his fellow knights and battled his way out through the surging throng of the enemy. Whether the swarthy, dark men he fought were Turkish Damascenes who had ridden out to send the invaders packing, or crack Muslim troops under the command of Nureddin, he did not know.

All he did know was that the enemy fought with an efficiency and a ferocity that he, a fighting man himself, could not help but admire. Professional soldiers, many used the bow – of a peculiar, curved shape – as a cavalry assault weapon, firing it from horseback with a skill born of long experience and endless training.

The effect on the Christian army was devastating. All around him Geoffroi saw men fall, some shot with the awful, penetrating arrows that flew off those strange bows, some dragged from their horses to be cut to death by knife or sword.

Geoffroi thought suddenly, I may be about to die.

As he thought this, a peculiar sense of detachment came over him. I cannot avoid what lies in store for me, he reflected fatalistically. I must do my best – of all things, a picture of his family sprang to mind, making sacrifice after sacrifice in order that he should be here, fighting before Damascus – and, if my best does not result in my escape, then I shall die and, with my sins absolved, go to Paradise.

Then he spurred his horse, screamed aloud and, with his sword held high, rode into the fray.

An unknowable time later – it could have been one hour or several – Geoffroi found himself in a press of Frankish knights fighting their way out of what appeared to be an attempted ambush. Some enemy troops had tried to corner them but, in this instance, it was the Christians who outnumbered the Turks, or Muslims, whoever they were, and the enemy soldiers were steadily being massacred.

Geoffroi, attracted by a sudden high-pitched wailing, spun round and saw the slight figure of a Muslim youth, quite short in stature, staggering into the path of a mounted Frankish knight who was bearing down on him.

In a peculiar moment of stillness, the youth turned his head and his terrified eyes met Geoffroi's. But he's a child! Geoffroi thought, aghast. He's nothing but a little boy! 'Wait!' he yelled, waving his sword towards the charging knight, 'stay your hand!'

The knight, who either did not hear or chose to ignore Geoffroi's appeal, spurred his horse.

The boy had been injured; a cut to the head was bleeding profusely, and the entire right side of his face looked as if it had been painted scarlet. In addition, he seemed to be concussed; he was running round in circles, stumbling, pushing himself upright only to fall again.

Geoffroi could see an obvious way out for him; if he turned sharp right, he would be facing the entrance to a sort of tunnel between two rocky outcrops where, for a precious life-saving moment, he would be out of the charging knight's reach.

Geoffroi waved at him, kicking on his horse and galloping towards him. 'Go in there, boy!' he cried. 'Quickly! Get under cover!'

But the boy's wide, panicking eyes looked blank; he had not understood.

The knight was almost on him.

Geoffroi, screaming now, yelled out, 'NO! He's a child; he's no soldier! Leave him! Leave him be!'

The knight charged on.

Drawing in his horse's head so sharply that the animal all but tripped, Geoffroi changed direction and flew forward on a path that would cross that of the knight. Passing in front of him so closely that he actually saw the knight's eyes behind the slit of his visor – dark eyes, narrowed, intent – Geoffroi then wheeled again and, bending down out of the high saddle and lowering his left arm more in hope than in expectation, scooped the child up and out of the knight's path.

Then, before the knight could slow down and turn, Geoffroi spurred his horse and, weaving and swerving, raced from the scene.

He was so charged up that, for a few minutes, all he could do was cling on to the child – whose terror seemed to have totally paralysed him – and urge his rapidly tiring horse onwards. So it was that, after some time, he suddenly realised that he had left the fighting behind.

The three of them, lathered horse, panting man and catatonic boy, seemed to be entirely alone.

They were in a shallow valley – little more than a depression – and cut off from the carnage they had left behind them by a short range of low hills. Hurriedly – this respite could last but moments, he knew – Geoffroi slid down from the saddle, still holding the child, and deposited him on the ground.

The boy immediately fell over.

Kneeling at Geoffroi's feet, face in his hands in the sand and small bottom stuck up in the air, he began to cry. Amid the tears he managed to splutter out a few words, but they were in a language that Geoffroi did not understand.

Squatting down beside him, Geoffroi said gently, 'I am not going to kill you, child! Is that likely, when I've just risked life and limb to save you?'

The boy raised his head. Cautiously, as if he were not at all sure it was wise. He said something, but, again, Geoffroi didn't understand.

Geoffroi stood up and went over to his horse, reaching up for a water bottle and a strip of cloth. Then, returning to the boy and sitting down beside him, he made gestures of face washing, pointing at the child.

The boy – he looked no more than six or seven – watched him out of terrified eyes. This, Geoffroi thought in exasperation, is getting us nowhere. Very gently, careful to make no violent move, he ran water on to the cloth and began to clean up the child's face.

The boy seemed to comprehend, at last, that this strange, sweaty man on the big horse was actually trying to help him. Submitting obediently to Geoffroi's ministrations, he sat quite still while Geoffroi wiped away what seemed like several cupfuls of blood.

The cut itself – on the boy's forehead just below the hairline – did not look too deep; in the manner of head wounds, the amount of blood was not indicative of the severity of the wound. By the time Geoffroi had finished mopping up, the bleeding had all but stopped, so he made a pad out of part of the cloth and tied it firmly in place with the remainder.

'That's the best I can do for you, young man,' he said, sitting back to study the results of his nursing.

The boy ventured a small smile; his teeth were very white and even. Some rich man's son, Geoffroi thought, if I do right to judge by the standards of my own people, for no poor child of the north has such a dazzling array of clean, white teeth. The child's clothes, too, under the blood and the dust, were of fine quality.

'What am I to do with you?' Geoffroi asked, knowing that the child would not answer. 'Take you into the city? No, they'd kill me long before they saw what I was carrying. Leave you here? No, for there is no guarantee that our forces might not arrive before your own people, whoever they are, and undo all my good work.'

He sat there, frowning, for some moments.

Then, for want of a better plan, he put the boy back on to his horse, swung up behind him and, keeping a very careful look out, rode along to a gap in the line of low hills and stared out over the plain before him.

The battle was still raging. The Christians, he saw clearly, were in retreat; the Turks and Muslims were chasing them ever faster from the walls of the city.

If he were to be very quick, it might just be possible . . .

Since further thought was probably a mistake – he might

come up with serious flaws in his plan – Geoffroi waited no longer. Kicking his horse to a canter, keeping as well within the feeble shelter of the hills as he could, he circled round in a wide sweep, behind the pursuing Muslims and in towards the city.

Then, again without pausing to think, he stopped, carefully lowered the child on to the ground, and pointed at the city.

'Go on,' he urged.

The child did not move.

'Go *ON*!'

Frightened by the sudden loud cry, the child, with one last look from those huge dark eyes, turned and ran.

Geoffroi, who had meant to keep his voice down and generally maintain a low profile, galloped off in the opposite direction. Quite sure that he could hear startled Turks yelling after him, that he could feel the drumming of their horses' hooves as they pursued him, notching arrows to the string as they did so, he made for the shelter of his hills.

And, in time, unsullied and probably even unnoticed by the enemy, he caught up with his own retreating army.

Many of the Christian army had been killed in the mêlée of the retreat from Damascus. Many more had been wounded; back in camp, Geoffroi saw that a large number of hospital tents had been prepared and were busy treating the worst of the injuries. Moans, cries and screams rent the air, and he could smell blood. The heat and the insects were turning the suffering of the wounded into torture; black flies kept alighting in swarms on open wounds, bringing with them at best a nightmare of tiny, stabbing pains as they repeatedly landed, were wafted away and landed again. At worst – and this the wounded must have realised – they brought the dreadful threat of infection.

Once the terrible yellow pus filled an open cut, as every crusader knew, it was but a short step to the hot, scarlet pain of inflammation, the sweet-sour stench of gangrene and, once that had set in, amputation.

Geoffroi had become separated from his own company, and, try as he might, he could not find them.

In the midst of his searching, he came across a familiar face: a short, swarthy knight from Lombardy – or was it Liguria? – with whom, lounging on the banks of a small tributary of the Danube, he and some fellow Frenchmen had once placed bets on who would be first to catch a fish.

A lifetime ago.

'Lost?' the dark knight asked. 'You certainly look it.'

Geoffroi explained.

'Ah, then you won't have eaten.'

'I'm not hungry.'

The dark knight took no notice. Grabbing Geoffroi by the elbow, he led him away to his own camp, where he fed him with slices of some salty meat and a hunk of dry bread, washed down with a thin, fairly sour red wine.

Then, when Geoffroi had thanked him, he pointed out the way back to the French troops' lines.

He got back to be told that Herbert of Lewes was dead.

He had been struck in the neck by one of those arrows. Although the wound in itself had not been fatal, Herbert had, in trying to pull it out, snagged its tip against a main artery.

Still astride his horse, he had bled to death.

Numb, Geoffroi whispered, 'I liked him. He was my friend.'

'Aye,' said the knight who had broken the news. 'I know that.' He hesitated, then said, 'We have a small packet of his belongings. Someone said he'd spoken to you of his home – where he came from, his family, that sort of thing. So we wondered . . .' He trailed off, as if what they had been wondering was too outrageous to be spoken of.

But Geoffroi was holding out his hand for the package. 'Of course,' he said quietly. 'I will see that they receive it.'

Then he crept away to grieve alone and to pray for the soul of his bluff and kindly Englishman.

Sleep did not come readily to Geoffroi that night. Although he was exhausted and sore from bruises, small cuts and aching muscles, his mind refused to switch off and allow him to rest. Images of the day flashed repeatedly before his eyes. A Turk's face, brown under the vivid purple and red of his headdress, teeth bared in a howl of fury as he charged. A French knight staring down, with a bemused expression, at the place where his right forearm used to be. A group of Muslim horsemen who seemed to move as one, galloping on such a beautiful, smoothly curved path that the movement could have been choreographed.

A child, lost in the midst of a battle, with wide brown eyes and half of his face stained bright red.

Herbert of Lewes bleeding to death from a severed artery in his neck.

For all that Geoffroi had not been a witness to the last scene, it was the one that haunted him most.

He had lain down to sleep a little apart from the other men; he had felt the need for solitude, or as near to that state as you could get in a camp full of soldiers. Now, listening to the steady breathing and the snores of those lucky enough to be fast asleep, and to the cries and muffled shouts of those in the throes of nightmare, Geoffroi turned his back on them all and closed his eyes.

He must have slept because, when some small sound alerted him, he woke from a dream.

He lay absolutely still and listened.

Nothing.

Hunching his blanket over his shoulder – the night was totally dark and quite chilly – he settled down again.

Then, shocking him so profoundly that he felt his heart leap against his ribs, a hand came down tightly and firmly over his mouth. He cut off short his instinctive lurch as he felt a steel point at his throat and a deep, hoarse voice, heavily accented, hissed right in his ear, 'If you move I shall kill you. If you do exactly as I say, I swear you shall come to no harm.'

Very aware of the knife's point, Geoffroi gave a very small nod. Then a hood or a bag of some sort was put over his head, his hands were tied behind him and his assailant took firm hold of his elbow and helped him to his feet.

He was led, he presumed, the short distance to the edge

of the sleeping enclosure, and made to exit it by rolling over on the ground so as to pass beneath the rope which cordoned off the area. Then, still with the knifepoint at his throat and his abductor's tight grip on his arm, he was taken to a horse and bundled on to its back. Somebody was astride it already, and this someone wordlessly hauled him up and settled him. Now another knife was at his throat; he did not, for the moment, see any way of escape.

So he just sat there.

The two horsemen quietly moved off. Geoffroi was aware of some small sounds – what had happened to the watch, for the good Lord's sake? Where were the guards? Why had nobody spotted two men on horseback abducting a Frankish knight? – but then, after a time, there was nothing but the sound of the horses' hooves cantering over the ground.

They rode for some time. Then Geoffroi was aware of a light ahead; it was no more than a glow that he could vaguely make out from beneath whatever it was they had used to cover his head. The light steadily grew in brightness, resolving itself into two, three and then four separate glowing patches.

Then the horses' hooves were clattering on stone. Someone called out – another added his voice – and the men on horseback called back. They spoke in a language or dialect that Geoffroi did not know. Geoffroi's horseman reined in his mount, and hands were suddenly around Geoffroi's waist and helping him – surprisingly gently – down to the ground.

He sensed the presence of other people, but none of

them spoke. His horseman said something to the man who had taken Geoffroi from his tent, and he answered. One of them laughed briefly.

Geoffroi thought, if they have brought me to my death, then they seem very relaxed and cheerful about it. He remembered the careful hands that had helped him off his horse and decided that it could just be possible that they *weren't* going to kill him.

But if not, why had they brought him here?

And where exactly was *here*?

Then the man who had come into the tent said, 'Come. You come with me now. I shall take you.'

Once again he took hold of Geoffroi's elbow and led him away. Their boots rang out on some hard stone floor, or at least Geoffroi's did; his companion seemed to be wearing soft-soled shoes. Geoffroi became aware of a scent . . . sweet, slightly spicy, not at all unpleasant . . . and he thought he heard the faint crackling of a fire.

They walked for some time, in darkness, in light, in darkness again. Then they must have emerged from a passage, perhaps, into a larger area, because Geoffroi was suddenly aware of a sense of space around him and a lot of light. He could hear the sound of running water. The sweet smell was stronger now, and slightly different . . . there was a tangy, musky element to it now . . . was it sandalwood?

The man beside him was saying something – a greeting? – and he pushed Geoffroi's head down so that he bowed.

That was the final indignity.

To be forcibly removed from his tent in the middle of the night with a knife at his throat and taken miles away on a fast, silent-footed horse was one thing. To be marched through long passages with a hood over his head was just about tolerable.

But to be made to bow to someone he couldn't even see, well, that was too much.

Geoffroi wrenched himself away from the pressure of the man's hand and stood up tall and proud. In a loud voice he said, 'Let me see who it is to whom you would have me bow, and judge with my own eyes whether I deem him worthy.'

There was a stunned silence. For a dreadful moment, Geoffroi thought he had gone too far. He could almost hear the soft scrape of a sword drawn from its sheath, the muted whistle as it descended to sever his head from his neck . . .

But then somebody laughed. A rich, happy sound.

And a deep voice said cheerfully, 'Quite right, sir knight. Why should a valiant man bow to an invisible shadow?'

He must have made some gesture, for immediately the rope binding Geoffroi's wrists was cut and the hood was taken off his head.

Blinking in the sudden bright light – there must have been thirty or more candles burning in glass lamps – Geoffroi stared around him. He was in a cool, marble hall, with arches along two sides open to the night air, and in the middle of it a fountain played. There was a small fire in some sort of brazier, and the sweet smell seemed to emanate from the soft coils of smoke rising from it.

There were about a dozen people in the hall. Some, standing perfectly still in the shadows, appeared to be servants, or perhaps guards. The two men either side of

Geoffroi, dressed in heavy hooded cloaks, must be the pair who had brought him here.

In front of him was a set of pure white marble steps, on top of which stood a divan covered in rich burgundy-coloured cloth. Extending down from the divan and down the centre of the steps was a runner of fine carpet, decorated with a geometric pattern in shades of purple, violet, rich yellow and dark red. Two more servants sat at the foot of the steps. Another stood at the top, beside the divan, holding a tray on which was a brass pot, a tiny cup and a plate containing small titbits of some sort of food.

On the divan, beringed hand extended to take one of the titbits, sat a plump man of perhaps sixty years. His round face under the elaborate, multicoloured headdress was beaming, making his small, dark eyes all but disappear behind the bulges of yellowish flesh around his eyelids. The wide skirts of his garments – made of rich, vivid silk, shining in the candlelight – had been carefully arranged on the divan around him.

He sat quite composed under Geoffroi's scrutiny for a moment or so. Then, the laughter clearly not far away, he said, 'Now you see me, sir knight.' His voice suddenly becoming serious, he said, 'But, indeed, it is not you who should do honour to me.'

With some effort, he slowly rose to his feet and, to Geoffroi's amazement, made him a low reverence.

Straightening up and flopping down once more on the divan, he said, 'I am Mehmed. I have had you brought here to thank you because, this afternoon, you saved the life of my grandson.'

8

—◆—

'Your *grandson*?'

'Yes. He is a courageous boy, like his father, but sometimes strong-headed. Yes? Is that the word?'

'Headstrong.'

'Ah, thank you. Headstrong.' Mehmed repeated the word a couple of times under his breath, as if committing it to memory.

Geoffroi said carefully – it seemed neither polite nor diplomatic to infer criticism – 'I was surprised to see a child in the field of battle.'

Mehmed sighed. 'Ah, sir knight, you ask yourself what sort of a people can we be, what sort of a man am I, to permit a little boy to do a grown man's job. Yes?'

'I – well, yes,' Geoffroi admitted.

'It was not done with my permission,' Mehmed said, in a tone of voice that allowed no argument. 'The child – his name is Azamar, incidentally – the child is disobedient.' The fat face crinkled into an indulgent smile. 'But then what spirited child of six is not? Azamar was confined with his mother in the innermost fastness of my house, told – *ordered* – to keep well away from any openings through which a Christian arrow or assault weapon might find him. Yet, so strong was his wish to fight the treacherous

Franks, whom we had believed to be our friends, that he slipped away from the vigilance of his mother and her ladies, made his sly way past my servants and my guard, found himself a horse that was far too big for him and rode out to do battle.'

Geoffroi said admiringly, 'He sounds quite a lad.'

Mehmed nodded. 'Quite a lad, yes. You must understand his great desire for our family to be seen to have at least one man on the field and I, alas, as you see . . .' He made a rueful face, extending a hand to indicate his large, unwieldy frame.

'You said he stole a horse,' Geoffroi began.

'He did not *steal*,' Mehmed rebuked him. 'The horses in my stable are ever at his disposal.'

Geoffroi was, he realised, going to have to be more careful how he phrased things; this grandfather, clearly, was so besotted with his grandson that, in his eyes, the child could do no wrong. Well, hardly any.

'He had no horse when I came across him,' Geoffroi said. 'He was on the ground.'

'On the ground.' Mehmed's face reflected his pain. 'Yes, so I have been told. On the ground, a six-year-old child, wounded, concussed, helpless. And a great Frankish knight about to – about to—' Unable to put such a horror into words, he closed his eyes and waved a fat hand, as if to push away the very thought.

Geoffroi, who could think of nothing to say, kept quiet.

After a while, Mehmed opened his eyes again and fixed them on Geoffroi. 'You saved him,' he said, his voice soft. 'You risked your own life to pick him up out of the path of that fury with the broadsword, and you rode off with

him until you found a quiet place where you could treat
his wound. Then you rode back with him and left him in
the safest place you could think of, right outside the gates
of his own city of Damascus.'

'It wasn't right outside,' Geoffroi muttered.

'Ah, honest as well!' Mehmed exclaimed. He waved a
hand around at the assembled servants, who all echoed,
'Ah!' sounding, Geoffroi thought, like the wind in the
poplars. 'But near enough, sir knight, for little Azamar
to trot up to the city walls and swiftly be brought inside
to safety.'

'Is he all right?' Geoffroi asked. 'That head wound was
bleeding profusely.'

'He is all right, yes. His mother and her nursing woman
have tended him, bathed him, fed him, cuddled and
coddled him, and now he sleeps.'

'I am glad of it,' Geoffroi muttered.

'*You* are glad?' Old and fat he might be, but Mehmed
had sharp ears. 'Think, then, how glad *I* must be, for
Azamar is the son of my only son, my jewel, who died
when the child was two years old.' Shadows of a great
grief crossed the round face and, for a moment, Mehmed
put up a hand to shield himself from Geoffroi's intent
stare. Then, recovering, he said quietly, 'Azamar is all
that I have. He would be precious in any event. Under
the particular circumstances that apply to my family,
he is doubly, trebly, four times precious.' A soft smile
crossed his face. 'Four times precious,' he repeated. 'Yes.
I like that.'

There was a short pause. Then, as if remembering
his manners, suddenly Mehmed clapped his hands and

shouted out a barrage of words in a language quite strange
to Geoffroi. At once, three of the servants leapt into action,
swiftly rushing to Geoffroi's side and proffering trays of
food, drink and something that looked like cloth, steaming
gently and smelling delicious.

At a loss, Geoffroi went to take one of the tiny cups.
But the servant, with extreme delicacy, withdrew his tray
a fraction, allowing the servant bearing the hot cloths to
advance instead. Geoffroi nodded his thanks and took one
of the cloths.

But what was he to do with it?

The servant – how subtly attentive they were! – immediately put down his tray, unfolded the tightly-rolled cloth
and, holding it out, mimed a quick, neat wiping of face and
hands. Understanding at last, Geoffroi took it from him
and gave his hands, face and neck a very thorough wash.

There were soft titters from behind him. Mehmed,
crushing them with a steely look, said something in his
own language. Then, as Geoffroi handed the now filthy
cloth back to the servant – he was ashamed of the black
dirt; he couldn't think when he had last bathed – Mehmed
said kindly, 'We are pleased that we may offer you this
small service.' Then he clapped his hands once more, and
the food and drink trays were offered again.

Geoffroi only ate a tiny amount – the delicacy was
extremely sweet, and in fact made him feel rather sick
– but he accepted two cups of the hot, spicy drink.
Then, when he had nodded his thanks, the servants withdrew.

He wondered what would happen next.

He wanted, more than anything, to be safely back in his

camp. Could he ask to be taken? Or would that break some rigid rule of Turkish hospitality?

Mehmed had clapped his hands again. This time, a servant from the shadowy far side of the hall advanced, bowing low before his master and holding out to him some object, wrapped in soft leather, laid on a velvet cushion.

Geoffroi, embarrassed, hoped very much that it was not going to be some unlikely, unsuitable gift; more of that tooth-rotting sweetmeat, perhaps?

Mehmed beckoned him forwards. He moved to the foot of the marble steps. Mehmed beckoned again; 'Come closer! I cannot reach you down there!'

Geoffroi did as he was bid.

He watched as the fat fingers unfolded the leather. Whatever was inside was not sweetmeats, that was clear, because, as it caught the light, rays shone out of it like bright stars in the night sky.

Mehmed was holding up a gold chain, from which hung a large, dark-blue stone. Round in shape, and about the size of Mehmed's thumbnail, it was set in a thick gold coin, the centre of which appeared to have been softened and hollowed out slightly, so as to hold the stone firmly. There was lettering of some sort around the edge of the coin, although Geoffroi could not read it.

Mehmed swung the stone on its chain gently, to and fro, to and fro. Then, in a hypnotic voice, he intoned, 'Behold the stone that men call the Eye of Jerusalem. Its mystical origins are lost in the past, and it came to my family when we were young and the tally of our days was yet brief.' He gave the deep blue stone a loving, almost yearning look. 'It is protector and friend to its rightful owner, keeping him safe from enemies both known and unknown,' he went on. 'Dipped in water, it will make a febrifuge that also has the power to stem bleeding. Dipped into a drink proffered by a stranger, it will detect the presence of poison.'

There was a long pause while Mehmed continued to swing the stone and everyone else watched it. Then he said, 'It was ever told, and the tale passed down from father to son, that the day would come when the Eye of Jerusalem, great treasure of the Mehmeds, would be given in exchange for something that we valued yet more highly. Until this day, we could not imagine what event this tale foretold.' He sighed again. Then, abruptly shooting out his arm and holding the stone out to Geoffroi, he said, 'Now we wonder no more. This day you saved my grandson, last male child of my line, and returned him safe to me. He is more valuable than all the sapphires and gold in the world and, in exchange for his life, I must do as long tradition orders me and give to you, sir knight, this precious jewel.'

Very slowly and cautiously, Geoffroi reached out and took the chain from Mehmed's fingers. The stone hung heavily; he could hardly bear to look at it.

'Take it,' Mehmed said, 'you are its rightful owner, and, from this day forward, it will acknowledge you as its master and protect only you.'

'But—'

'There is no but,' Mehmed said gently. 'Even if I had the courage and the foolhardiness to countermand a thousand-year-old tradition and hang on to what is now yours, it would advance me nothing, for the Eye knows a new master now and would do me nothing but harm.'

His small, dark eyes went back to the great jewel as if it drew them. Then, breaking his gaze away with an obvious effort, he picked up the leather wrapping still lying on the cushion, held it out to Geoffroi and said, 'Put it away, sir knight. Wrap it up and hide it well.'

With one last look at the stone, Geoffroi folded it up inside the soft leather and pushed it deep inside his clothing. He could feel it, hard against his chest.

Mehmed, who seemed to be overcome, said from behind the hand he was pressing to his face, 'That is all, sir knight. My men will take you back to your camp although, I am sorry to say, once more they must cover your head. I regret the mode of your transportation to my home and from it, but I would not have my dwelling known to the Franks.'

'I understand.'

Before Geoffroi was quite ready – he would have liked a long last look around the extraordinary hall and its rich fabrics and furnishings – the hood was once more pulled down over his head. This time his wrists were bound in front of him, which was easier.

But, just as the two horsemen began to lead him away, Geoffroi broke free of them. Turning to where he thought Mehmed sat on his divan, he said, 'Sir, I had no thought of reward when I went to the aid of your grandson, and I would have asked for none. He was a child, and we – I do not kill children.' He paused, trying to think of an appropriate form of words, then said, 'I wish you a long and happy life and, for Azamar your grandson, I wish the same, with the hope that he weds a fair wife and begets a quiver-full of sons.' Then he made a very deep bow and finished, 'Mehmed of Damascus, I thank you.'

From in front of him and slightly to the right came Mehmed's voice. He said, 'I thank you for your wishes and I extend the same sentiments also to you. It is for me to thank you, which I do with a full heart. Farewell, Geoffroi of Acquin. May Allah turn a kind face upon you.'

Then the two horsemen took Geoffroi's arms and marched him out of the hall and back along the maze of passages to the stables.

It was only as they were cantering away through the silence of the dark night that he realised.

Mehmed's spy network must have infiltrated right to the heart of the Frankish camp. Because he had known Geoffroi's name all along.

With the humiliating failure of the siege of Damascus, the crusaders had, in Muslim eyes, turned themselves into incompetent, hapless fools.

With no clear purpose in Outremer, the continued presence there of what remained of King Louis's great army seemed pointless. As the August days passed and the year proceeded into September, then October, the King acceded to pressure from his men – many of whom had already deserted – and issued orders that those who were still there should be provided with funds and allowed to return home.

King Louis himself, it was rumoured, was to remain in Jerusalem, and Queen Eleanor would stay at his side. Nobody quite knew why; Geoffroi, for one, could not bring himself to care very much.

The army was moved up to the coast, at Acre. Preparing to depart – the ship that would take him at least part of the way home, as far as Constantinople, was due to sail in the morning – Geoffroi thought back over the sixteen months that he had been away. He still wore his crusader's cross; had he fulfilled his vow? He had seen the Holy City, Jerusalem, yes. But could he put his hand on his heart and say that he had fought for God's cause, and thereby gained the longed-for remission of his sins?

He was not sure.

He tried to ask some of his fellow knights and, when they shrugged and said, of course! what else? he asked a priest. But the priest, also due to sail for Constantinople in the morning, clearly had other things on his mind and paid Geoffroi even less heed than the knights had done.

In the morning, sailing away from Acre in the pale dawn light, Geoffroi stood at the ship's rail and stared at the dry, dusty land until it was nothing more than a faint smudge on the eastern horizon. Then, with a sigh, he turned his back on Outremer and began to think of home.

On the long march overland from Constantinople, Geoffroi met up with the dark-haired knight from Lombardy, who had come seeking him out. Both were affected by the pleasure of seeing a familiar face in a friendless place, and they fell into the habit of riding together. In the perils of that endless journey, it was an advantage to have a companion; conditions on the northward march were very different from how they had been when the great Christian army had ridden south. Then, they had been a vast force, unassailable, invulnerable, taking what they wanted, unmindful of the feeble protests of the weak and the unarmed.

Now, riding in small bands, it was they who were vulnerable.

Afterwards, Geoffroi could not help but wonder whether the Eye of Jerusalem had played any part in his survival. Certainly, the fact that he finally reached home largely unhurt and reasonably healthy was something of a miracle. Marking the daily tally of misfortunes – horses gone lame, falling sick, having to be slaughtered for meat; men using up their last particle of energy and collapsing by the roadside; fevers, sickness and injuries; theft, assault and even murder among the men as their supplies and their hope ran out – Geoffroi began to believe that his survival must have something supernatural about it.

He first put the Eye to the test when, in a small village on some desolate Bulgar plain, he and three of his companions were approached by a pair of ragged, foul-smelling herdsmen and offered some sort of fermented, milky drink in exchange for coin. One of the knights eagerly reached into his pouch to take out a coin, and was on the point of putting the cracked wooden cup to his lips when Geoffroi murmured, 'Wait. Let us retreat a few paces first.'

Angrily the knight – a tall, rangy Burgundian – cried, 'Wait? What for?'

But Geoffroi did not answer, instead walking away from the herdsmen and moving a little apart. The Burgundian followed him.

'Give me the cup,' Geoffroi said quietly.

'No! It's mine, I just bought it!'

'Let me test it,' Geoffroi insisted. 'It may—'

The Burgundian paled. 'You think they try to poison us? The bastards, wait till I—'

Geoffroi grabbed at him. 'Wait,' he repeated.

Then, turning away from his comrades, he took the Eye from the secret place under his shirt where he kept it safe, unfolded the leather cover and held the jewel over the wooden cup.

Nothing happened.

Then he gently lowered the sapphire in its gold coin into the milk.

And, after an instant, there came a sort of fizzing sound. A wisp of yellowish smoke floated up from the surface of the liquid. Hastily Geoffroi withdrew the Eye.

Turning back to the Burgundian, he said, 'It's poison. Don't touch it.'

The Burgundian glared at him. 'You are sure?'

'I am.'

The Burgundian took back the cup, dashed it and its contents to the ground, then drew his sword and, in the blink of an eye, one after the other cut off the heads of the two herdsmen.

Geoffroi, horrified, stared at the headless bodies, their blood at first fountaining and then seeping into the dusty ground. Looking up, he met the Burgundian's eyes.

He was wiping his sword prior to returning it to its sheath. With a faint lift of his shoulders, he said, 'It was them or us. Would you have me leave them alive to poison more poor, thirsty knights?'

Geoffroi made no reply.

★　　★　　★

He tested one of the Eye's other claimed virtues a month later when the Lombardy knight went down with a fever. Hardly crediting what he did – his friend was raving, sweating profusely and thrashing about in his makeshift, insubstantial bed – Geoffroi heated some water, cooled it and then, again ensuring that he was unobserved, lowered the Eye into it and stirred it a few times around in the cup. Then, supporting the Lombard's head, he trickled a few drops on the cracked lips. The Lombard ran his tongue over his mouth, taking in the liquid. Geoffroi repeated the exercise, then again. On the fourth attempt, the Lombard sucked up and swallowed two decent mouthfuls.

His fever broke that night.

In the morning, he was weak but fully conscious. Two days later, they were able to resume their journey.

It was the water itself that restored him, Geoffroi told himself. Everyone knew that fevers dried a man out, and that water was the way to make him better again. So, the Lombard had drunk, and he had recovered.

That had to be the way of it.

The alternative – that Geoffroi truly did have in his possession a miracle-working jewel – was almost too awesome to contemplate.

Protective jewel or not, Geoffroi's luck appeared to desert him in the spring of the following year. Their progress over the winter months had been very slow; some days, the weather had been so foul that it had seemed the safer option to remain in whatever meagre shelter they had found for the night.

With their food supplies all but non-existent and their

funds running dangerously low, the four knights – Geoffroi, the Lombard, the Burgundian and the latter's kinsman – were ambushed in a mountain pass. The Burgundian was killed outright by a rock dislodged from the mountainside as the assailants charged down from the heights. The remaining three knights, penned into a narrow file whose width made the use of a broadsword difficult, if not impossible, were swiftly overcome.

There were enough men in the band of assailants for some to pin down the knights while others went through their garments and their belongings. Geoffroi, fully believing his end had come, silently mourned his home and his kinfolk, neither of which he would ever see again.

The band of thieves attended to the Lombard and the Burgundian first. Then, just as they leapt up and prepared to approach Geoffroi, there was a shout from somewhere up above and a horn was blown three times in quick succession. To a man, the marauders stood up, jumped nimbly over the knights and ran off, scrambling back up the steep side of the gorge as if it were a flight of steps.

Geoffroi's initial huge relief quickly evaporated. He had retained his weapons, his small parcel of food and what little money he had left, yes. But, unless he now abandoned his companions and went on alone – which was unwise as well as ungallant – he faced the prospect of supporting the three of them on his own rapidly-dwindling supplies.

It was hopeless.

They ran out of food two days later. Starving, seriously dehydrated, ragged and filthy, they presented themselves at a reasonably prosperous-looking farm and threw themselves on the farmer's mercy. When their crusader's crosses failed to impress, they offered their labour. Finally, when a promise had been extracted from them to work until the harvest was gathered in exchange for food and water, they were given a meal. Not much of a meal, but it was the best food Geoffroi had ever tasted.

They set out on the last leg of the long road home in the late autumn of 1149. Again, misfortune struck; they were at the foot of an Alpine pass when a life-threatening snowfall occurred. They had food enough now, and there was nothing for it but to descend down the pass, find shelter and camp until the weather relented.

They finally came down on the northern side of the mountains at the beginning of March. They had been snowbound, they had got lost, and the Burgundian's kinsman had taken a bad fall. But they were alive.

As they rode on, Geoffroi constantly expected that the Lombard would announce he was leaving them; his home must now lie to the west, and the direction in which the trio was travelling was north-west. But the Lombard said nothing.

Finally, Geoffroi asked him.

With a rueful glance at him, the Lombard said, 'My friend, I would, if I may, travel on with you.'

Amazed, Geoffroi said, 'Haven't you had enough of travelling? As God is my witness, I have!'

The Lombard smiled. 'Ah, Geoffroi, but you probably do not have a young woman waiting for you at home, whose formidable mother will insist becomes my wife the moment I have got my boots off.'

'You are promised in marriage?'

'Yes. Oh, she is fair, and I dare say will make me a splendid wife. But not just yet. I wish to spend a little more time free and single before I am forced to settle down and chained to the house for ever more. I would dearly love to travel the road home with you, if you will have me.'

Moved by his friend's honesty, and flattered by the fact that he obviously enjoyed Geoffroi's company sufficiently to desire some more of it, Geoffroi agreed.

They bid farewell to the Burgundian's kinsman on the road from Beaune to Vézelay. Then, hearts high and singing as they went, they marched on north and, in the fine spring weather of 1150, they came at last to Acquin.

PART THREE

France and England, 1150–1165

9

As Geoffroi led the way along the Aa valley towards home, the Lombard held back.

Turning to him, believing his sudden slowness to be due to fatigue, Geoffroi said encouragingly, 'Have heart, my friend! We are almost home!'

'Yes, so I suspected,' the Lombard replied. With a grin, he added, 'You have been increasing your pace steadily all morning. I reasoned that, like a weary horse at last come close to his stable, the scent of home is hastening your steps.'

'I hadn't realised.' Geoffroi grinned back. 'Will you not step out beside me so that we may march along together?'

'No.' Now the Lombard came to stand by him, resting a hand on Geoffroi's shoulder. 'My friend, you should go in to your kin alone. They may still have faith that you will return safe to them, they may have given you up for lost. Either way, your homecoming will be an emotional time, and best for family eyes alone, not witnessed by a stranger.'

Geoffroi regarded him with affection. 'Not a stranger to me,' he said quietly.

The Lombard bowed his head in acknowledgement.

'No. But to them, I am unknown and, in the instant that you step once more over your father's threshold, unwelcome.'

'But—' Geoffroi, frowning, met his companion's dark eyes. And realised there was no need to say more.

'Go on,' the Lombard urged. 'I will not be far behind.'

Geoffroi gave him one last look. Then, unable to restrain himself, he turned and headed away, at first walking but quickly breaking into a run, up the track that led to home.

As always, it was the tops of the watchtowers on the outer corners of the great Acquin courtyard that came into view first. As he hurried on, the long, low roofs of the main buildings became visible, the warm spring sun beating down on them and catching blueish glints and shimmers from the flint; it was lavender coloured in the bright light.

Now he was almost there.

He ran through the small village that surrounded the manor, aware of curious eyes peering out at him but not wanting to stop. Past the church, where someone called out to him. He ignored the cry.

Then at last up the path to the gates.

Slowing down, stopping, he stood and gazed into the courtyard.

He could hear voices from somewhere within; they would be preparing the noon meal. Somebody laughed. Was it Esmai? He thought so. Another female voice responded, full of affection. His mother.

He felt as if a slow and gentle hand were squeezing his heart.

Then a man appeared from one of the storerooms, heading towards the family accommodation, head down, lost in contemplation.

Geoffroi said, 'Father?'

The man turned. Caught sight of Geoffroi, standing in the gateway. Instantly his face lit with love and happiness and, crying out 'It's Geoffroi! Geoffroi's come home!' Robert d'Acquin tripped and stumbled across the courtyard to take his son in his arms.

The joy of being home again was so great that it seemed there could never be enough celebration and thanksgiving.

Geoffroi had been away for almost three years. His family, with no idea of how long he would be gone and therefore no yardstick by which to judge whether or not he was overdue, had spent the months of his absence alternating between bright optimism and the darkness of despair. Their parish priest, Father Herluin, had encouraged the former and gently reprimanded them for the latter, reminded them that despair was a sin against the Holy Spirit. Being a human being as well as a priest, however, he had understood a mother and a father's anxiety and grief for a missing son and he had imposed but light penance.

They had never stopped praying for him. Father Herluin told him so, in a quiet moment when Geoffroi had sought out the priest to ask how they had fared while he was away. Nor had their belief in the rightness of his crusade ever wavered; not, at least, according to Father Herluin. He added, however, as, after hearing Geoffroi's confession, he walked with him out of the church and saw him on his way, 'I trust, my son, that there will be no more crusading in the immediate future?'

And Geoffroi, understanding what it was that lurked unspoken behind the words, said, 'No, Father Herluin. There will not.'

He could see for himself, once the euphoria of home-coming had begun to wane, what his long absence had done to his family. His father, who bore by far the greater part of the weighty responsibility of Acquin, had aged by more than the three years that Geoffroi had been away. It could not be the work and the heavy duty that had worn him down, Geoffroi reasoned, for he had been accustomed to those burdens for all of his adult life, since inheriting Acquin from his own father. And it was not as if Sir Robert had missed Geoffroi's contribution to the labour of running the estate because, as a page, a squire and finally a knight, he had always lived away from home and never *made* any contribution.

He talked it over with the Lombard, now a popular and honoured guest at Acquin. ('Any man who travelled, fought and suffered with my son,' Sir Robert had told him, 'is as welcome here as Geoffroi himself.') The Lombard, who, it seemed to Geoffroi, observed much but spoke little, gave the matter due thought before replying.

'I think, my friend,' he said eventually, 'that what ails your father would have come to him anyway, for he suffers from the pains in the joints and the narrowing of the chest that afflict many men as they begin to grow old.'

'He is not all that old,' Geoffroi protested.

The Lombard shrugged. 'Maybe not. But he has lived a demanding life, would you not say? A life of hard work, out in all weathers, so that the damp of autumn and the chill of winter have entered his bones and taken up permanent lodging there?'

'But—' Geoffroi began. Then, lapsing into silence, he gave a brief nod.

The Lombard reached out to touch his arm. 'Do not take the burden on to yourself,' he said softly. 'Whilst the long absence of a loved son might not do much to assuage an ageing man's pains and ailments, it certainly is not a primary cause of them.'

As always, Geoffroi reflected, his friend spoke good sense.

'I worry about my brother Robert as well,' he said, the words bursting out of him in the relief of actually speaking his concerns out loud. 'He does not look healthy. He coughs – have you heard him at night? – and he has a pallor that is not natural in a man who spends much of his day out of doors. And there is the matter of Adela.'

Geoffroi's brother Robert, they said, had fallen in love with a neighbouring lord's daughter, adoring her from afar while he plucked up courage to court her. But he dallied too long, and she married another. Robert, according to his sister Esmai, had been heartbroken. Still was, for all that Adela was now a wife of a year or more and expecting her first child.

The Lombard sighed. 'For some men, it is like that. They love, they lose, they are hurt beyond comfort.'

'But there must be other girls, if Robert has set his heart on a wife and a family!' Geoffroi protested.

The Lombard looked at him steadily. 'For some, yes, there is recovery and then the joy of a new love. For others . . .' He let the sentence trail away.

And Geoffroi, grieving, found no comfort.

The Lombard, sympathy in his face and in his tone, said, 'My friend, to ease your torments over how you find your father and your brother, think now about your mother.'

With relief, Geoffroi did so. And – as he suspected the Lombard had intended – his expression lifted.

The lady Matilda, Geoffroi's mother, uncomplicated soul that she was, had spent the years of her son's absence keeping her hands busy with her wide daily round of tasks, her mind occupied with the care and duty she owed to her family and to her husband's tenants, and her heart with God. Or, more likely, with Geoffroi, which, since he was away on God's business, amounted to the same thing. To have Geoffroi home safe and sound had caused her such joy that she had wept for at least half an hour, before turning to practical matters such as arranging a bath for him, attending to his small hurts and beginning on the huge task of washing and mending his clothes.

She moved now, Geoffroi had noticed, with a permanent smile on her face.

But there were also Esmai and young William.

His sister Esmai, he had noticed, had become very thin. Her small face had still a childlike look, and her figure was boyish, with hardly any breast development. She ate sparingly, and appeared to need a lot of sleep. When Geoffroi had broached the subject with his mother, she had said, with a small sigh, that Esmai had not come into her womanhood as she ought, and that she was therefore probably doomed to the life of a spinster. 'No man wishes to wed a barren wife,' Matilda said sadly, 'no matter how pretty and bright she is, no matter how lively her conversation nor how deft her hands when she plies the needle.'

Geoffroi, understanding, had given his mother a hug. 'She does not need a husband and a home of her own while she has us and Acquin,' he said stoutly.

But his mother, returning his hug, made no reply.

William, fifteen years old and a quiet, studious boy, had set his heart on becoming a monk.

Geoffroi was only partially comforted by his conversation with the Lombard, and he sought out Father Herluin to talk it all over with him.

'The trouble, you see,' Geoffroi concluded, after outlining his worries in considerable detail to the patient priest, 'is that, not really having studied them all that closely before I went away, I cannot say how much these changes that I observe are to be laid at my own door.'

'Not your door alone,' the priest said mildly. 'You did not answer the call to go on crusade for your own good, now, did you?'

'I was greatly relieved and comforted by the knowledge that taking the cross would earn me remission of my sins,' Geoffroi said honestly.

'Which of us would not be?' Father Herluin instantly replied. 'But God provided this great opportunity for you and for all crusaders, and you must not think there is any blame or guilt attached to having answered God's summons.'

'But my father looks so old!' Geoffroi cried. 'My elder brother sickens, my sister does not thrive and William wants to be a monk!'

The priest waited a moment while Geoffroi collected himself. Then he said, 'My son, these are things that happen to men and women. God has a pattern and a plan for us all, and you must not think that what you have done, in all good faith, has altered what the Almighty had in store for your family.' When Geoffroi made no answer, the priest said gently, 'Geoffroi? Do you understand what I am saying?'

Geoffroi nodded.

But he was not sure he felt very reassured.

With the honourable aim of trying to make amends to them all for his absence, Geoffroi threw himself into the life of the manor. Dutifully he presented himself to his father every morning to hear the plan of the day's work, and obediently he waited for his elder brother to say which tasks were his to see to. Then Geoffroi, always deferring, always humble, would offer to take on the remainder, never too proud to ask for help, never missing an opportunity to ask his father or his brother how *they* would go about whatever job he was tackling.

To his amazement, he discovered that he loved it.

The Lombard, helping him both by his capable hands and strong back and by his moral support – he seemed to understand without being told that this was something Geoffroi just had to do – told Geoffroi that he was a farmer now, not a soldier. And Geoffroi, agreeing with a happy smile, found that he did not have one single regret for the life he now seemed to have left behind.

In the autumn of the year in which Geoffroi came home, his father, Robert d'Acquin, finally succumbed to his long illness and the pain it caused him. He died peacefully, shriven of his sins and surrounded by his loving family, three days before the feast of All Saints.

The family's grief was mixed with a certain relief, entirely on Sir Robert's behalf, that he was now out of his agony and safe in the arms of the Lord.

The younger Robert, inheriting the title and the estate, seemed to grow more pale and weary under the load. Geoffroi, suffering for his brother even while he mourned his father, worked even harder, offering his strength to compensate for Robert's weakness. But, whatever he did, nothing seemed to remove the look of miserable resignation from his brother's pallid face.

Out hunting with the Lombard one bright winter morning – the Lombard insisted that Geoffroi allow himself a few pleasures amid his toil and his worries – the pair of them drew rein on top of a small knoll overlooking the Aa river. It was swollen with late autumn rains, and sang so loud a song as it hastened along that they had to shout to be heard over the noise.

'You know, my friend,' the Lombard said, 'there is something you should be thinking about.'

'Aye? And what is that?' Geoffroi's voice sounded terse, even to his own ears, but it was difficult not to be short with people implying that he was being negligent, when so many cares constantly pressed down on him.

'Your brother is sinking,' the Lombard said baldly. 'And when he dies, you will inherit Acquin.'

'Do you not think that has occurred to me?' Geoffroi replied crossly.

'Yes, of course it has.' The Lombard's tone was soothing. There was a pause, then he said, 'Do you recall what I said when I first rode on north with you instead of making for home?'

Geoffroi turned his mind back, with some difficulty, to those days of the long, hard journey home; they seemed half a lifetime away. 'Aye. You said you wished to have some more time of freedom before going back to take up the responsibilities of home, hearth and family.'

'Indeed,' the Lombard agreed. 'Responsibilities which you, my friend, have had thrust upon you whether you sought them or not.'

'I do not mind!' Geoffroi protested. 'Would you have me desert my family when they need me most?'

'No, Geoffroi.' The Lombard wisely waited while Geoffroi's brief anger spent itself. Then he said, 'For the moment, Robert is able to cope with the demands of Acquin, relatively slight as they are in this winter season. I suggest, my friend, that you and I grasp this opportunity that presents itself for the pair of us to have one more small adventure together.'

Geoffroi managed a grin. 'Not another crusade.'

The Lombard laughed. 'No, not that. But what I propose relates to our crusade, in a way.'

Illogically, a picture of the Eye of Jerusalem flashed into Geoffroi's mind. He wondered why that should be; he had hidden the jewel safely away on his return home, in a place where nobody could possibly find it, and, apart from occasionally going to have a furtive look at it, he left it alone. There had been no call to use its peculiar powers; here in Acquin he had no enemies – none that he knew of, anyway – nobody had tried to poison him, no one had suffered a bad wound, and his father's sickness would not have been helped by a febrifuge.

If he were honest with himself, the whole business of a magic jewel with supernatural powers now seemed a little far-fetched. Against the mundane problems of getting in the harvest, coping with floodwaters that threatened tenants in the lower-lying areas, and the normal aches, pains, grumbles and moans that were the usual human lot, a magnificent sapphire set in gold that had belonged to a Turkish emir seemed somewhat irrelevant.

So, what had the Lombard in mind?

Turning to him, Geoffroi said, 'Explain.'

'You had a friend, an Englishman, yes?'

'Yes. Herbert of Lewes. He died.'

'I know. You told me about him. You also told me that you had been entrusted with his belongings, to take home to his kin.'

'I have not had a chance!' Geoffroi cried. 'Have I not been occupied, every waking minute since my return, with my own kin? They have first call on me, you must realise that!'

'I do, I do,' soothed the Lombard. 'What I propose is that we travel to England together, you and I, and seek out Herbert of Lewes's home. By so doing, you will fulfil your undertaking and, at the same time, afford yourself a break from your cares and your labours here in Acquin.'

'But—' Objections rose in Geoffroi's mind. It was winter, and no season for travelling. How would his mother feel if he went away again? And what about poor Robert, having to bear full responsibility for the estate all by himself? Should Geoffroi even be thinking of what amounted to a jaunt, when all was said and done, when his father had not been dead much more than a month? Would they even be able to find Herbert of Lewes's kin?

Still, he had said he would return his friend's belongings to his kin. And that had been a solemn promise.

Turning to the Lombard, already feeling the faint stirrings of excitement that the prospect of a journey always brought, Geoffroi said, 'All right. We'll go.'

IO

Despite the winter season and the normal unsuitability of its weather for travelling, Geoffroi and the Lombard journeyed the short distance up to the coast, and then across the Channel, without mishap. The wind strengthened and turned round to the south-west as they took ship for England, which, while making the crossing rough enough for both men to succumb to seasickness, also had the effect of speeding up the ship's progress and so lessening the time spent at sea.

Neither man having set foot in England before, they had no idea where Lewes might be. They were relieved to be told it was not much over a day's ride away from the port – there were inns, apparently, where they could put up overnight if necessary – and that the way was easy to find. Follow the track that runs along the top of the downs, they were told – up there, on the cliffs; it would be drier and easier at this time of year than the road that ran along the foot of the downs – and descend into the valley of the Ouse river once you have passed Firle Beacon and the Caburn.

They had no idea what these last two features would look like, and they set off trusting to their luck that the landmarks would prove unmistakable.

They were entranced by the track along the cliffs. In that cold, frosty December, they seemed to have the land to themselves, and they rode along together in good spirits. They knew somehow, without having been told, that the way they trod was ancient, perhaps dating back to the very first inhabitants of this green and misty land; for one thing, the track was etched deep in the chalky soil, and for another, there were strange and puzzling relics which suggested earlier populations that had now vanished. There were the remains of stout walls; built so close to the cliffs that their outer sections had vanished, they had fallen away, as the very cliffs themselves had crumbled, into the restless, hungry grey sea below.

Who had lived there? Why had they felt the need to build so close to the cliff edge? Against whom had they felt driven to defend themselves?

There were signs of magic, too. Signs that those early inhabitants of Britain, whoever they were, had worshipped a very different God. In a grove of mighty oaks on the top of a summit they saw balls of mistletoe, and into the aged trunk of the host tree was carved a small figure that looked like a pregnant woman. And, close by, there was what appeared to be a broken stone altar.

Early on the second day they saw, on the hillside away to their left, the figure of a white giant. Hugely tall, he held spears in each of his outstretched hands. There was a faint hint of facial features – the giant looked stern, solemn – and he seemed to be wearing a plumed helmet.

'Who is he?' Geoffroi asked in an awed whisper, as if the giant might overhear and resent the question. Resent Geoffroi's ignorance. But the Lombard merely shrugged.

The Caburn was a prominent, rounded hill with the marks of ruined, circular walls. Firle Beacon was covered in humps that suggested ancient burials. Both locations made the travellers edgy, so that they looked uneasily over their shoulders and seemed to feel unseen, secret eyes on their backs.

It was a relief to come down off the lonely cliff-top track and follow the road that led along the Ouse to Lewes.

The town was bustling, and there was any number of people of whom to ask directions. Herbert of Lewes? Ah, yes, brave knight that he was, he lived down that-a-way. Follow the stream, over the bridge, on for a while and you'll see his manor up on the rise.

The manor was a compact stone house, its outer court-yard wall decorated with bisected flint stones, whose grey-ish sheen made a pleasing contrast with the reddish-gold of the stonework. A wooden gate stood open; Geoffroi and the Lombard rode through it, drawing rein just inside.

Two men, one young, one old, were bending over a brindled hound that lay on his back at their feet. The younger man was scratching the hound's belly, making the dog wriggle and howl with pleasure.

Geoffroi called out, 'Good day to you both! I seek the household and kin of Herbert of Lewes. Am I come to the right place?'

The older man instantly stood up – as far as his bent spine would allow – and said, his face suddenly grave, 'Aye. This is Sir Herbert's house. And just who might you be?'

Geoffroi slipped from his horse's back; the Lombard held out his hand and took the reins.

'I am Geoffroi d'Acquin,' he said. 'I would speak with Sir Herbert's family.'

The old man studied him for a silent moment. Then, with a brisk nod, he said, 'Follow me, please.'

Geoffroi turned to exchange glances with the Lombard, who shook his head minutely and said quietly, 'You go in alone – it was you who knew the man. I will wait here.'

Geoffroi followed the old man up a shallow flight of steps that led to the entrance to the house. The main living accommodation seemed to have been arranged at first-floor level, over an undercroft. Inside, they entered a wide hall with a fire crackling in a hearth at the far end. The furnishings were few – a table pushed against one wall, on which stood some rather elegant candlesticks; a chest or two; some benches – but they were solidly made, from good English oak, Geoffroi guessed, with the deep shine that comes from many years of diligent polishing.

Three people sat on a bench facing the fire, their backs to the entrance. Two were women, one a boy. The younger woman had just said something – in a pleasant, light-toned voice – that had set them all laughing.

The old man cleared his throat and, having gained the trio's attention, said, 'Here is a visitor, my lady. He is called Sir Geoffroi of Acquin, and he comes seeking the kin of Sir Herbert.'

Instantly, the mirth faded from the three faces.

The older woman stood up and approached Geoffroi. She said, 'I am Ediva, wife to Sir Herbert. What tidings do you bring?'

There was the shadow of pain in her blue eyes, and her handsome face seemed suddenly to have taken on downward lines. Stepping towards her and taking her outstretched hand – held out in greeting or to ward off whatever he was about to say? – in both of his, Geoffroi knelt before her and said, 'My lady, I was with Sir Herbert in Outremer, and I fear to tell you that I bear grim news. He was—'

But already she was nodding. 'He is dead, yes, sir knight, this we know. Have known, indeed, for many months, since his kinsman returned home and told us.'

Much of the tension left Geoffroi. Feeling himself slump, he bowed his head.

The woman hurried to crouch beside him. 'Sir Geoffroi? Are you sick? What ails you?' Her voice was kindly, solicitous.

Quickly raising his head, he said, 'Nothing, my lady, nothing!' He managed a smile. Looking up into her concerned face, he added frankly, 'I must admit to being relieved, that is all. Throughout the journey I dreaded breaking the news of Herbert's death to his widow and his family, and here you are already aware of it.'

The other woman and the boy had crept over as well now, and they, too, knelt down on the floor beside Geoffroi and the older woman. The boy said, 'Have you come far, sir?

'He has come from Acquin,' the younger woman said; hers was the sweet-toned voice. Glancing at her, Geoffroi took in that she was young – fifteen, sixteen? – and had her mother's bright blue eyes.

And that she was extremely lovely.

He would have liked to extend the glance into an all-out stare, but the lad was plucking at his sleeve.

'I know *that*,' he was saying, 'but I don't know where *Acquin* is. *Do* I?' he turned to hiss at the girl. 'I suppose you do, miss know-it-all,' he added in a cross whisper.

The older woman – surely the mother of what just had to be a sister and brother – said mildly, 'Enough, you two.' Then, still kneeling on the floor, she called up to the old man, who had retreated a respectful distance and was now hovering by the door. 'Symond? Will you fetch refreshments, please?'

There was a muttered, 'At once, my lady,' and the old man quietly let himself out of the hall.

The blue-eyed girl opened her mouth to speak, but her mother held up her hand. 'A moment,' she said softly. 'I would ask first, sweet.'

The girl dropped her eyes.

And Ediva, an anxious hand resting on Geoffroi's shoulder as if it were he, not she, who was in need of comfort, said, 'We know he is dead, but no more than that, for his kinsman had the tale from another and could give us no details of the circumstances.' She paused to take a shaky breath and then said, 'Will *you* tell us, Sir Geoffroi?'

And, sitting on the clean rush-strewn floor of a small Sussex manor house, Geoffroi did so. He spoke of how Herbert and he had become friends – he made light of their period of convalescence in Antioch, dwelling on the light-hearted rather than the distressing or crude aspects – and of how they had each valued the other as a friendly face in a vast army far from home. Then, sensing that this anxious family wanted to get the worst over with, he hurried on to what had happened outside Damascus.

'I was not beside him when he died,' he said, looking in turn into each pair of eyes; the lad, too, had inherited his mother's shade of bright, almost lavender blue, 'but I spoke the same night with a man who was. He told me—' He paused. Could he – should he – tell them the bare truth?

But, reading him right and understanding his hesitation, Ediva said, 'Please, sir, continue. We have imagined such dreadful things that surely the truth can be no worse.'

So, simply and quickly, he told them.

'He was in the press of knights before the city,' he said. 'He was fit, well, sound, full of enthusiasm. In the midst of his vibrant life, he took an arrow in the neck. The wound itself was slight but, in his haste to be rid of it and return to the fray, he dragged it out and tore some vital organ. He bled to death, even there as he sat his horse.'

There was a silence. Then Ediva said shakily, 'It was swift, then? He did not suffer?'

Geoffroi took her hands. They were icy. 'My lady, I think not. He was dead so quickly and, if I know anything of battle wounds, I would guess that he felt little pain.' He paused, then added, 'It is in the nature of fighting. At the time, the emotions run high, like a fever in the blood, and even a severe wound can go almost unfelt. It is only afterwards, when the battle is over, that the pain sets in. And Herbert—'

'Herbert did not live to suffer an afterwards,' Ediva finished for him.

He met her eyes. For a moment, neither spoke. Then he said quietly, 'No, my lady. He did not.'

A sob broke from the girl. Ediva put out her arms

and the girl threw herself against her mother. Crooning gently, lovingly, Ediva soothed her daughter as if she were a frightened, hurt animal. The boy, after a brief and unsuccessful attempt to hold back his tears, gave way; Ediva, sitting there on the floor, extended her arms to include her son. Meeting Geoffroi's eyes over the girl's head, Ediva said, 'They loved their father dearly.'

'He was a lovable man,' Geoffroi replied. 'And, believe me, my lady, he loved all of you, too. He was so proud of you, and his tales of happy family life were a comfort when we were all so far away from our own kin.'

Ediva smiled. 'Yes, I can imagine. He liked to talk, did my Herbert.'

She sat gazing into the distance at something only she could see. But, Geoffroi thought, it was a cheerful scene, for the small smile continued to lift her lips.

Suddenly Geoffroi could hear Herbert's voice, quite clearly in his head.

There's my wife – lovely, she is, comely, welcoming, capable – and there's my boy, Hugh. Ah, Geoffroi, my lad, but you should see my girl, my Ida! Hair like autumn leaves, rippling right down to her waist – why, she can sit on it! Imagine that! Eyes like the summer sky, and a waist you could encircle with your two hands!

This, then, this girl sobbing out her grief for her lost father, was Ida.

Gradually the sounds of weeping lessened and, eventually, ceased. The four of them went on sitting on the floor; it was actually quite pleasant, Geoffroi thought, relaxing in the warmth of the fire, except that there was a spiteful little draught coming from somewhere . . .

He was just craning round to see if he could find its source when abruptly Ida sat up, wiped her wet face with her hands and said, with a surprised laugh, 'Look at us! Why are we all crouched down here like a band of beggars when we have perfectly good benches to sit on?' Rising swiftly to her feet, she pulled her mother up after her and, glancing over her shoulder at Geoffroi with what he was quite certain was a flirtatious look, she added, 'Come, sir knight! Come and warm your toes.'

Geoffroi was taken aback at the sudden change from tears to light-hearted humour. His puzzlement must have shown on his face; Ediva, watching him, said, 'Ida! Hugh! Go and find Symond, if you please. I cannot think what has happened to the refreshments I ordered. Tell him to hurry up, will you? Our guest would like his ale and food now, not tomorrow.'

When her children had gone, she said quietly, 'Sir knight, do not think badly of them. They mourned their father deeply and sincerely when news came of his death, believe me. What you saw today was, I think, the final outburst. It may have appeared brief, but it should be viewed for what it is; a part, merely, of their whole sorrow, to which I hope – I pray – that your timely visit has now put an end.'

Geoffroi, highly embarrassed that she should imagine he criticised them, hastened to reassure her. 'Please, my lady, it is not for me to judge! I would not dream of telling anyone else how to go about coping with the loss of someone as dear as Herbert clearly was to all of you.' Out of the blue, he remembered; how, indeed, had he forgotten, even momentarily? And, knowing he wanted to share his memory with this kind, sensible woman, he said, 'I have just lost my own father. I know what it is like.'

Now Ediva's arms were around him, motherly, reassuring. 'There, there,' she murmured. 'And yet, despite your loss, still you take the trouble to visit us, in this winter season, to bring your message of comfort? Sir Geoffroi, we are in your debt.'

Geoffroi's conscience pricked him as he recalled that there had been another reason for this excursion. He said, 'Well, to be honest, I was glad to make the journey for my own sake as well. It – I – that is, things can get depressing, at home, and it was—' It was useful to have an excuse to get away for a while? No, heaven forbid! He couldn't say that!

But Ediva, as if she understood, said softly, 'Of course. And why not?'

He was saved further awkwardness by the arrival of Ida bearing a tray of food and mugs, and Hugh with a jug of what smelled like mulled ale. Belatedly remembering the Lombard, presumably still patiently waiting outside, Geoffroi said, 'May I summon my companion? He waits out in the courtyard.'

Ediva said, 'Of course! Why did you not tell us that you were not alone?' With a shake of her head as if to say, men! she nodded at Hugh, who hurried outside, and soon the Lombard was being introduced to the family and urged to sit right up close to the fire and have some ale to take the chill out of his bones.

It seemed, Geoffroi thought later, that this was a celebration. He could not work out precisely why it should be so, and concluded that the reason might have been implied in what Ediva had said: his visit, or rather the tidings he brought, had helped this likeable, friendly family by answering their final questions regarding Herbert's death. Now they could put aside their fearful imaginings, abandon for ever those dreadful mental pictures of him suffering, bearing some terrible wound, crying out in the agony of a long drawn-out death.

For it had not been that way, and now they knew it.

Was that not worth a celebration?

The hours passed quickly in cheery conversation and, when Geoffroi went out to see that the horses were comfortable, he was surprised to see that the short winter daylight was drawing to a close and darkness was falling.

Back inside the hall, he said to Ediva, 'My lady, I regret that we must be on our way. It is almost dark, and we have to find lodgings.'

'Nonsense,' she replied briskly. 'You are our guests. You have come all this way – yes, where *is* Acquin, exactly? – and you must stay with us. Yes, children?'

Ida and Hugh said, 'Yes!' Ida, Geoffroi couldn't help but notice, flashed him a brilliant smile.

He realised, with a strange leap of the heart, that the very last thing he actually wanted to do just now was to ride away.

Geoffroi and the Lombard stayed in Lewes for a week. They would have extended the visit longer, and were certainly pressed to do so, but Geoffroi was very aware of his own family back at Acquin. The Christmas season was fast approaching, and he must be home for the feast. It would be the first one that his family would spend without Sir Robert, and Geoffroi knew he must be there to help them all through it. Indeed, to have them help him.

It was amazing, though, how much better he felt now. He felt guilty, as if he should not be feeling so happy when his father had been dead for less than two months. He prayed for forgiveness and confessed himself humbly to the local priest who said, with what sounded like a smile, that God had sent love and happiness as precious gifts and that no man should question them when their flowering stemmed from all that was honest and honourable.

All the way back to the manor house, Geoffroi puzzled over what precisely the priest could have meant.

Later he heard that Ida had visited the priest shortly before he had done.

And he began – very tentatively and wonderingly – to think he might have stumbled on the answer.

By the time Geoffroi and the Lombard left for the journey back to Acquin, Geoffroi knew he had fallen in love with Ida.

She was bright, brave, funny, capable and, given that she was still only sixteen, mature and quite sensible. Sensible, anyway, when she wasn't poking fun at people – Geoffroi in particular – and hooting with laughter.

He was sure – almost sure – that she felt something for him, too.

But he dared not ask. Dared not approach either Ida herself or her mother. For one thing, he had come here on a very different mission from courting Herbert's daughter, and his sense of what was fitting did not allow him to turn the one purpose into the other. For another thing, he was quite terrified that Ida, informed that this large foreigner who had crusaded with her father had fallen in love with her and wished to ask for her hand, would fall over herself laughing.

So Geoffroi kept his peace.

He found a private moment just before his departure to present Ediva with the small parcel of Herbert's belongings. He was about to leave her on her own to open it, but she shot out her hand and caught his sleeve.

'No, Geoffroi, please stay,' she said. 'You have carried this packet so long and so far, and I would prefer you to be with me when I uncover its contents. If you will?'

'Aye, lady,' he said softly. 'Gladly.'

He watched as she unfolded the cloth wrappings and took out her last mementoes of her husband.

They were not many.

A heavy gold signet ring. A fine undershirt, the fabric so soft and worn that it folded up into a small bundle. A knife. A belt.

Geoffroi had realised, when first given the package, that it could not possibly hold all that Herbert had worn and owned; clearly, his body must have been robbed while he lay dead on the battlefield. Some opportunist hand had helped itself to Herbert's sword. To his helmet, breastplate and armour. And the clothing he had been wearing when he died, heavily bloodstained as it must have been, had presumably been buried with him.

A sudden stifled gasp brought him back to the present. Glancing quickly at Ediva, he saw that she held in her hands a carefully folded square of linen, which she unwrapped to reveal three locks of hair.

The brown peppered with strands of grey had to be her own. The short, dark auburn curl – just like Herbert's, Geoffroi remembered – would belong to Hugh.

And the long tress with a wave running through it, its bright chestnut colour catching the light and shining like the sunset, could only have been cut from one head.

Staring at it, Geoffroi felt something – some strange new emotion – take up its place in his heart. And Ediva, as if she perceived and understood, held out Ida's lock of hair.

'Take it, Geoffroi,' she said. 'Guard it safe, as dear Herbert did. Let it serve to keep her in your heart until you come back to us.'

I I

Geoffroi returned to Lewes in the spring.

The Lombard insisted on accompanying him; a man who stood fair to lose his heart (if indeed he had not already lost it), he maintained, ought to have a companion when he went a-courting, in case he lost his head as well and did something foolish that would land him in trouble.

Geoffroi, happy to have his friend's company, gave way to the insistence with a smile.

He was much easier in his mind over leaving Acquin this time than he had been last December. The family had grown used to Sir Robert's absence and it seemed to Geoffroi that, in some ways, life was now simpler and less painful for his mother, at least, now that she no longer had to live with the anxiety of caring for a sick and fast-sinking husband. His brother, Robert, seemed to be coping well with his new responsibilities. Geoffroi felt that Robert would not miss him if he were to go away on even a prolonged visit, since he clearly preferred to set about things quietly and alone, introspective as ever, and without going to the trouble of asking his younger sibling what *he* thought.

The night before he was due to leave, Geoffroi woke from a strange and intense dream. He was standing in a small, round room, a fire burning in a brazier and a woman all in white by his side. She wore a veil of some fine cloth which, while obscuring the detail of her features, yet revealed that her expression was one of grave concern.

In a narrow bed lay a sick person. When the dreaming Geoffroi tried to bend down to see who it might be, the woman shook her head and drew him away. Then she pointed at Geoffroi's chest and said, *Where is it? Do you carry it in the accustomed place?*

And in his dream he felt – just as he had felt it as he carried it for those endless miles – the Eye of Jerusalem, pressed close against his breast.

He drew it out and held it out towards the woman in white. But instead of taking it from him, she stepped back, bowed her head and made way for him now to approach the figure on the bed.

Inside his head someone said, with absolute clarity, *the Eye is yours to command. You know what you must do.*

He was in the very act of holding the Eye over the burning forehead of the sick person – he thought it was a woman, or perhaps a youth – when a jolt ran through him, throwing him into a panic and waking him up.

Sweating, heart pounding, he shot up in bed.

It was a dream, he told himself, willing courage back into his veins. Just a dream.

But he found it impossible to lie down again with any hope of getting back to sleep. No matter how he tried to distract his thoughts, he kept seeing the Eye of Jerusalem; it was as if, having brought itself so dramatically to his attention, it was not going to let go.

Eventually, and with a weird and rather unpleasant

feeling that he obeyed another's whim, Geoffroi got out of bed and, tiptoeing so as not to disturb his brothers and the Lombard, crept out of the chamber and outside into the courtyard.

Even in the dark, he went unerringly to the place where he had hidden his treasure. He moved the concealing stone aside – not without difficulty, for it was some time since he had been out to look at the Eye – and put his hand inside the secret aperture. His fingers found the leather bag, and he drew it out.

He had to have a look.

He opened the bag and held out the Eye, suspended on its chain and gently turning.

Aye. It was as beautiful – and as strange – as it had been in his dream.

He had intended to put it back in its bag and hide it away again. That was his intention; he was quite sure of that.

He was therefore quite surprised when, getting back into bed, he felt the hard shape of the Eye in its bag beneath him as he lay down.

In the morning, he would have put the whole experience down to a febrile dream. Except that there was the Eye, against his heart where he had borne it for so long. Very well, then, he thought. I shall take it with me on my travels. Why not? I can keep it concealed, that I know well enough. I brought it safely home all the way from Damascus, through all the perils of that journey. In comparison, a short visit across the Channel to Lewes is nothing.

Nevertheless, he resolved to attach a new, stout piece of

leather thong to the Eye's bag, by which to hang it around his neck.

He also resolved never to let anyone else see it.

Geoffroi and the Lombard set out, with a spring in their steps, later that morning. It was May, the sun was shining and there was a light, refreshing breeze; perfect travelling weather. They crossed the Channel (this time without being sick) and, once again, followed the now familiar route to Lewes.

They covered the miles from the port to the town in a day. Their boat had arrived very early in the morning and, the month being May and not December, there was more daylight in which to ride.

They went round the edge of Lewes, not needing to ask directions now, and, a little before sunset, rode into Herbert of Lewes's courtyard.

As if she had been waiting for them, Ida came rushing out. Geoffroi's smile of delight froze as he saw that she had been crying; sliding off his horse and hurrying towards her, he was about to ask what was the matter when she threw herself into his arms.

Even his acute awareness of her distress could not entirely rob the moment of its sweetness.

But she was sobbing now, and he made out the words, 'Oh, you're here! I'm so glad, I've prayed and *prayed* for you to come! It's Hugh – Hugh has a fever, and Mother and I have tried *everything*, and he still burns as if he's on fire!'

Geoffroi froze.

She felt it, poor lass, even in her anguish. Pulling away

slightly so that she could look up into his face – he was a lot taller than she was – she said, 'Geoffroi? What is it? What's the matter?'

Instantly he recovered himself. Now was not the moment to go numb with terror at the thought of just what it might be that he carried around his neck, if, indeed, there ever was such a moment. Perhaps, he thought, in a swift burst of practicality, I should just thank God that I *do* carry it.

It was only later – a long time later – that it occurred to him to wonder just which, or whose, God he should thank.

Now, giving Ida a little shake, he said firmly, 'Nothing is the matter. Take me to Hugh – it may be that I can help him.'

A smile broke through her tears, and, with a touching faith that he hoped – prayed – he was worthy of, she said, 'I *knew* you'd save him.'

She took his hand and ran with him inside the hall, up a stair, along a narrow passage and past what appeared to be a small family chapel. Then into a chamber – not round, like the one in Geoffroi's dream – where Hugh lay on a wide bed, his mother sitting beside him pressing a cloth to his forehead.

She looked up at Geoffroi.

She did not speak, but he read in her eyes, as clearly as if she had spoken aloud, *my daughter believes in you, sir knight. Now let us see what you can do.*

He said, 'Greetings, my lady.'

'Geoffroi.' She bowed her head.

Hesitating only an instant, he said, putting all the authority he could summon into his voice, 'I shall need water. Drinking water, if you have it.'

Ediva rose from her stool and fetched a jug and cup.
'Here. Fresh from our own spring, cool and pure.'

He nodded. Very aware of the two pairs of eyes on him
– Hugh lay as if asleep, except for his violent restlessness –
he poured out half a cupful of water. Then, feeling foolish
and unconfident – what if it fails? – he reached inside his
tunic and beneath his undershirt and took out the leather
bag. Removing the Eye, he held the jewel concealed in
the palm of his hand. Then, keeping his movements
hidden, he dropped it into the cup and swirled it around
in the water.

Then, approaching the bed, he slid his hand and forearm
beneath Hugh's head, raised him a little from his damp
pillows, and held the cup to the boy's lips. Hugh took a
sip, then another. Then, to Geoffroi's surprise, he brought
a hand out from beneath the bedcovers and grabbed the
cup, gulping down the remainder of the water as if he
hadn't drunk for a week.

Then, the small effort having exhausted him, he slumped
back on his pillows. He closed his eyes. After a few
moments, he emitted a faint snore.

Into the stunned silence of the room, Ediva said, 'Well!
What have we here, Sir Geoffroi? A knight or a wizard?'

Not entirely sure that the remark should be taken as a
joke, Geoffroi turned to her. He met her frank blue eyes,
so like Ida's. And made up his mind.

'I was given a precious jewel,' he said quietly. 'In
Damascus. I – I was able to render a service for an
Emir and, although I swear to you that it was not done
with reward in mind, he chose to make me this gift.'

For the first time since it had been in his possession,

Geoffroi held up the Eye. He showed it first to Ediva, then to Ida, who gave a gasp.

'And this jewel allows you to feed water into a sick boy who has refused a drop for the last two days?' There was distinct irony in Ediva's tone.

Geoffroi said, 'I do not know, my lady.' He hesitated. 'That it has the power to assuage a fever is indeed one of the claims made by the man who gave it to me. And this is not the first time it has helped someone who was burning up.'

Ediva raised one eyebrow, but made no comment.

Desperate, wanting only to say the right thing and not alienate the mother of the young woman he loved, Geoffroi blurted out, 'But you will have been praying, my lady, you and Ida both, and also there is the natural resilience of youth, and really I make no claim for the Eye, since it is far more likely that Hugh here was ready for a good drink, and that he—'

Surprisingly, Ediva began to laugh. 'Geoffroi, my dear man, stop,' she said, coming to stand beside him and placing her hand on his. 'Who knows, ever, what brings about recovery – or the hope of it – when a loved one is sick? All that we know is that, for the instant, Hugh has at last drunk some water and seems a little better.' She glanced down at her son. 'Now, if you will stay with him, I wish to go to give thanks to God that my prayers have been answered.'

Geoffroi and Ida stood side by side as Ediva swept past and headed down the passage towards the chapel.

When she had gone, Ida said very softly, 'There! I knew you'd come and I knew Hugh would get better.' There was such certainty in her voice that his heart gave a lurch. In a whisper that he barely heard, she added, 'I knew you wouldn't let me down.'

Not thinking, letting his intuition guide him, he turned to her and took her little hands in his. 'Ida, I will *never* let you down,' he whispered back.

He would have said more – quite what, he did not know – but at that moment they heard a footstep out in the passage. In case it might be Ediva, on her way back, they sprang apart. Geoffroi went to the bed to lay a hand on Hugh's forehead – sweating freely now, and correspondingly cooler – and Ida went to pour out some more water.

The respite gave Geoffroi time to collect his thoughts. As his racing heartbeat gradually slowed down, he closed his eyes and sent up a swift but sincere prayer of gratitude that he had been in the right place at the right time.

The mood of the visit improved daily from then on. Hugh remained weak and unwell, although the fever, having broken, did not return. His mother judged that he was on the mend, and set about presenting him with a variety of dainty little dishes to tempt his appetite, accompanied always by draught after draught of water, one cupful of which each morning was subjected to the Eye's blessing.

Ediva, after the shock of their original reunion, now treated Geoffroi much as she had done before; whatever thoughts she might have on his possession and use of the Eye, she kept to herself. Ida, however, was far less reticent; in fact, she was not reticent at all.

'I would lay odds that you have captured her heart,' the

Lombard teased Geoffroi as they settled down for sleep on the fifth night after their arrival. 'Would that every man who went a-courting could effect a miracle cure on his sweetheart's little brother!'

Geoffroi had not told his friend of the Eye's role in Hugh's recovery, which made him uneasy since it meant he had to take credit for a healing skill that he did not actually possess. 'Better to have no sick little brother in the first place,' he said soberly.

Faintly he heard the Lombard chuckle but, to Geoffroi's relief, he did not pursue the matter.

The next day, Ida and Geoffroi went out riding together.

It was the first time that they had spent any length of time entirely in one another's company. Geoffroi felt the joyful hours of that fine May day etch themselves so deeply in his memory that he knew he would never forget one moment of them. And, looking at Ida's happy, laughter-filled face, illuminated to beauty by her love, he guessed she felt the same.

He went to speak to Ediva one evening, while Ida was sitting with the fast-recovering Hugh.

They sat facing one another in front of the fire in the hall; Geoffroi imagined that she knew very well what he wanted to say, and did not waste her time by hesitation.

'I have fallen in love with Ida,' he said simply, 'and I would like to ask her to be my wife.' Before Ediva could speak, he rushed on, 'I have a home to offer her – Acquin is not grand or even very large, but it is the household of a proper family, secure, full of affection, and it is set in the midst of fertile, productive land. For all that I cannot offer her great wealth, jewels or fine clothes, Ida would not want for any necessity, you have my word on that. My mother, my brothers and my sister would welcome her and embrace her as one of the family and, as for me, well, I will not cease to work to make her happy as long as I live.' He cast around in his mind to see if he had left anything out; he didn't think so. He raised his eyes from their studied concentration of the fire and met Ediva's.

She was smiling.

'Geoffroi,' she said gently, 'Although I now know the whereabouts of Acquin, and appreciate that it is not too many days' distant from us here at Lewes, I must say that my hope has always been that Ida would marry a man who lived close by.'

Heart beating fast even as it appeared to plunge down towards his boots, Geoffroi said, 'But—'

Ediva held up her hand for silence.

'I had in mind,' she went on, 'some kindly, honourable, courteous man who loved her deeply and whom she loved in return, who lived close by so that I might have the pleasure of seeing my beloved daughter grow in beauty as she embraced the joys of being a wife and, in time, a mother.' She paused, looking steadfastly into Geoffroi's eyes. 'But,' she went on, a smile quirking her lips, 'I think I always knew that was asking for too much. This paragon of virtues who lived but a stone's throw away just does not seem to exist' – she gave a small sigh – 'so I suppose we shall have to make do with you.'

Geoffroi, mouth open, closed it and then said again, 'But—'

Ediva began to laugh. 'Geoffroi, my dear man, I am teasing, and it is very wrong of me.' She got up and came to sit beside him. 'What I just said is, in essence, true. But what I did not say is that, in all important respects, you are what I should have chosen for Ida, and I am quite sure dear Herbert would have thought so too.' There was a brief pause – her voice had broken a little as she spoke of Herbert – and then she said, 'What woman, after all, sees her daughter establish her own household on the doorstep of her mother's? My girl will be happy with you, Geoffroi,' she added firmly. 'Go and ask her if she will have you. And, if she will, you have my blessing.'

He asked her. So eager was she to say yes that she had thrown herself on him, shouting 'I will! Oh, I will!' even before he had finished getting the words out.

Geoffroi d'Acquin and Ida, daughter of Herbert of Lewes, were married on Midsummer's Day of the following year. The seventeen-year-old bride, who did not seem to be able to keep her adoring eyes off her tall husband, wore a garland of flowers on her auburn hair; Geoffroi, gazing down at her as she clung to his arm, thought, eyes as blue as the midsummer sky. Aye, now I see it for myself.

Herbert, I thank you.

12

From the start, Geoffroi and Ida were happy together. Ida took to Acquin as soon as she saw it – country girl that she was, the landscape and the quiet rural setting suited her well – and she quickly grew to love the lady Matilda, Geoffroi's mother. She became, to a greater extent than Geoffroi had dared to hope, given her youth, a dependable, capable and beloved member of his family. If she missed her own mother and her childhood home, she never said, and Geoffroi did not ask.

Geoffroi's brother Robert was not well. They all realised it and, it seemed to Geoffroi, they all made private preparations for what rapidly began to seem the inevitable. The poor man, skeleton-thin, and racked with pains in both his stomach and his chest, lasted through the summer and saw the harvest in, although he himself had no hand in it.

Satisfied that he left Acquin in Geoffroi's good hands – 'You really have had enough of soldiering, haven't you, Geoffroi?' – Robert d'Acquin died in the warmth of a golden September evening, three months after Geoffroi had brought home his bride. And, with his passing, Geoffroi took up the title and the responsibilities of Acquin, and his new life truly began.

He had the firm support of his mother; and the lady

Matilda probably knew as well as, if not better than, anyone did how to run the estate. But she could not go out herself to order and command the busy daily round of the farmer, and neither could frail Esmai nor young William, about to leave Acquin and enter a monastery near Rouen.

Geoffroi, feeling the weight of Acquin descend on to his back, was more grateful than he could say for the presence of the Lombard. 'I know you want to go home,' he said one day to his friend, 'and I know, too, that I am wrong to detain you here, but—'

'You do not detain me,' the Lombard said calmly. 'I choose to stay.'

'—but if you'd just agree to remain with us for another few months, just while I get used to everything,' Geoffroi continued as if he hadn't heard, 'I should thank you with all my heart and keep you always in my prayers.'

The Lombard said, with the faintest irony, 'How kind.'

The Lombard was true to his word and remained at Acquin through that winter and the following spring and summer. Geoffroi gradually ceased to consult him before making big decisions, and the time finally came when he didn't consult him at all, instead merely informing him once a decision had been made, and then more from courtesy and habit than from necessity.

By early autumn, it was apparent that Ida was pregnant.

The state became her; Geoffroi thought she had never looked lovelier and he fell in love with her all over again.

It was perhaps their very apparent happiness together –

and the attendant redundancy of anybody else – that made the Lombard finally decide that, at long last, it was time for him to head for home. Perhaps, as Geoffroi remarked to Ida, he had started to think that a wife and family of his own would not be a bad thing.

They saw him on his way one dull September day, just short of the first anniversary of Robert's death. Both Geoffroi and the Lombard were feeling the effects of the farewell feast which Matilda, Ida and their serving women had prepared the night before; the wine had flowed in almost as lively a manner as the Aa now rushed along between its banks.

Geoffroi wished for a swift final parting; sentimental man that he was, he hated saying goodbye. Especially to such an old friend, and especially when that friend was hardly likely ever to come back to Acquin. It seemed that the Lombard, too, was affected by the emotion of the moment; he must have had tears in his eyes, Geoffroi thought, as, deeply moved himself, he stood watching the distant figure ride away. For why else, unless it were to hide them from me, would he not meet mine?

In the months that followed, the Acquin region – indeed, much of north-east Europe – saw some of the worst weather it had known for years. Cold followed rain, persistent damp and fog brought chills and ailments, animals fell sick, and then people did, too. Strangers were seen: a dark man and his companion, furtive, skulking in the shadows like Death himself.

In February, the plague came.

At Acquin, where the family and the villagers were a

reasonably self-sufficient unit, they were safe; as safe, anyway, as anybody could be. But it did not stop them from suffering sleepless nights of terrible anxiety. It did not stop them praying long and hard for others; the local priest saw to that. Father Herluin, who did not spare himself in striving to save the living, care for the sick and comfort the dying, stressed upon his parishioners that it was their duty to go down on their knees to pray for God's love for the suffering and, each day that they themselves were spared, thank Him for His mercy.

As he worried over what was happening in other, less fortunate households, it occurred to Geoffroi to wonder if the Eye of Jerusalem could be of any help; to wonder, indeed, if he dared propose the use of such an infidel thing to Father Herluin. But the Lord helps those who help themselves, Geoffroi reminded himself; and, besides, why had God allowed the Eye to fall into Geoffroi's hands if he was not supposed to use it for the good of his fellow men?

And Father Herluin was a compassionate and broad-minded man. Unlike other churchmen whom Geoffroi had encountered, both on crusade and afterwards, the local priest did not subscribe to the entrenched belief of the average western cleric that all Christians were good and all non-Christians were terrible sinners, debauched and vicious and beyond God's mercy. Geoffroi had seen too much evidence to the contrary to support such a view and when, on returning to Acquin, he mulled over such matters with Father Herluin, he had been heartily relieved to find that the priest did not brand men as sheep or goats, preferring to obey Christ's teaching and leave such judgement to God.

Talking the matter over with Ida as they lay in bed one night served to make up Geoffroi's mind; he would offer his services with his magic Eye and, if the priest thought he could be of help, he would go with Father Herluin to try out the jewel's healing powers.

In the morning, choosing a moment when the household was occupied elsewhere and the courtyard was empty, he crept through the stables and the disused storeroom and across to the wall in which he had hidden away the Eye.

It was not there.

Stupidly, for it was a very small hiding place, he felt all around the aperture that he had hollowed out between the stones. Then he looked on the floor, then up at the rafters over his head. It was only when he found himself down on hands and knees, feeling all over the cobwebby, dusty flagstones, that he had to admit the truth.

The Eye had vanished.

In that first instant of horrified reaction, he almost believed that the jewel had disappeared of its own volition. He had always thought of it as something awesome, something that answered to laws known only to itself. And he had always half-believed that it was only on loan; that, someday, somehow, Mehmed would regret his generous gesture and come to fetch his prize back again.

Was that it? Slowly he rose to his feet, brushing dust and old, dead leaves from his knees. Had the Eye gone home again?

The shock wore off as he walked slowly back to the house. Of course it hadn't, he told himself firmly, don't be so foolish! Somebody had stolen it.

This logical conclusion led to another thought which,

in its way, was even more dreadful than imagining the Eye to have made off all by itself. Because, when Geoffroi thought it through, he realised that, with the possible exception of one person, nobody in the world knew where he had hidden the Eye. He had not even told Ida; oh, he had wanted to, but she had not let him. 'The Eye is yours, my love,' she had said firmly, 'and I wish no part in it, no, not even to know of its whereabouts. For, who can say, I might be tempted one day to try to use it, and that would not be right.'

He had wondered afterwards if she might be afraid of the Eye. He would not have blamed her if she had been; he was a little afraid of it himself.

No, he thought as he made his way to where Ida would be finishing dressing, preparatory to descending from their bedchamber. No, my Ida can neither have moved the Eye herself nor have told anyone else where it was concealed. And no other soul at Acquin even knows that I possess it.

Except possibly one.

And he is no longer here, but now back home in Lombardy.

With a muffled moan, Geoffroi slumped down on the cold stone step and put his head in his hands. And, against his will, a picture formed in his mind. Of himself, on his return from that second visit to Lewes when, on the prompting of a dream, he had taken the Eye with him and helped to heal Ida's little brother. Going out to the hiding place at dusk the day that he and the Lombard had returned to Acquin, he had heard a small sound as he dusted off his hands after replacing the Eye in its hiding place. Looking around him in alarm, he had seen a pair of doves on the stable roof, cooing and fluttering as they settled. You are too nervous! he had reproached himself, crossing the courtyard back to the house. Where the Lombard stood, just inside the door and slightly breathless.

Did I deliberately put the awful suspicion from my mind because I felt us to be so close? Geoffroi wondered now. Did I tell myself that to believe him capable of *spying* on me was an insult to our long friendship, to the many hardships we had shared, to the support we had given each other over so many miles and so many months?

With another groan, he realised that it was true. He *had* believed, that night, that the Lombard might have crept out to see what his friend was up to. Which raised the further, equally disturbing question: had the Lombard known what Geoffroi took to Lewes with him and so secretively brought home again?

Needing the comfort of his wife, Geoffroi got to his feet and went on up to their chamber. There she was, now noticeably rounded with pregnancy, her lovely face serene and happy; hurrying towards her, he knelt at her feet and told her what had happened. And what he suspected.

She said nothing for some moments, merely stroking his head with a gentle hand while his anguish subsided. Then she said quietly, 'You are sure, my love? There can be no other explanation? Can it not be possible that someone else in the household witnessed you either fetching the stone from its hiding place or putting it back?'

'I have tried to think that there might be some other culprit,' Geoffroi replied, 'but in my heart I know there cannot be. The occasions on which I have taken the Eye out of concealment are so very few that I can remember every one with clarity. Each time, Ida, I made sure I knew beforehand where everybody was; I cannot have been observed, I would stake my life on it!'

'There, there,' she comforted, 'do not distress yourself.' Her hands continued to stroke his head. 'Then if, as it seems, the Lombard truly is the thief, then we must ascribe his action to unbearable temptation, and we must pray for him.'

Her charity did not surprise him, but nevertheless he was stung to protest. 'Ida, he has robbed me of a thing of great beauty and value! And you say we must *pray* for him?'

'Indeed I do,' she insisted. 'For he was your true friend, Geoffroi, of that there is no doubt. We must pray for him because the evil one tempted him, and he had not the fortitude to resist.' He was about to make a sour comment but she overrode him. 'He deserves your pity, my love. How do you think he feels, knowing that he has stolen from his great friend and has no means of making recompense? How, Geoffroi? Will he not feel like the worst cur on God's earth?'

But Geoffroi, who had no idea, made no answer.

When he was calm again and he and Ida prepared to go and join the household, she said, practical girl that she was, 'What a good thing it is that you had not yet mentioned the magical stone to Father Herluin. As it is, you have not raised his hopes for nothing.'

Ida and Geoffroi's first child was born in April that year, 1154. The baby was a girl, and they named her Eleanor.

Their delight in her was tempered by anxiety, however; she did not thrive.

Ida's mother came over on a prolonged visit, and she and the lady Matilda put their experienced heads together and tried various remedies and therapies. Sometimes the baby responded, usually not. She was pale, disinclined to feed, and her breathing had a distinct rattle.

'If I only had the Eye,' Geoffroi said to Ida one sleepless night, 'then I could make her well.'

'You do not know that, my love,' Ida replied. 'There is no real proof that your magical stone ever did anybody any good. Is there?'

'But—' No. She was right. 'No. It could all have been mere coincidence.'

'Just so,' she agreed, adding lovingly, 'Do not torture yourself with what might have been.'

Torture myself? he thought, looking into her deadly white face, eyes circled with darkness, their lids perpetually pink from her secret weeping. Oh, Ida, I would give the entire world, my own self included, if I could only make our child well and make you smile again.

The baby gave up her brief struggle in October.

Geoffroi, wondering how anyone could grieve as Ida did and still live, entered a time of grey misery from which, for a while, he almost believed he would never emerge. Shouting at the priest one day, histrionically he demanded that God tell him what terrible sin he had done, that Ida and he should now be so punished.

Father Herluin let him rage. Then, when he was quiet, said gently, 'There is no answer to your question, Geoffroi. And the only comfort I can give you is to say that you *will* be better, in time. Ida will recover. And so will you.'

But Ida was sick. The light in her eyes had gone out, and she was listless, unenthusiastic. Geoffroi took her over to England for a stay with her mother and Hugh, and the change of scene seemed to do her good. But then they came home again, and the loss of her child was once more right there before her.

Father Herluin suggested privately to Geoffroi that another baby might serve to take her mind off her grief. But Ida seemed disinclined for lovemaking, and Geoffroi, loving her as he did, would not force her.

Then, in the September of 1156, the lady Matilda succumbed to a brief but violent fever and joined her husband in death.

With William gone to Rouen and Esmai now a semi-invalid, home seemed a quiet, empty place of unremitting hard work and little else. Geoffroi wondered if there could ever be any happiness at Acquin again.

Then at last, on a bright spring day when he persuaded Ida to ride out with him and see the beauty of the sun on the new green grass, things changed. They spotted a small clump of primroses sunning themselves at the top of a low bank, and Geoffroi, too eager, hurried over to pick one for her and slipped, sliding all the way down the bank and landing with one foot in the muddy sludge at the edge of the Aa river. Ida, sombre face creasing into a wide grin, burst out laughing.

The laughter released something in her; holding her in his arms, he felt her mirth turn to tears, and she wept as she had not done since the baby's death. But then, when she dried her eyes, she turned her face up to him and said, 'Oh, Geoffroi, I feel better. I do! It's as if—' She frowned. 'As if I've turned a corner and, although she's still there, I don't have to look at her every moment. Is that terrible?'

He fought to control his voice. 'No, my sweet, not terrible at all. Natural, I would say. And—' He wondered if he should say what had come to mind; it was something Father Herluin spoke of, prayed for.

'And what?'

He stared down at her, bending his head to kiss the tip of her nose. 'Father Herluin would say it's a sign of God's compassion.'

'God's compassion,' she repeated softly. Then, standing on tiptoe, she reached up and kissed him full on the mouth.

Their second child was born on 10th October 1160, six years after they had lost their first.

He was a strong, healthy boy who suckled enthusiastically, slept deeply and peacefully and seemed to grow under their very eyes. They named him Josse, and he healed his mother's sore heart.

Geoffroi often wondered, as the years went by and the family grew, whether the tragedy of their first, lost child had been because she was a girl. For Ida, who soon became as efficient at motherhood and child-rearing as she was at everything else, gave birth to four more sons in fairly quick succession, each as lusty and as healthy as their eldest brother. Yves was born in the early autumn of 1162, Patrice in November of the following year, Honoré in March of 1165 and Acelin in the heat of August in 1166.

Even the thin spinster Esmai responded to a houseful of boys; summoning from unsuspected depths a voice worthy of a warrior, she ruled her young nephews, whenever they were left in her care, with a firm hand that only they knew hid a loving heart and a mouth just made for laughter.

Acquin responded to the happiness of the family. Year after fruitful year saw good harvests, healthy stock, contented tenants. Geoffroi, walking one evening with his old friend the priest, was not in the least surprised when, stopping to admire the peaceful scene of the manor standing serenely at the top of the valley, Father Herluin said with forgivable smugness, 'There! I told you so!'

The boys grew. Josse, it became clear, was exactly like his father and wanted nothing from life but to be a soldier. He was sent away, just as his father had been, to the household of Sir Girald de Gisors, although the head of the household there was now the son of the man who had instructed Geoffroi.

Ida, who never forgot her English home, insisted that each of her sons spend time with their Uncle Hugh in Lewes. Her own mother, the lady Ediva, died peacefully a couple of years after Acelin was born. She had lived to enjoy not only her five grandsons but also the three little girls born to Hugh and his wife; as she had apparently said shortly before her death, what more could any woman ask?

Yves had inherited his grandfather's love of the land and, with the encouragement of his parents, he took an active part in the running of Acquin from a young age. While the thirteen-year-old Josse was moving in the exalted circles of the Plantagenet court – even meeting the young Richard, on one memorable occasion – Yves, at eleven, was already a very valuable part of the Acquin management.

Geoffroi, watching his beloved Ida grow in stature, girth, confidence and serenity, shared with her a joy in their sons that he would have not thought possible. I have been given so much more than I deserve, he thought; I am thankful, to my very bones, for everything.

He barely gave his hectic past a thought unless it was at the prompting of his sons. Josse, naturally, whenever he came home would plague his father to tell him about the crusades and the infidel and what weapons they used and how the Christian army won, and Geoffroi was only too happy to comply. The younger boys would creep towards their father as he sat by the fire, his eldest son at his feet, and listen wide-eyed to Geoffroi's tales. They preferred it when he passed on the stories he had picked up from other men, closer to the heart of the great ones' lives; in their shrill little voices they would plead, 'Tell us about the kings and the queens! Tell us about the rich people, the lords and the ladies, and the king's sorcerer!'

Sometimes Geoffroi would tell the tale of how he saved a little infidel boy, and how a grateful grandfather gave him a sapphire the size of your fist in thanks. From her quiet corner the other side of the fire, Ida would say mildly, 'Your fist? *I* would say, closer to your thumb.'

And sometimes, when wine had made him maudlin, Geoffroi would mention the Lombard. But even then, he could not bring himself to admit his suspicions about his old friend. Once, when Yves asked what had happened to the Eye of Jerusalem, Geoffroi said, 'Eh? What became of it, you ask? I don't know, son. I suppose I must have lost it.'

And, in the end, he half-believed it himself.

The boys' beloved Aunt Esmai died in the cold winter of 1173. And, in a hot July three years later, Geoffroi himself died, as a result of falling from the top of a laden wagon bringing in sheaves of ripe, golden corn.

Cut down, like the Corn King, with the harvest.

Ida, who lost a part of herself when he died, nevertheless knew it was too soon for her sons to be robbed of both their parents. Yves was still but fourteen, and Acquin too heavy a burden for him alone just yet, even with the support of his younger brothers. And Ida did not want Yves to put pressure on Josse to come home, not when Josse was just beginning to throw himself – with no small success – into his military career.

She lived until February 1180. Then, sad to leave her children but overjoyed at the prospect of joining Geoffroi, she died.

One after another, the younger brothers married and, in time, sons and daughters were born to them. While Josse followed his own star, his kin guarded and tended Acquin.

Geoffroi's home, which he had loved and to which he had returned after his great crusading adventure, where he had taken his beloved Ida as his wife, was in safe hands.

PART FOUR

England, Autumn 1192

13

Josse and Yves had talked for hours.

Some time towards the dawn, Josse awoke from his first deep sleep. He felt restless. Too many memories had been stirred up, and his mind did not want the calm peace of sleep. He glanced across at Yves, who was fast asleep, on his back with his mouth slightly open and snoring gently. Josse grinned. Dear old Yves. It had been a rare pleasure, that long night of reminiscence. So vividly had the memories flowed back that, at one time, Josse had looked up and thought that he saw Geoffroi and Ida standing in a dark corner, smiling down on their two eldest sons.

They weren't there, of course. Although Josse would hardly have been surprised if they had been.

Closing his eyes once more and settling down to try to sleep, he saw in his mind's eye his father, sitting in his accustomed place by the fire, with Ida opposite him suckling a newborn baby. Acelin, would it be? Or Honoré? There at Geoffroi's feet sat Josse and Yves, and on his lap, half-asleep, thumb in his mouth and fingers playing delicately with the hair on his father's forearm, another small child. From time to time Geoffroi would place a gentle kiss on the top of the little down-covered head nestling into his neck.

Geoffroi was talking. His voice came quite clearly to Josse; half-awake, half-dreaming, he heard his father say, *'and do you know what the emir gave me? It was a huge sapphire, as big as your fist, set in a golden coin! There was writing etched into the gold, but I did not know how to read it — they told me that the words were in a language called Aramaic, which was the language of the Persians. They had an empire, you know — they were conquerors with a vast army, and when they marched they were invincible. They took Babylon, and Assyria, and Turkey, and Syria, and even Egypt, and they would have gone on to expand into Greece except they came up against Alexander the Great, and he had an even mightier army than the Persians. But that's another story — I was telling you how I came by the stone that they call the Eye of Jerusalem, which a fat old man too large to ride into battle gave to me, because I saved the life of his little grandson. The sorcerer said it was a magical stone, you know, and would always warn me when a secret enemy approached, so I carried it safely, all the way home from Outremer to Acquin, and it saved the lives of many of my companions. It even saved the life of your Uncle Hugh, when I took it to England with me when I went to court your mother.'* Josse smiled, watching as his father sent a loving glance across the fireplace to his mother, who smiled equally lovingly back at him. *'And it was so beautiful, boys, that I loved just to hold it up and look into its depths, where, if you were very careful and caught the light just right, you could see an eye, the jewel's very own eye, staring out at you . . .'*

Aye. The Eye of Jerusalem. That had been Father's best tale of all. And it had been a tale that did not have a satisfactory end.

Josse thought on. Worrying at half-resolved ideas, trying out theories until they began to clarify, slowly he drew a tentative conclusion. Then, as sleep finally won him over, he dreamed that his father had grown a long milk-white beard and carried a tiny girl in arms suddenly grown like the limbs of a tree.

As they were eating the simple breakfast brought to them by Brother Saul the next morning, Josse said, 'I've been thinking, Yves.'

Yves grinned. 'Thought you might have.'

'Aye.' Josse laughed briefly. 'Plenty to dwell on, in all those memories we brought up last night.'

'Go on, then.' Yves reached for another piece of bread. 'What have you been thinking?'

'You remember how Father used to tell us of that wondrous, magical sapphire he was given in Damascus?'

'The Eye of Jerusalem. Of course, it was always the story that I liked the best.'

'Remember what he would say when we asked where the stone was now?

'Aye. He'd say he'd lost it, and he always looked so sad.'

Eager now, Josse sat forward, face close to his brother's; for some reason that he did not stop to query, he lowered his voice to a level that only Yves could have heard.

'What do you think of this?' he whispered. 'That friend who travelled home from Outremer with Father and stayed on with him at Acquin—'

'The Lombard?'

'Aye, the Lombard. Supposing it was not friendship that

kept him so long with Father? Supposing he had caught a glimpse of the Eye on one of those occasions that Father used it, and decided he would not rest until it was his?'

'You're suggesting he *stole* from Father?' Honest, decent Yves was clearly shocked at the idea. 'From his friend? When he was Father's *guest*?'

'Aye, I am,' Josse said tersely. 'The way I see it is this. Maybe the Lombard even knew about the Eye right from the start, from the very night Father was given it. You wouldn't know, Yves, because you're not a soldier, but, believe me, it's not easy to keep anything a secret when the men of an army eat, rest, exercise and sleep side by side, together every moment of every day. Even when they're not fighting.'

'Father used to say that Grandfather Herbert was the best source of information in all of Outremer,' Yves said, a smile on his face.

'Exactly!' Josse pounded a triumphant fist on the planks of the table, making it bounce on its supports. 'Just what I mean! I shouldn't be surprised if they all gossiped ceaselessly. When not engaged in fighting, there's little more tedious than being a soldier stuck in camp with nothing to do but moan and speculate. A good bit of rumour-mongering always serves to lighten the mood.'

'You ought to know,' Yves said.

'Just supposing,' Josse went on, 'that the Lombard got wind of some magical jewel given to Geoffroi of Acquin. For all we know, it might have been all round the camp; maybe everyone was whispering and muttering about it. So perhaps the Lombard goes a step further and thinks it would be a good idea to work on making friends with the man. I do not wish to undermine their affection for one another, which might well have been perfectly genuine. But I think it entirely possible that, because he was forewarned and looking out for it, the Lombard managed to spy on Father on one of those occasions on the journey home when he used the Eye. And after that, he couldn't give up till he'd achieved his end.'

Yves was frowning. 'He knew of the Eye – at least, he knew Father had *something*. So he kept close to him, all the way home, and watched out to see if he could catch a glimpse of whatever it was. He managed to do so, and whatever it was that he saw convinced him that he couldn't turn for home till he'd stolen it from Father.' A pause. 'From his *friend*!'

'I know,' Josse said gently, 'it's not what you would do, honest fellow that you are.'

'Nor you!' Yves cried hotly. 'Nor any decent man!'

'Hush!' Josse glanced around him, but there was nobody within earshot. 'But my speculations do not end there, Yves. I'm thinking that, if we are right and the Lombard did steal the Eye, then perhaps he, too, realised he had gravely offended against his friend. Perhaps, as he grew old and sick, he made up his mind that there was one thing he must do before he died.'

'He travelled back to Acquin to return the Eye!' Yves finished for him. 'Only to find that Father was dead, so he tried to take it to you instead.' His excited expression faded. 'Except he didn't get to you. He died, right here at Hawkenlye, before he could reach you.'

Josse was watching him. 'Not entirely bad, was he?' he said gently. 'He was sorry for what he had done, and he died in the very act of trying to make amends. We should not judge him too harshly, Yves.'

'Hmm.' Yves did not sound completely convinced. He sat frowning, chewing on his lip, for a while, then said musingly, 'We can give him a name, now. The Lombard was Galbertius Sidonius.'

'Aye.' Josse, too, was frowning. There was something . . . something had been nagging at him yesterday, when he and young Augustus had been talking to the Abbess. Augustus had made some remark – about not everybody in the world being Christian – and a thought had half formed in Josse's mind, only to be overwhelmed with everything else that had been going on.

It was still nagging now, whatever it was, and it concerned the Lombard. Or Geoffroi. Or probably, Josse thought with a flash of frustration, both of them.

There was silence between them for some time. Then Yves said, 'What should we do now, Josse?'

Josse looked at him with deep affection. I wonder, he thought, just how many times I've heard him say that. From when we were tiny, and trying to decide where to run away and play, to as recently as last year, wondering what to do about the field at Acquin that always floods with heavy spring rainfall.

He reached out and clasped his brother's arm. 'I don't know yet,' he said with a smile, 'but just give me time, and I'll come up with something.'

Sooner than he had expected, he broke the contemplative silence again. 'You recall I told you that Prince John came to see me, using the excuse of trying to extort rent for New Winnowlands out of me?'

'Aye, I do.' Yves smiled. 'Hardly something I'm likely to forget, when a prince of the realm honours my brother with a visit.'

'He has a certain charm,' Josse mused, 'and, for all we hear tell of his cunning, conniving ways, I cannot help but like him. But, to return to the point, Yves, he came looking for Galbertius. Remember?'

'Aye. And you ask yourself how it comes to be, that Prince John is going to considerable efforts to find the very man who came north to seek Father and you.'

'I may well ask myself,' Josse said, 'but I give no answers.'

'What exactly did the Prince say?'

'He asked if I had news of a stranger, Galbertius Sidonius, and to be sure to send word if I came across him.'

'And the old man, John Dee, did he add anything to that when you went to see him?'

'No, I can't say that he did.' Josse scratched his head, thinking hard. 'He confirmed that the Prince and his party had gone to London, and he informed me that Sidonius was not a young man, and so could not be the victim found here in the Vale.'

'And?' Yves was looking at him expectantly.

'I think that was all.'

'Yet you still appear to be racking your brains over something.'

'Aye, I am, but it does not concern my visit to John Dee. No, all that he said in addition to what I have just told you was that he seemed to know how and when Father died.'

'He's a sorcerer,' Yves said with calm acceptance.

'People like him are meant to know impossible things. Ordinary men do well not to question the ways of sorcerers.'

'Quite,' Josse agreed. 'He also said that the stranger would come to me – I suppose he meant Galbertius – or someone who represented him.' He tried to think, but the image was unclear. 'It's all rather vague – it was almost as if he had put me in a trance.'

'That's sorcerers for you,' Yves said knowingly, as if he knew dozens and was familiar with their little ways.

'And he confirmed that he is descended from the John Dee that Father used to talk about – you know, the magician in the court of the first William and his sons, Rufus and Henry.'

'I recall being frightened out of my wits when Father told tales about him,' Yves said in a hushed voice. 'There was one about him going out by the light of the full moon to collect the silver berries of the mistletoe from a great oak tree, a golden knife in his hand and—'

'The knife!' Josse shouted.

'The knife? It's only a fable, Josse, an old legend to entertain the children round the fire!'

'Not *that* knife.' The elusive fragment had returned to Josse. 'The knife that was found in the corpse discovered down there' – he waved an impatient hand – 'had a curved tip. It was young Augustus saying not all folk were Christian that did it!' He grinned broadly at Yves.

'Did what, Josse?'

'Made me remember, of course! Father had a knife like that – I only saw it the once, when Mother was going through his things after he died. It wasn't the sort of knife he'd have had much use for – too small – and Mother probably refused to let him give it to us boys to play with in case we accidentally cut our own fingers or each other's ears off. It had a curved tip.'

'So?' Yves sounded bemused.

'He brought it home from Outremer!' Josse cried. 'It was a Saracen knife.'

Enlightenment dawned on Yves's face. 'Which was why the lad's comment about people not all being Christian made you think about it! Father met Muslims – met and fought them – and brought home one of their weapons as a souvenir.'

'And a very similar weapon has recently been used to kill a young man here at Hawkenlye,' Josse finished. 'Just what, Yves, are we to make of that?'

'You think it is important?' Yves whispered.

'I do, although I cannot yet say why.' Frowning, Josse got to his feet. 'A man from Lombardy steals a precious Outremer jewel from our father, dies trying to return it and, at the same time, another man is murdered with a knife that gives every appearance of being of Saracen origin. Aye, Yves, I *know* it is important.' He strode over to the doorway. 'Are you coming?'

Yves hastened to join him. 'Where are we going?'

Josse gave a brief sound of annoyance. 'I am sorry, Yves, I forgot. You do not know her as I do.'

'Her?'

'Aye. We're going to talk to the Abbess Helewise, if she can spare us the time. We will tell her of all our conjecturing, and ask her to turn her considerable mental powers on to the problem and give us the benefit of her opinion.'

'And that will help us?'

Josse gave him an almost pitying look. 'Oh, yes, Yves. Undoubtedly it will.'

14

Helewise had been expecting a visit from Josse and his brother, and she managed to find space in her busy day to receive them.

Studying them as they stood before her in her room, she noted both the similarities and the differences between the two men. Yves had his elder brother's dark eyes and thick brown hair, and there was the same suggestion of lurking humour in his face. But he was built altogether on a smaller scale than Josse: he was shorter (but then most men were) and less broad framed.

But Josse had begun to speak. 'My lady Abbess, we wish to share with you our thoughts concerning this Galbertius Sidonius and what compelled him to seek out the family d'Acquin, if you would hear us?'

'Gladly,' she replied, as, tucking her hands away in the opposite sleeves of her habit, she settled to listen.

When they had finished – Josse had been the main speaker, although, as he gathered confidence and lost his apparent awe of the novel surroundings in which he found himself, Yves had increasingly joined in – she said, 'You have worked long and hard on this mystery. And the fabric that you weave out of these many disparate strands is sound, I think.' She paused and, into the brief silence, she heard Josse murmur, 'Thank you.'

Then, expressing a thought that had struck her as they told the tale, she went on, 'This theft of the Eye of Jerusalem by the man he knew as the Lombard may be, perhaps, why your father always seemed sad when he spoke of how the jewel was lost. Because he suspected – but could hardly bring himself to believe – that his friend had stolen it from him.'

Yves, meeting her eyes, said, 'He was a kind, honest, man. Perhaps he was too willing to look for the good in people and not see the bad.'

Helewise studied him. His earnest, slightly bashful expression suggested he might be a little ashamed of his late father's naivety and, wishing to comfort him, she said, 'Would that we were all made that way. It is a noble fault, if, indeed, fault it is.'

He gave her a brief bow, and she saw a faint flush colour his cheeks. Then, looking from one brother to the other, she said, 'One question, however, you do not appear to have addressed.'

Josse grinned. 'Only one? I fear there are many more than that.'

She smiled back. 'The matter that I have in mind is this: where, do you think, is this precious jewel now?'

There was a silence. She guessed, from the look that passed between them, that it was a question they had not thought about at all.

Since neither brother appeared to have anything to say, she spoke instead. 'You were asked by Prince John,

Sir Josse, to inform him if you heard tell of Galbertius Sidonius. Yes?'

'Yes.'

She indicated Yves with a slight inclination of her head and a lift of her eyebrows; Josse, understanding, added, 'Aye, I've told him all about the Prince's visit, and my own journey to speak to John Dee.'

'Very well. I am thinking that, now that we believe we have identified Galbertius as the old man who died here in August, should you not go to the Prince and inform him?'

Again, she observed, there was that exchange of glances between the brothers. Then Josse said, 'I am not entirely convinced of the wisdom of that, my lady.'

She thought she could guess why. But nevertheless she asked, 'And your reason for that lack of conviction?'

Josse had the grace to look abashed; he was, after all, speaking of a man of royal blood. 'Er – because I fear that Prince John's interest in Galbertius may not have been so much in the man himself as what he bore.'

'Ah,' she said softly. 'The Eye of Jerusalem.'

'Quite so.'

'The Eye that belonged to your father and is now rightfully yours.'

She saw a brief flash of cupidity at war with the genial expression of open, honest decency that he habitually wore. And he said, after a moment, 'Er – aye.'

'Sir Josse,' she said quietly, 'at present an old man with no name lies in our graveyard. If a visit to the court of Prince John can help us to identify him with a further degree of certainty than we already have, should you not make that visit?'

'But—'

'Besides,' she interrupted craftily, 'as we established earlier, the present whereabouts of the Eye is unknown. The Prince, you speculate, is greatly interested in this jewel and knew, so it seems, that Galbertius had some connection with it. Is it not possible that he may have some idea where the Eye is now?'

Josse said, 'My lady, if we are right in assuming that it was the Eye that Prince John came seeking when he asked after Galbertius, then surely it can only be that he heard tell of it from rumour, from crusader gossip. And I cannot think that, other than the one whispered name, he can possess any more details than—'

Abruptly he broke off. Yves, turning to him, said with slight anxiety, 'Josse?'

And Helewise, able to see his face quite clearly from where she sat, observed that his eyes had widened in what looked like mild shock.

'Sir Josse?' she prompted. 'What is the matter?'

'I—' He looked at her, glanced at Yves, swallowed with an effort and went on, 'I have thought of another way in which the Prince may be gaining information although, in these hallowed surroundings, I hesitate to mention it.'

'Pray do,' she said briefly.

She saw the shadow of a smile cross his face. Then he said, 'We told you earlier, Abbess Helewise, that our father used to tell us tales of the old kings, of William that they called the Conqueror, and his sons William Rufus and the first Henry. Of how, according to some, anyway, the religious rites that they practised, especially Rufus, were – that is to say, it's probably only rumour, but they say – er, it's said the rites may well have been—'

He seemed unable to go on, so she supplied for him, 'Pagan?'

He said, 'Aye.'

She understood his discomfort and, wanting to alleviate it since it was unnecessary, said calmly, 'Sir Josse, I, too, have heard the old stories of how the first Norman kings were meant to associate with witches, and I was once told that the very name Rufus was given to the second William not because he was red-haired, since he wasn't, but because red, the colour of life, was sacred to the Old Religion.'

'I am quite certain it is not so,' Josse said with dramatic conviction.

'Are you?' She stared at him coolly. 'I am not so sure.'

'But you,' Yves began, apparently unable to contain himself, 'you're an Abbess!'

She wanted to laugh. 'Indeed I am,' she agreed. 'But I have ears, Yves, and I hear what is said. That William Rufus, dying in such puzzling circumstances on Lammas Morn, was a sacrificial king. That he may have intention-ally given up his life in honour of the Old Gods and their ways.'

Yves, she noted, looked horrified; Josse, who knew her better, merely appeared intrigued. 'Can it be so?' he murmured.

She shrugged. 'I do not see why not. We know that William Rufus had little time for our faith, and that as a consequence he was thoroughly disliked and disapproved of by the monks of his time.' With an effort, she recalled what had started this line of thought and she said firmly, 'But we were speaking of other matters. Sir Josse, you said your father used to tell stories of early court life that included a pagan element. Please, continue.'

'Yes. Right.' He seemed to be having some difficulty in gathering his thoughts together but, after a moment, said, 'Well, Father used to talk of a sorcerer who lived back in those days, a man also by the name of Dee, so I imagine he was an ancestor of the Prince's John Dee. Maybe the role gets passed down from father to son, I don't know. Anyway, Father used to say the old magician could look into a sphere made of black glass and see things that were happening far away, and it set me to wonder if Prince John's man – they call him Magister, by the way – has something similar. Perhaps the same sphere, even, inherited from his forebears. And that, staring into it, he sort of saw the Eye of Jerusalem.' Suddenly he shook his head, quite violently, and said, 'I apologise. I am getting carried away and mired down in pagan superstition, and I am talking utter nonsense.'

As the echoes of his raised, angry voice died away, Helewise said quietly, 'Sir Josse, I do not think that I have ever heard you talk nonsense.'

'But far-seeing glass spheres, Abbess! In heaven's name, how could they possibly work?'

'I have no idea,' she said. 'Although I am told there is evidence that they may do. We should not always strive to understand the how, Sir Josse,' she pressed on, overriding his protest, 'for many things in this world are known only to God. It is how He has ordered it.'

The two brothers were staring at one another now, and she was amused to see that Yves still wore his shocked face, as if an Abbess who expressed interest in such wild, outlandish and frighteningly heathen things as sacrificial kings and far-seeing spheres had no business being in charge of such a grand foundation as Hawkenlye Abbey.

She knew she should not tease them further, but she could not resist it; she said helpfully, 'Those spheres you speak of are known as scrying glasses, you know.'

Yves opened his mouth as if to speak, closed it again, then, as if at a loss to know quite what to do, gave her another of his little bows. Josse made a sound that seemed to indicate a mixture of surprise and disbelief.

She said, 'Gentlemen, if you lived here as we do, so close to the ancient Wealden Forest that when we rise in the dawn we can smell its very airs, you might not be so shocked to hear a Christian woman, an Abbess, indeed, speak of pagan things.' She fixed her eyes on to Josse's. 'There are folk within the forest's wide boundaries who see life very differently from the way in which we do, and who hold very different beliefs.'

Josse gave a faint nod, as if to say, I understand what you say. Then, turning to his brother, he murmured something that Helewise didn't catch; she thought she heard '. . . not quite the same, here in England . . .' and then there was another brief sentence. Whatever it was, it served to reassure Yves; turning to her, he said with great courtesy, 'My lady Abbess, I would not question anything you said.'

'That is magnanimous of you,' she murmured, resisting the urge to add, almost dangerously so. Then, once again directing their thoughts back to the matter in hand, she said, 'So, Sir Josse, you suggest that this John Dee is using his ancestor's scrying ball one day when he sees a wonderful jewel called the Eye of Jerusalem, borne by one Galbertius Sidonius who is apparently searching for someone of the family of Acquin. Understanding the powers of the stone, he informs his lord, Prince John, and they set off to find it. Or, failing that, to seek out this man d'Acquin and keep a watch on him until someone brings the Eye to him. Yes?'

'I told you I was speaking rubbish,' Josse growled. 'It is hardly likely, now, is it, Abbess Helewise? Far more sensible to go back to our original thought, that the Prince knows of Father, of the Eye, and of Galbertius because of the gossip of returning crusaders.'

'You must, of course, believe what makes most sense to you,' she replied, refusing to be drawn. 'But I urge you to consider seeking out Prince John, not only to aid me in identifying our unknown dead man, but also to help you find the Eye. Now, if you will excuse me, I must go. There are matters awaiting my attention.' She stood up.

Instantly the two men remembered their manners, thanking her profusely for giving up her time to listen to them, for her helpful comments, for offering them Hawkenlye's hospitality. Almost falling over himself, Yves rushed to open the door for her, and Josse gave her a low bow.

As she walked out of the room between them, she asked, 'So, you will go to seek out the Prince and tell him what you now know?'

After the briefest of pauses, they both said, 'Aye.'

They set out from the Abbey a little later. They had eaten a good meal before leaving; Sister Basilia, the nun in charge of the refectory, told them they must fortify themselves against whatever they might meet, which sounded quite ominous. As they rode off, Yves said with a rueful grin, 'She is all that you said of her and more.'

'Who is?' Josse asked, although he knew very well.

'Your Abbess Helewise.'

'Hmm.'

He heard Yves laugh softly. 'I know that sound,' he remarked. 'It means you are not going to say another word on the matter.'

'Quite right. I'm not.'

They were just starting on the descent down Castle Hill towards Tonbridge and the river crossing when they saw a party of travellers coming towards them.

As the two groups approached one another, Josse realised, with a sinking of the heart, that the other party was headed by Sheriff Pelham. As dishevelled and grim-faced as ever, he strode out in front of a quartet of men bearing between them a large piece of sacking, clearly containing something heavy. Each man held one corner of the sack, which dipped down almost to the ground as they lugged it along.

The four men were scarlet in the face and sweating from the effort of carrying their burden up the long slope. 'How typical,' Josse murmured, 'that he does not help them.'

'You know him?' Yves asked.

'Aye, I do. He is Harry Pelham, and he is the Sheriff of Tonbridge.'

'You do not like him.' Yves was certain enough to make it a statement.

'I do not.'

'Why is that?'

'I will leave you to work that out for yourself. Good morning, Sheriff Pelham,' he called. 'What have you got there?'

The sheriff put up his hand and his men halted, instantly dropping the sacking down on to the muddy track and standing there puffing and blowing as they began to recover their breath.

Pelham was glaring up at Josse. 'What's it to you?'

'Mere curiosity, I admit,' Josse said easily.

'I know you!' Pelham said accusingly. 'You're that Josse d'Acquin!'

'I am,' Josse agreed. 'And this man is my brother.'

'Your brother, eh?' The sheriff appeared to be thinking whether there was some rude remark he could make in response, but he didn't seem to be able to come up with one. 'Well, *Sir* Josse, what d'you reckon to this?' He gave one of his men a curt nod, at which the man drew back the sacking to reveal what was inside.

It was a body. And Josse thought that it was very probably dead.

He slid off his horse's back, flinging the reins at Yves to hold. Hurrying forward, he knelt down on the track beside the body. He put his ear down over the mouth, at the same time touching his fingers against the cheek.

There was neither the sound nor the feel of breath, and the cheek was icy.

He sat back on his heels and studied the corpse.

It was that of a youth, fourteen, fifteen years old. He was thin – almost skeletally thin – and his dirty body bore the sores, scratches and bruises suggestive of a life spent out in the open, without benefit of shelter or water to wash in.

He was naked.

Lifting the limbs one by one, brushing the long, tangled hair away from the face, Josse searched for some wound or injury that might indicate how the lad had met his end. Nothing. Then – with rather more trepidation – he looked for signs of disease; again, nothing.

Letting the heavy mass of hair fall back so that it concealed the face and neck and part of the skinny shoulders, Josse said, 'Where are you taking him?'

'Where d'you think?' Pelham replied sarcastically. 'To the Abbey, a'course.'

'You know that he is dead?'

'Er – aye, he's dead all right.' The sheriff's brief hesitation seemed to Josse to suggest that he had known nothing of the kind. 'We found him down there.' He indicated with an outstretched thumb; it had a blackened nail. 'In the undergrowth beside the track. One of my men had gone in for a – well, he'd gone in, and there he was. The lad, I mean. The *dead* lad.'

'Why take him to the Abbey?' Josse demanded.

'Well, er—' The Sheriff cast around as if for inspiration. 'To get him washed and prepared for decent burial, a'course! Them nuns are good at all that.'

'Aye, they are.' Josse spoke softly, staring down at the

dead boy. They will take care of you, he said silently. And, when Sister Euphemia has tidied you up, they will bury you and say prayers for your soul.

He closed his eyes in a brief prayer of his own. Then, standing up, he said, 'My brother and I will come back to Hawkenlye with you.'

He silenced the sheriff's protest with a look. And Yves, who appeared to have taken the measure of Harry Pelham and not been overly impressed, nodded and said quietly to Josse, 'You have made the right decision, Josse. Our business with the Prince must wait.'

Back at the Abbey, Josse directed the men to bear the body to the infirmary while he went to seek out the Abbess. He found her in the herb garden, where she had gone to speak to the herbalist, Sister Tiphaine; as he approached, the two of them broke off their conversation and gave him what seemed momentarily to be guilty looks, almost as if they had been talking about him . . .

But he pushed that thought aside and, quickly and with few words, told the Abbess about the dead body.

He accompanied her back to the infirmary. Sheriff Pelham and his men were standing outside, no doubt shooed out by Sister Euphemia; the sheriff greeted the Abbess with a mere nod, then said shortly, 'We've taken him inside and that nurse woman's taken over. You'll bury him, Abbess?'

'Naturally,' she said frostily.

'Then I'll bid you good day.' He sniffed, hawked and would have spat the product on the ground, except that Josse, predicting what he was about to do, intervened.

'You stand on holy ground, Sheriff Pelham,' he said, his voice as cold as the Abbess's had been. 'Remember it.'

Pelham shot him a fierce glance. Then he turned on his heel and strode away, his men falling into step behind him. Josse watched until they had gone out through the gates, then he followed the Abbess into the infirmary.

Sister Euphemia had got the men to carry the dead boy to a cubicle curtained off from the rest of the infirmary. In this private corner, she had lain the body on a clean sheet and was already washing it down.

'Mother-naked, like that other poor soul,' she was muttering as, sleeves rolled up to reveal her muscular forearms, she continued her work. 'I suppose someone robbed this sad wretch of his clothes and his possessions, such as they were, while he lay dead.'

'Perhaps they did,' Josse said absently.

The Abbess turned to him. 'Sir Josse?' she said softly. 'Do I detect that you have another thought in mind?'

She's quick, he thought. She misses nothing. 'My thoughts echoed those of Sister Euphemia,' he murmured back. 'I was thinking of that other naked body.'

'And wondering if there was a connection,' she finished for him. 'Yes. So was I.'

They watched as Sister Euphemia washed the dirt and the dust from the corpse. Then, with a gentle hand, she swept the hair back from the white face, gathering it up and twisting it into a knot which she pushed beneath the back of the head where it rested on the clean linen.

She gave a soft exclamation and said, 'Sir Josse? What do you make of this?'

He stepped forward and she took his hand, guiding his

fingers to the back of the dead boy's neck. He felt an indentation . . . Quite deep, and extending from beneath his left ear to just past where the spine made a raised bump under the skin.

'Could he – is this the mark of a garrotte?' he wondered aloud.

'You think he was *murdered*?' Sister Euphemia breathed. 'Strangled with some cord or rope wrapped tight around his throat till it throttled him?

'I am not sure . . .'

'It is possible,' the infirmarer said. 'Indeed it is, for I can find no other mark upon him that can have led to his death.'

Josse stood in silence for a moment. Then he said decisively, 'I am wrong. He cannot have been throttled. The marks go only around the back of his neck, whereas to throttle someone, the front of the throat must be constricted. And here' – he lightly touched a finger on to the Adam's apple – 'although I see faint discoloration, I see the mark of no garrotte.'

The Abbess had moved forward and now stood at his side, gazing down at the boy. She was holding the pectoral cross that hung around her neck. She said quietly, 'Sir Josse?' Then, having attracted his attention, she raised the cross on its cord and pulled at it.

After an instant, he understood.

'Aye,' he breathed. 'Aye.'

The infirmarer said quite sharply, 'What?'

The Abbess turned to her. She was still holding the cross. 'Look,' she said. 'Someone has grabbed hold of this, wishing to rob me of it.' She pulled hard on it. 'They tear it from me and, before the cord breaks, it digs into the flesh on the back of my neck.'

Sister Euphemia was already nodding before the Abbess had finished her demonstration. 'Of course,' she said. 'I see it now.'

She turned back to the dead youth. 'Murdered for what he wore around his neck?' she asked, of nobody in particular. 'May the good Lord have mercy on us.'

Although he did not believe that it would serve any useful purpose, Josse went along with the Abbess's suggestion that they ask some of the monks in the Vale to come and see if they could identify the corpse. Glad of the chance to get out of the infirmary and into the fresh air, he beckoned to Yves, who had gone to find shelter from the soft rain that had begun to fall, and led the way out of the rear gate and down into the Vale below.

Brother Saul and Brother Augustus were in the shelter beside the shrine, helping a visitor repair a damaged wheel on his handcart. Abandoning the task immediately – Saul muttered something to the disgruntled peasant, who seemed to object at the sudden withdrawal of Saul and Augustus's help – they leapt up to follow Josse and Yves back to the Abbey.

It was clear, as soon as the two lay brothers stood looking down at the dead boy, that they recognised him.

Brother Saul spoke. 'It's the lad that arrived with the old man, the one that had a cough and died. Back in August.'

Augustus looked at Josse. 'We told you about him,' he said. 'When you asked Saul, me and Erse. We thought—'

He swallowed, his distress evident. 'We all wondered if the body that the little girl found was him. The old man's servant, I mean. But it can't have been, because *he* is.' His eyes fell back to the boy on the bed and, as Josse watched him, his lips began to move in silent prayer.

You're a good lad, Augustus, Josse thought.

And, her warm tone suggesting that she shared his opinion, the Abbess said quietly, 'Be comforted, Brother Augustus. He is out of his pain now, whatever it was. And we will do our utmost for his soul, I promise you.'

Augustus flashed her a grateful look. Then he returned to his prayers.

Saul, too, was studying the dead body. He said tentatively, 'Was it a natural death, Sir Josse? Only – I don't like to think of the poor lad, running away when his master died and falling foul of some murderous villain.'

'I cannot yet say, Saul,' Josse replied. But, busy with a thought sparked off by Saul's words, he was hardly aware of what he said. Turning to the Abbess, he muttered, 'The boy can't have been dead long – I warrant the sheriff believed he was still alive. So—'

'So he has been surviving out there, living rough, for – let me see – for six weeks or more.'

'Only just surviving, by the look of him,' Josse said. 'No flesh left on those bones, is there? He was close to starving.' Another thought struck him. 'Could that have caused his death?'

'Sister Euphemia thinks not,' the Abbess said.

'Do you reckon,' Josse said, continuing with his earlier thought, 'that he was on his way back here?' Excitement coursing through him, he went on, 'You asked earlier, my lady, where we thought the Eye of Jerusalem was now. Well, what about this? Galbertius Sidonius bore it as far as Hawkenlye but, back in August, he died. Then his young servant – this lad here, we know that – stole it. Ran off with it, abandoning his dead master. But out there in the world, friendless, nowhere to turn, nothing to eat, nowhere to take shelter, he is overcome with remorse, and he sets out back to Hawkenlye to return what he stole. Only he never gets here, because he dies on his way up out of Tonbridge.'

'And his master's precious burden, which he now wears around his own neck, is torn from him,' she finished. 'Oh, Sir Josse, you may well be right. But how does it advance us when, yet again, we are one step behind the theft of your jewel?'

He shook his head, his face grave. Mistaking his emotion, she said, 'Have heart! We shall resolve this, somehow.'

He turned to her, grateful for her kindness. 'My lady, I was not sorrowing over my lost treasure. It is not lost to me, never having been mine in the first place. No, I am sad for this boy.'

He stepped up to the bed again. Hardly thinking what he was doing – he was very aware of the Abbess just behind him and, on the opposite side of the corpse, the watchful eyes of Saul and Augustus. But, as if someone else were guiding his hand, he stretched out his fingers and touched that strange discolouration on the dead boy's throat.

And out of nowhere came a memory. Of a stocky, tough and incredibly strong little man who had trained Josse and his fellow soldiers, all those years ago.

To accompany the memory came words . . . *you can kill a man with your bare hands, aye, with one bare hand, if you know where to strike. Harden your hands, my boys, hit the outer edge of your palm against a stone until it's as hard as that stone, and you've got yourself a killing weapon.* Flash of a hand, lightning-fast, swinging up through the air with the energy of the man's whole body behind it. *One blow to the front of the throat, and your man's down, dead as a pole-axed ox.*

Coming out of his reverie, Josse thought, it is the method of an expert. Of one who excels at killing.

He looked at the Abbess, then at Saul and Augustus. 'I'll tell you what increases my sorrow,' he said softly. 'The boy was murdered. And I can show you exactly how.'

15

The Abbess was preparing to see Josse and Yves on their way the next day when, for the second time, their mission was thwarted, this time before they had even left Hawkenlye.

Sister Ursel, the porteress, was standing at the gate, all ready to form part of the valedictory guard, when, hearing the sound of hooves, she turned to look down the road.

'There's a band of horsemen approaching,' she reported to Helewise. 'Twelve, fourteen of them at least.'

Helewise went over to where Josse was about to mount up. 'Sir Josse? Can it be that we are about to receive another visit from Sheriff Pelham?'

'Not if there are fourteen men mounted in the group,' he replied. 'I once saw Pelham astride a tired old cob, but I doubt that his men have mounts.'

She walked to stand beside Sister Ursel. 'They are well mounted,' she said, as the company drew nearer. 'Well dressed, too.'

She sensed Josse at her side. Looking down the track, he said neutrally, 'If you have a fatted calf, my lady, I suggest you order it killed straight away. The Abbey is about to receive a visit from Prince John.'

★   ★   ★

The Prince was travelling with what, for him, was a small retinue. Nevertheless, Helewise experienced several moments of alarm – and one or two of downright panic – as she set about organising her nuns to cater for a royal visitor and fifteen courtiers.

Observing the reaction of the sisters as the news spread swiftly through the Abbey, she knew that, above all, she must retain a serene demeanour, and act as if visits from princes were all in a day's work. My nuns will look to me, she told herself as she tried to listen to two sisters talking at once, one reporting on stocks of the good wine, one saying anxiously that the refectory roof had developed a leak and was the Abbess quite sure it was all right to entertain the Prince in there? Then, like a blessing, she had a sudden image of Queen Eleanor, who was a frequent visitor to Hawkenlye and who neither expected nor wanted any fuss made of her.

We do not entertain Prince John's mother so lavishly that we have to be on short rations for weeks, she reminded herself. Nor would the Queen dream of complaining if a drip or two of autumn rain found its way through the roof and landed in her soup. Why, then, should we do more for her son?

Turning to the cellarer, she said, 'Sister Goodeth, you may draw one jug of the good wine, for the Prince and his immediate circle. Otherwise, serve the wine that we drink.'

Sister Goodeth's mouth opened in a 'But—' Then, looking at her Abbess's resolute expression, she bowed her head and said meekly, 'Yes, my lady.'

'And, Sister Anne, we shall organise a repair of the

refectory roof when Brother Saul and Brother Erse can spare the time. For now, Prince John and his men will have to take us as they find us.'

Sister Anne's round eyes were fixed on Helewise as she spoke; Helewise had the sudden unsettling notion that Anne was memorising her words to repeat them to the rest of the kitchen staff.

Ah, well. There was nothing she could do about that.

As she left the refectory, Josse materialised at her side. 'Abbess Helewise, what can I do to help?'

She turned to him gratefully and, as she had done so many times before, offered up a swift and silent prayer of thanks for his strength and his reliability. 'We need time to prepare a meal. Would you care to entertain them while we do so?'

Josse grinned. 'Gladly. Yves and I will take them down to the Vale, and Brother Firmin can show them the Holy Water shrine. By the time he's finished telling them every last detail and fact, you and the good sisters could have a week's worth of food prepared.'

'I sincerely hope it will not come to that.'

He leaned towards her and said quietly, 'It will not. I think we know why he is here, and the sooner he finds out what he wants to know, the sooner he'll be gone.'

Watching him as he strode away, calling out to Yves, who hurried to his side, she hoped he was right.

The hastily prepared meal, if not a feast, was adequate. Prince John thanked the Abbess and her nuns in a rather flowery speech – Helewise observed Sister Anne watching him intently, no doubt recording every word of *that* utterance, too – and one or two of the younger and more impressionable of the novices, affected by his looks and his charm, simpered with delight.

He *was* a handsome man, Helewise had to admit. Nevertheless, charming and handsome though he might be, she was heartily relieved when, drawing her aside for a private word, he said that he would not dream of imposing his company on her further and was therefore dispatching the majority of his companions off to where they lodged, with one of his knights whose manor was nearby.

'As you wish, Sire,' she replied.

'But I would stay on, my lady, if it does not inconvenience you.' The blue eyes bored into hers.

'Of course not,' she said quickly. 'I will arrange quarters for you.'

'No need for that.' Now the smile spread across his handsome face. 'I note that Sir Josse and his brother lodge with the monks in the Vale, and that will be quite good enough for us.'

Wondering if 'us' was a sudden use of the royal 'we' or denoted a party consisting of more than the one person, she said, 'We?'

'The Magister will remain with me, as will two of my knights.'

'Very well, Sire.' She made him a graceful bow and, noticing as she straightened up that he was already walking away, presumed herself dismissed.

You could not, Helewise realised, raise an item for discussion with a Prince; you just had to wait, biting your nails with impatience, until you were summoned to the presence and the matter was introduced by him.

Finding a quiet moment to speak to Josse, she found that he was as tense as she was. 'He probably enjoys seeing us stew,' he growled. 'What's he up to? He *must* be aware that we know as well as he does why he's here. Why doesn't just he get on with it?'

'He will,' she said soothingly. 'In the meantime, why not come and pray with us?'

To her faint surprise, he did.

They received word in the late evening that the Prince wished to speak with them. The Prince, who had been offered the use of the Abbess's private room and instantly accepted, had installed himself in Helewise's chair. As Helewise and Josse entered the room – only the two of them, it appeared, had been summoned – the Prince sat at his ease, John Dee positioned at his shoulder.

Standing side by side with Josse, Helewise found she was holding her breath.

Don't be absurd, she told herself firmly. He is but a man, like any other. Being born royal does not turn a man into a god.

She lifted her chin and looked the Prince right in the face.

She saw a faint smile cross his face. Then, turning to Josse, he said, 'We discommode the lady Abbess by our presence, and so I will come to the point of our visit straight away.'

Since he spoke the truth, she did not contradict him.

He noticed that, as well; there was a definite edge of

amusement to his voice as he went on, 'Sir Josse, when last we met, I asked you if you had come across a man named Galbertius Sidonius. A few days later, you came to seek out the Magister here' – he indicated John Dee – 'who reported to me that you wanted to discover if a dead man found here at Hawkenlye could be the man we seek. It was decided that he could not be, since the dead man was younger than Sidonius.'

He paused. Josse, apparently thinking he was expected to respond, said, 'Aye, Sire. All of that is so.'

The Prince stared at him. Eventually he said, 'You see, Sir Josse, the problem is this. We are no nearer to finding Sidonius, and you are still our only lead.'

'But I don't – that is, I have never met the man!' Josse protested. 'Why, Sire, are you so certain that I can help you?'

The Prince, who had been relaxing in his seat and idly inspecting the nails of his right hand as if finding the whole business impossibly tedious, suddenly shot upright, turned the lazy hand into a fist and banged it down hard on the arm of the chair. 'Because you know exactly who he is and why he will come seeking you out!' he cried. Eyes blazing, he added in a tone that could have frozen wine, 'Do not play with me, d'Acquin.'

Helewise sensed Josse's reaction. Far from being frightened into submission, he was, she knew quite well, almost as furious as the Prince.

'I have a suspicion that I do know the identity of this Galbertius Sidonius,' he said, his voice tightly under control. 'And, although a suspicion is not a certainty, nevertheless I was on the point of setting out to find you,

Sire, to tell you what I know, when your party arrived this morning. As the Abbess Helewise here will verify, and she does not lie.'

'I am glad to hear it,' the Prince murmured. 'And so? Tell me, if you please, what tidings you were bringing me.'

But, to Helewise's surprise and admiration, Josse stood his ground. 'I will, Sire, but may I have leave to ask a question, too?'

She thought the Prince might flare up in a rage. But instead he gave a bark of laughter and said, 'Very well. But you must answer me first.'

'We believe Sidonius to be a man who fought and travelled with my late father, Geoffroi d'Acquin,' Josse began. 'My father knew him as the Lombard, and they were good friends. Or so my father believed. The Lombard returned to Acquin with my father when they came back from Outremer and, when he finally set off for his own home, stole a precious object from my father. Earlier this year, my family at Acquin received a visit from an old man and a boy. The old man was seeking my father, and expressed a wish to keep faith with him. The boy was overheard referring to his master by name; it appeared he called him Galbertius Sidonius. The old man came here, to Hawkenlye, seeking the healing waters, but he died before the monks could help him. His servant had disappeared, but has recently been found dead. His body even now lies in the crypt awaiting burial.'

The Prince, who had been listening intently, now turned to John Dee. They murmured together for some time; once or twice Dee shook his head emphatically. The Prince did not look pleased.

Eventually, Prince John turned back to face Josse. 'You believe the old man to be Sidonius,' he said, his tone giving nothing away. 'Can you prove it?'

'I believe so, Sire,' Josse said eagerly. 'Although, as I said, I never met him, others did. My brother, Yves, for one, who is at present here in Hawkenlye. Some of the monks in the Vale, too, encountered the old man. Perhaps if they were to describe him to you, in as much detail as possible, you could say whether we speak, indeed, of the same man.'

'A sound plan,' the Prince said, 'but for one thing. We have never met Sidonius either.'

'We—?'

The Prince gave a tsk! of exasperation. 'The Magister and I.'

'But the Magister told me he was old! Ancient, in fact! I thought that meant he must know him!' Josse exclaimed.

The Magister spoke. 'No. I do not.'

'Then how do you know he is ancient?' Josse demanded, turning to glare at Dee.

'There are ways,' Dee murmured. 'One receives . . . an impression.'

As if he did not want the Magister to proceed with that line, the Prince spoke sharply. 'You said you have a question for us, Sir Josse. You may ask it.'

Helewise was almost sure, judging by the long pause, that Josse had forgotten what he had wanted to know. She was about to whisper a reminder when he said, 'Aye. I would ask you, Sire, how *you* come to know of Galbertius Sidonius.'

Once more, there was a brief exchange between Prince

John and the Magister. Then the Prince said, with credible nonchalance, 'The story of your father and his jewel was well-known in court circles, d'Acquin. The returning crusaders brought home many tales, and the one of the modest and unassuming knight who rescued a little boy and was awarded a valuable prize was ever a favourite.' He leaned forward, stopping whatever Josse had been about to say before he could begin. 'You may like to know that the little boy grew up into a warrior who begat many bellicose sons and who is still a much-respected military authority in his own land. My brother and his knights have not always been entirely happy that his life was saved; a considerable number of Christian soldiers would still be alive today if your father had left Azamar where he was.'

'He was a *child*,' Josse said softly. 'Surely it is not in God's orders that we kill children.'

The Prince shrugged. 'War is unpleasant, d'Acquin. Do you not recall?'

Josse made no reply, but Helewise felt the anger ripple through him. Thinking that he might be glad of a moment to get himself under control, she said, 'May I speak, Sire?'

The Prince waved a hand heavy with rings. 'Of course, my lady.'

'I wondered how you came to connect the tale of Geoffroi d'Acquin and his jewel with Galbertius Sidonius. Geoffroi's family remember that his father always referred to his friend as the Lombard, and I was curious to know how you managed to identify him with the man you seek.'

The Prince stared at her. It was not, she discovered, a

pleasant experience; against her will – she was determined not to be cowed – stories of his famous temper came to mind. I am Abbess here, she told herself. He is sitting in *my* chair, and I am not going to stand here before him quaking like some child postulant caught out in a minor misdemeanour.

She straightened her shoulders and stared back.

From behind the Prince, she heard John Dee emit a brief, soft chuckle.

As if the small sound had broken some contest going on between the Prince and the Abbess, the Prince relaxed, smiled and said, 'My lady, these things happen, do they not? A man's deeds are mentioned, someone says, oh, you mean old so-and-so, and there you are, an unknown person suddenly has an identity. Is that not so?'

She wondered why she should feel so strongly that he very much wanted her to swallow this explanation, which was so flimsy as to be almost non-existent. She said meekly, 'Yes, Sire. Indeed it is.'

She caught Dee's eyes on her; even if the Prince thought she believed him, John Dee certainly did not.

She went on staring at Dee.

Was it her imagination, or did she sense a warmth from him, a sense that he meant her no harm? That – surely this was taking it too far! – he just might be on her side. Which, since she and Josse stood shoulder to shoulder, made it Josse's side, too.

In the face of the power that seemed to come in waves off the person of the Prince, to have the Magister as an ally seemed something greatly to be desired.

16

Josse retired to bed that night feeling exhausted. He had told Yves every last detail of the interview with the Prince and John Dee, and they had talked it over for a long time. The problem is, he thought as he lay trying to relax sufficiently for sleep, that, for all those words that were exchanged, we are no nearer to a resolution to this puzzle. Nor – far more importantly – any closer to finding what hand, or hands, was behind those two murders.

As he lay there in the darkness of the shelter, he hoped fervently that both killings had been carried out by the same man. The thought of having *two* cold, professional killers around was just too awful.

It was quiet, down there in the Vale. Josse and Yves were the only occupants of the pilgrims' shelter that night; the monks and the lay brothers had their own quarters, a short distance away. And the Prince, despite his protestations that he would be quite happy to put up in the clean but basic lodgings in the Vale shelter, had changed his mind when the rain refused to let up. The Abbess had arranged an area of the chapter house as a makeshift guest chamber, organising the laying-out of shakedown beds and the provision of a small brazier, and there Prince John, the Magister and the Prince's two personal attendants were, presumably, now enjoying a good night's sleep.

Unlike me, Josse reflected.

It was no use; sleep was proving frustratingly elusive. He got up – quietly, so as not to disturb Yves – and, having made sure his knife was in its sheath on his belt, left the shelter.

It was still raining, although the downpour that had flattened anyone unwise enough to be out of doors in the late evening had moved off. The rainfall was soft now, and the wind had dropped. Hunching into his travelling cloak, Josse moved out from under the eaves of the shelter and strode off along the path that led down to the lake at the bottom of the valley.

Then, under a group of chestnut trees that stood a little way back from the track, he saw a light.

He stopped dead, staring at it. For it was in a place where surely no light should be . . .

Was it a lost group of travellers, making for Hawkenlye but overcome by the early falling darkness of an overcast, rainy night? Aye, perhaps so; and, poor souls, they were seeking comfort from the deep shadows with a lantern.

But the light did not look like that of a candle in a lantern; it had no soft, golden, flickering glow, but burned with a steady intensity and a faint bluish tinge.

Josse put his hand over the hilt of his knife. Fool that I am, he thought, why did I not bring my sword?

He had, as always when he visited, handed it over to Saul for safe keeping, out of respect for the holy ground of the Abbey and the Vale. It would have taken but a moment to slip into the monks' quarters and retrieve it; Saul, knowing that Josse would not take his weapon unless he had dire need, had made no secret of where he had put it.

Josse was angry with himself. There was a trained killer around; he knew that full well. And there he was, armed only with his knife.

He drew it from its sheath. It was sharp, sturdy, and he was well used to wielding it. Ah, well, it would have to serve; curiosity had overcome him, and he was moving stealthily up towards the strange light even as he tightened his grip on his knife.

He crouched low as he approached the trees. He could see the light more clearly now; it came from a small ball of some substance that burned inside a small iron cup. The cup was set on top of a spike, stuck firmly into the ground.

Entranced, Josse crept closer. And closer. Until he was under the canopy of the chestnut tree, deep in the black shadow cast by the brilliant light.

He stopped, staring down at the unnatural steadiness of the flame; it seemed to be one flame, which burned with a fervour that almost hurt the eyes.

What, in God's holy name, could it be?

As if he had asked the question out loud, a voice from the shadows answered softly, 'It is known as Greek fire, my friend. Do not be alarmed, for it will not hurt you unless you touch it.'

Josse had spun round at the first words, as swiftly as if a spark of the fire had indeed leapt out and burned him; now, holding his knife before him, he said, 'Who are you? Come out and show yourself!'

And out of the darkness came John Dee.

His milky hair was partly concealed by a hood, but his beard seemed to glow silver in the light, merging into the luminous pallor of his face. The dark eyes, intense, deep, were fixed on Josse with a power that seemed to hold him still.

With an effort, as if breaking out of an enchantment, he said, 'What are you doing out here in the rain, Magister?'

Dee, with a faint air of surprise, held out his long hands, palms uppermost. Josse caught a glint of brilliant pale blue as the light of the fire caught the large aquamarine. 'But it is not raining,' he observed.

'Yes it is, I—' But as Josse, too, put out a hand, he realised that it was staying quite dry.

But he could still hear the rain, hissing down out of the black sky, drumming down on the ground!

Dee laughed. 'There is no magic involved in that, Sir Josse,' he said. 'We stand under the generous branches of a chestnut tree and, for all that it is autumn, she still has sufficient leaves to shelter us.'

Feeling foolish, Josse bent his head and carefully put his knife away in its sheath. Then, raising his eyes and glaring at Dee, he said, 'You did not answer my question. What are you doing out here?'

'I am waiting for you,' Dee replied calmly.

'But how did you know that I would come out and find you?'

'You did, didn't you?'

'Er – aye, I did.'

'Well, then.' Before Josse could make a comment – before, indeed, he had thought of one to make – Dee said, 'I wanted to see you, Josse. May I address you so? Thank you. Yes, I wanted – needed – to speak to you privately, with no fear of being overheard.' As he spoke, he turned and did something to the fire that quietened its brilliance to a gentle glow which, Josse reckoned, would scarcely be visible from the track. 'There. The fire has done its job and brought you here. I have softened it so that it will not bring anyone else.'

Josse went to stand beside him. 'Greek fire, you said?' He was intrigued.

'Yes. It is an invention of the Byzantines. They use it as a weapon, and it is a fearsome, terrifying one for, although when inert it has the appearance of a harmless lump of mud, it leaps into life when water touches it. Imagine, Josse, what that flame could do when stuck like a second skin to a man's body.'

Josse preferred not to imagine that. 'Fearsome,' he muttered. 'Aye, that it is.'

'I have never used it to harm a living being,' Dee said. 'But I find that, as a light on a moonless night, it is incomparable. I have added a few ingredients of my own to the Byzantines' formula,' he went on, eagerness creeping into his voice, 'and this modified fire suits me well.' He waved a hand over the iron cup, and the flame quietened further. 'Now. To business.'

He turned to face Josse, tucking his hands away in his wide sleeves; fleetingly, Josse was reminded of the Abbess. 'What did you wish to say to me that must not be overheard?' he asked.

The Magister studied him for a few moments. Then he said, 'I admired your restraint when you asked your question of Prince John earlier. You merely wondered how he came to know of Sidonius. It displayed wise forbearance, if I may say so, not to have demanded what was really in your mind.'

'And what was that?'

'Why, how he knew about the Eye of Jerusalem, of course. You surely realise that it is the jewel he is after?'

With a long sigh, Josse said, 'Aye. It does not take any great intelligence to work that out, when it is commonly said that the Prince is trying to raise cash and support against the likelihood that he becomes king.' He scowled at Dee. 'And I reckon I already know how he found out about the Eye.' He hesitated for an instant – was it wise to hurl accusations at a sorcerer, out in a lonely valley with nobody about and a magical fire glowing steadily? But his anger burned more hotly than the fire; he leaned closer to Dee and said, 'You told him about it. You use the scrying glass that your forefathers passed down to you – aye, I know about it, my own father used to tell us tales of the first two King Williams and their court magician – and you saw Galbertius Sidonius carrying the Eye into England, looking for me.' He paused for breath, then went on, 'That was why the Prince came seeking me out at New Winnowlands. When I said I had never heard of Sidonius, you knew I spoke the truth, and so you turned the search elsewhere. And, eventually, you came here.'

He heard the echo of his final words on the still air. The intensity of the Magister's stare was disconcerting; for the first time, Josse felt the stirrings of fear.

But, as if he were aware of it, Dee put out a hand and lightly touched Josse's arm. 'I mean you no harm, Josse,' he said. 'You are an honest man, and I have no quarrel with one such as you. Indeed, I – But no.' Briefly he shook his head, as if casting aside whatever he had been about to say. 'In essence, you guess rightly,' he said instead. 'Although we had heard tell of a magical stone of power brought home from Outremer, there are many such tales and few are worth credence. However, the story of Geoffroi d'Acquin and the Eye of Jerusalem did seem particularly persistent, and the Prince suggested that enquiries should be made. Even the best of his spies, I'm afraid, came quickly to a dead end.' He paused. Then added, compassion in his voice, 'Literally to a dead end, I fear, in one instance. We are almost certain that the dead body that you told me about, the one discovered here in the Vale, was that of one of the Prince's agents.'

'The rotting corpse with the knife stuck in his ribs?' As soon as he had said the words, Josse regretted their bluntness. 'I am sorry,' he said. 'I speak of a rotting corpse, whereas you, Magister, perhaps knew the living man, and regret his death.'

'I knew him, yes, a little,' Dee said. 'And I do indeed regret his death, both for its brutality and for the fact that it was a sheer waste.'

'A waste?'

'The young man did not stand a chance,' Dee murmured. Then, once again, he stared into Josse's eyes. Instantly Josse had the sense that what they had just been speaking of was now obscured by a cloud of smoke; although he tried, he could not remember what it was.

Dee said firmly, 'But we were discussing your father. I was explaining how it was known that Geoffroi set out from Outremer to head for home, but nobody seemed to be able to say whether or not he made it. Except that there was you.' The dark eyes held Josse's.

'Me?'

'Yes. Your name was known – are you not a King's man? Did not Richard give you a task to do, and award you the manor of New Winnowlands in gratitude?'

'Aye, that he did.'

'So. Josse d'Acquin, who came from northern France. You see how the assumption was made, that you could very well be of Geoffroi's line?'

'Aye. Which led to the conclusion that he must have got home, married, and had a son.'

'Exactly!' The Magister looked pleased. 'So, assuming that Geoffroi returned to Acquin, we further guessed that he brought the Eye with him. And then, when you came to see me that day, you told me that your father was dead.'

'You already knew.'

'Did I?' There was a definite twinkle in Dee's eyes. 'Perhaps I did. As I was saying, knowing that your father was dead, it was natural to reason that the man you call Sidonius would bring the Eye to you, his heir, and so—'

'You *did* know that Father was dead!' Josse interrupted. 'You came to New Winnowlands to ask me about Sidonius several days before I told you! You would only have done so had you known full well that I now hold the Acquin title!'

'Very well, then.' Dee sounded amused. 'Yes, I knew of your father's summertime death, and I regret to say that I guided the Prince's steps to you.' Sounding serious now, he went on, 'I serve the Crown, as John Dee has always done and will always do, as long as his services are required. King Richard, however, has no time for my talents; his brother is a different matter. My master's need, Josse, is for wealth; as his loyal servant, is it not my duty to assist him in its acquisition?'

'Perhaps.' Josse was not going to be seduced into an unreserved agreement. 'But what if Prince John acquiring wealth means stealing things from other people?'

Dee made no answer for a moment. Then, eyeing Josse steadily, he said, 'There you have it. My dilemma, as bluntly expressed as any man could wish.'

Josse, wanting to be entirely sure that he had understood, said slowly, 'Let me be clear about this, Magister. You knew of the Eye, you told the Prince it was valuable, you tracked it to the house of Acquin, you brought the Prince to me. You aim to help steal it from me, but the problem is that I do not have it.'

'I know that, Josse. I can see full well that the Eye has not come to you. But that is not the problem, for I assure you that the stone is on its way. My problem is that I no longer believe the Prince should relieve you of it.'

Stunned, Josse could only manage, 'Why not?'

'Because you are an honest man,' Dee replied simply, 'like your father before you. And as powerful a tool as the Eye of Jerusalem is will ever be safer in the hands of those whose moral fibre is straight, strong and incorruptible.'

'I don't know about all that,' Josse began. But then, realising what Dee's comment implied about his master the Prince, he stopped. Confused, vaguely uneasy, he did not know what to say.

'I see much that the Prince is not aware that I see,' Dee said, his voice taking on a hypnotic tone. 'I see that he is clever – oh, yes, highly intelligent – and that he has some fine qualities. But I also see what seethes below the surface; he has all the energy and thrust of his redoubtable parents but, perhaps typically of a last-born, he has a strong sense of survival. He is able, I believe, to put aside what he knows to be right and best for the majority in favour of what is right and best for himself. He is not' – now the voice spoke out clearly – 'the right guardian of the Eye. And you are.'

Josse said in a whisper, 'Are you sure of that?'

'I am,' Dee said. 'It was given to your father – freely given, in thanks for a brave deed of rare loving kindness – and, as your father's eldest child, it is now rightfully yours.'

'I had an elder sister, but she died when she was a baby,' Josse murmured.

'Yes. Had she lived, the stone would have been hers.'

'It does not have to be passed to a son?'

'No.' The Magister laughed. 'The Eye is old, Josse. It comes from a time long ago when, before men elbowed women out of the seats of power, the female was accorded the greater honour. And the Eye holds ancient magic from the land of its birth, far away, whose northern borders touch the trade routes that wind out of China and lead to India and into the west, joining the great Silk Road in the mountains to the east of Persia. It was in Persia that jewellers worked the uncut stone, and skilled goldsmiths fashioned the Eye's casing; they wrote a magic inscription in their own language.'

'Aramaic,' Josse said dreamily.

'Aramaic,' Dee agreed. 'Do you know what the words say, Josse?'

'No.' He was bewitched by the Magister's deep, dark eyes, and had the sense that, as he stared into their depths, he was being drawn down a long, shadowed tunnel.

'The stone is a sapphire, which the Persians call *saffir*,' Dee's dream-voice went on. 'They believe that the stone is formed from the elixir of immortality, the *amrita*. It is the life-giving milk of the Great Goddess whom they know as Ishtar, although she has many names. You see, Josse? Long ago, when mankind was in his infancy, the deity was adored in her female role. So, to answer your question, naturally the Eye does not ignore the Goddess's daughters in favour of her sons. There is nothing to suggest that a woman may not inherit the stone.'

'I see,' Josse murmured. Then, recovering from his dream state, ashamed that this old sorcerer should have found him such an easy victim, he blurted out the first thing that came into his head. 'This Abbey is ruled by a woman.'

'A fine woman,' Dee agreed. 'I confess I am greatly impressed by Abbess Helewise. She refused to be intimidated by the Prince, didn't she? Even when he was on the point of erupting into a rage, she stood firm. I admire that in anyone, but it is as rare as to be virtually unique in a woman.' He chuckled. 'The only other lady who looks him straight in the eye is his mother.'

'Do you have a wife, Magister?' Josse asked, interested.

'I? No, I regret not. Wedlock and sorcery do not sit comfortably together.'

'But you like and admire women?'

'Oh, yes. Our age does not value them as it should, and

the world is the poorer for it. Power in the female form is our only hope,' he murmured.

'How so?' Josse demanded.

The Magister's eyes took on a clouded look, as if he were staring at something in the distance. 'The power of men is a selfish power,' he intoned. 'It is a base and naked force which, once discovered, is akin to that of a small boy who finds he can cut off the head of a cat with his father's sword. Because he can is no reason to assume that he should. Do you see?'

'Er – aye.'

'There is no future for us unless we acknowledge the female force,' Dee went on. 'The spark of the Great Mother, the nurturer, exists in all of us, would we but recognise it.'

Some hope of that, Josse reflected.

Dee, as if picking up on Josse's unspoken thought, said, 'One day, Josse – a day not far off in terms of the long history of this world of ours – one day it will change.' The dark eyes suddenly turned to Josse, piercing him with a stabbing stare that was almost painful. 'There will sit on the great throne of England a monarch who will be the greatest of them all.' He spoke the words as if he were chanting. 'Wise, astute, learned and just, beloved of the people, this monarch will be the child of a philanderer and a witch with eleven fingers.' He paused. 'And she will be a woman.'

For an instant Josse was sufficiently carried away by the Magister to believe him. But then, with a slightly uneasy laugh, he realised Dee must be joking. 'That,' he said, grinning, 'would indeed be something to behold.'

Dee, regarding him with faint irony, did not answer.

'So, Magister' – Josse tried to sound business-like; there had surely been quite enough of this whimsical talk, and Dee, after all, must have brought him out here for a purpose – 'what do you suggest we do now?'

Dee, appearing not to resent Josse's lead back to the matter-of-fact, said, 'As I told you, I do not believe that the Eye should fall into the hands of my master the Prince. Therefore I shall not let that happen.'

The Magister in his day-to-day form was, Josse realised, a different matter from the powerful sorcerer of the shadows; he found that it was quite easy to say to the former, now standing before him, 'And just how will you prevent it?'

Dee smiled. 'The Eye will come to you. I told you that, also. Provided you do not rush away to tell the Prince and offer your treasure to him, he will not know that you possess it.'

'And he will cease demanding it of me?' It sounded highly unlikely.

'He will.' Dee, it seemed, could see that Josse did not believe him. Smiling, he added, 'It is not in his best interests to have the Eye. He has perils enough ahead, without the added danger of attracting the malice of a powerful amulet.'

'But—'

'I wish that you would pay attention.' A mildly peevish note had entered Dee's soft voice. 'The Eye only works positively for its rightful owner, which is you. And your descendants. Unless, of course, you give it away of your own free will, which you may choose to do, although I do not advise it.' He paused, then added, even more quietly, 'I certainly do not advise giving it to Prince John.' His eyes on Josse's, he murmured, 'If anybody steals the stone, removes it from your possession without your consent, it will do them no good; its unique powers will become inert, and it will be no more than a pretty bauble. Worse than that, I suspect it may actually work against a man who purloins it. So, Josse. Do you understand?'

Slowly Josse nodded. 'Aye. But—'

Dee sighed faintly. 'But? Go on, you may as well ask.'

'You said that the Prince faced perils ahead,' Josse whispered, as if the very trees in the Vale might try to overhear. 'What did you mean? Will he succeed Richard and become king?'

Dee paused, then said, 'King Richard has no child. If he does not beget a healthy son on Berengaria his wife, then the laws of our land state that he must be succeeded by his brother.'

'Aha!' But Josse's brief moment of excitement was swiftly curtained as he realised that Dee had told him nothing that he had not already known. 'If Prince John should reign,' he said, wondering if he might be able to trick the Magister into a confidence, 'will it be a dreadful disaster?'

Dee stared at him, his face impassive. Then, with the shadow of a wry smile, he said, 'Wait and see. Just wait and see.'

17

---◆---

In the morning, waking to the sheer normality of Yves yawning and stretching beside him, laughing at some light-hearted remark made by Brother Saul as he brought them mugs of some hot, pleasant-tasting drink, Josse wondered if the experiences of the previous night had been a dream.

In some ways, he would have been relieved if they had been. But he knew better. And, besides, his cloak was still soaking wet from the drenching he had received as he saw the Magister safely back to the Abbey gates.

In retrospect, surely it had been unnecessary for a man armed only with a knife to presume to safeguard a powerful magician. Dee, Josse was quite sure, was more than capable of looking after himself.

But the old man had accepted Josse's gesture with grace and a courteous 'Thank you'. He had even deigned to take Josse's proffered arm as they climbed up the slippery path.

I like the man, Josse decided, blowing on his herbal drink to cool it. If indeed man is what he is . . .

But that thought was disturbing, even in the sunshine of early morning. He put it aside, instead announcing to Yves that they must go and seek an audience with the Abbess because he had something important to tell her.

*　　*　　*

Helewise, once over the shock of learning that Josse had been abroad in the night and consorting with a sorcerer, discovered that she was not surprised that John Dee had declared himself for Josse. Watching his earnest, honest face as he repeated to her what Dee had said, she thought, I, too, would place my trust in dear Josse over the Prince. What a pity it is that Josse cannot ascend the throne if King Richard leaves it vacant.

But that thought, she was well aware, was treasonable. She said a quick and silent apology, and turned her full attention back to Josse.

'We have, if nothing else, now managed to identify the poor young man murdered in the Vale,' she observed when, after quite some time, he finally finished all that he had to say. 'An agent of Prince John's, did Dee say?'

'Aye, he did. And—' Josse frowned, apparently thinking hard, but, after a moment, gave up and said with a shrug, 'There was something else he said, but I can't seem to bring it to mind. Something about the young man not standing a chance . . .' Turning to Yves and then back to Helewise, he added, half-apologetically, 'It's an odd experience, talking to a sorcerer. He – well, you get the feeling that he makes sure you only recall what he wants you to recall.'

Yves made a faint sound of awe. Helewise, managing to control her reaction, merely said, 'He is a powerful man, this John Dee.'

'That he is,' Josse agreed fervently. 'And knowledgeable! Why, he told me things about this Eye of Jerusalem that only the very wise could know!'

'Yes, you said,' Helewise interrupted. Fascinated though

she had been with Josse's tale of the Eye's history according to John Dee, she did not want to hear it all over again. 'And he is going to ensure that the jewel comes to you, its rightful owner.'

'That's what he said, aye. And I believe him.' Josse stuck his chin up.

'I am sure you are quite right to do so,' she said soothingly. 'Although, of course, that presupposes that the Magister is right and the Eye is indeed on its way to you.'

'All this talk,' Yves put in, sounding as if he had had to steel himself to speak, 'it unnerves me.' He addressed his brother: 'Josse, you make it sound as if this here Eye has a mind of its own. As if – as if—' With a shrug, he gave up. 'I don't know. But, like I say, I'm – well, I'm afraid. We seem to be dealing with matters outside the normal, everyday world that *I* know.'

Helewise could feel his unease, and she both understood and sympathised. 'Do not forget, Yves,' she said gently, 'that your brother here has spent the night in the company of a great magician. Fortunately for Sir Josse – indeed, for all of us here – it seems that Dee approves of the family of Acquin, and means them no harm. Whether or not Dee does in fact have power, I think we can be fairly confident that he does not intend to turn it against us.'

'Thank you, my lady,' Yves said, bowing to her. 'Your words reassure me. But if this Eye turns up, what then?'

'I suggest,' she said, as calmly as she could, 'that we worry about that when, and if, it happens. Now, Sir Josse, to return to the matter of the poor dead young man. Did Dee supply a name?'

'No, he said he did not know it, but he promised to speak

to Prince John this morning. I think, my lady, that, come evening, we shall have an identity for the body buried out there.'

'I am glad of it,' she replied. She was silent for a moment as she thought, then she said, 'I don't know if you agree, but to me it seems likely that the Prince's man must have picked up the trail of Galbertius Sidonius and followed him here to Hawkenlye. Perhaps he intended to steal the Eye from him, perhaps he was merely intending to report back to the Prince that Galbertius was here, and await further instructions.'

'I imagine his instructions were quite clear,' Josse put in. 'The Prince probably said, find the man, steal the stone and bring it to me.'

Helewise watched him. He was, she thought, becoming quite possessive about the Eye of Jerusalem. Which, although in many ways understandable, did not entirely seem to accord with what she knew of his generous, open-hearted nature.

It was, perhaps, something to watch out for.

'If that is so,' she said, 'then we can only assume that someone else was already on the Prince's man's trail. And that he killed him before he could carry out his intention of stealing the Eye.'

Yves said excitedly, 'But then, before the killer could creep up on Galbertius and take the Eye, the old man died and his own servant stole the stone and made off with it!'

'Then, for some reason, the lad was making his way back here when the killer caught up with him and murdered him!' Josse cried. Then, the light fading from his face, he concluded, 'So this skilful, brutal murderer now has the Eye.'

'But Dee is convinced that the Eye will be brought to you,' Helewise said. 'Which can only mean that the killer, whoever he is, intends to redress the original theft of the Eye by the Lombard – or rather Galbertius, to call him by his name – and give it back to you, Sir Josse, whom he sees as its rightful owner.'

Josse's eyes met hers, and his distress was evident even before he spoke. 'If an assassin who can slay two innocent men wants to give me the Eye, I am not so sure I want it.'

It was exactly what Helewise had been thinking. But she said smoothly, 'Wait and see, Sir Josse. We do not know the whole tale yet – far from it – and we should not prejudge.'

'You speak sense, as always, Abbess Helewise,' Josse said with a grunt. 'But, just the same . . .' He left the sentence unfinished.

Suddenly Yves said, 'My lady, Josse told me that the first victim was killed with a Saracen knife.'

Helewise looked enquiringly at Josse. 'Indeed? How so?'

'My father had a similar knife, my lady,' Josse explained. 'I am certain that the murder weapon was of Outremer origin.'

She was thinking hard. Could her conclusion be right? There was little to support it, other than her strong feeling that she had hit on the truth . . . Raising her head to look at the brothers, she said, 'What if the killer did in fact acquire his knife in Outremer? Can we deduce that he, too, was on crusade with Sir Geoffroi and the Lombard? That he is driven simply by the desire to possess the Eye of Jerusalem, which he has followed all the way north to Acquin and thence here to Hawkenlye?'

Josse stared at her with his mouth open for a moment. Then he said, 'Your proposal is sound, my lady, up to a point. But we must not forget that Dee says the Eye will come to me. Why should a former crusader go to such lengths – travel all that way, kill two men – to steal the jewel, then give it away?'

She shook her head. 'You are right, Sir Josse. Why indeed.' But the thought would not go away, even in the face of such a credible undermining; she said tentatively, 'Unless there were some great compulsion, some higher motive . . .'

'We speak here of a killer, a cruel, efficient murderer,' Yves put in. 'Can such a man have a higher motive?'

She looked at him and smiled. 'No, Yves. Probably not.'

'But yet—' Yves began, only to be interrupted by a vexed sound from Josse. 'Josse? What ails you?'

'I keep thinking that I am beginning to see this whole mystery clearly, that the solution is almost to hand, but then it seems as if a mist, or a fog, rises up suddenly and obscures my sight,' he said, frustration evident in his angry voice. He shook his head violently. 'I try and I try, but it's as if that sorcerer has put an enchantment on me. As if his one desire is to make quite sure I do *not* see the solution.' He glared furiously at Helewise but then, as if remembering where he was, abruptly dropped his eyes. 'I apologise, my lady. And to you, Yves.' He touched his brother's shoulder. 'I *hate* men who take out their bad temper on innocent bystanders.'

'It's all right, Josse, we understand,' Yves said.

But Josse, who did not seem to have heard, spun on his heel and headed for the door. 'I'm going out for a ride,' he announced. 'I'm bad company, I have no useful thoughts to add to this discussion, and I am a trial to those who would try to muster some up. Perhaps some fresh air will clear this accursed fog in my head!'

He was out of the door before either Helewise or Yves could say anything to detain him. As the echoes of a violently slammed door died away – it was fortunate, Helewise mused, that the door and its hinges were stout and strong – Yves said quietly, 'Oh, dear.'

She looked up at him, feeling a genuine affection. 'Don't worry,' she said, 'he'll soon be back.'

Yves gave her a grin. 'Aye,' he agreed. Then, more sombrely, 'He drives himself hard, my lady. He takes everything on those broad shoulders of his, and carries responsibilities that in truth belong elsewhere.' She was about to agree with him when, flushing slightly, he said, 'I implied no criticism of *you*, Abbess Helewise.'

'I did not imagine that you did,' she murmured.

'But should not that sheriff – what was his name?'

'Harry Pelham,' she said tonelessly.

'Aye, Pelham. Should he not be hunting down this killer?'

'He should, yes,' she agreed. 'But, Yves, if we sat back and waited for him to solve every crime that occurred in this region, we should still be waiting when the Last Trump sounds.'

'He is not – oh. I see.' Yves' face reflected his comprehension. 'That's why Josse feels so driven?'

'I imagine so, yes. He has helped us many times before, you know, Yves. We at Hawkenlye treasure him.'

'Mmm, so I gather,' Yves said. Then, as if he were afraid of saying more than he should, he firmly changed the subject and said, 'If you will excuse me, I will go and see to my horse and, I think, perhaps follow Josse's example and take him out for some exercise.'

With a low bow, he backed out of the room and closed the door carefully – and quietly – behind him.

Leaving Helewise to wonder just what Josse had told his family back at Acquin about Hawkenlye Abbey and what they made of the goings-on there.

In particular, what they made of the Abbess.

But such speculation was, she firmly told herself presently, both a waste of God's good time and a temptation to vanity; getting up, she strode out of the room and headed off towards the church for some private prayer. We need your help, Lord, she thought as she hurried along the cloisters; we have a murderer at large, and we must bring him to justice.

Then not only those two dead men, but also the rest of us, may find some peace.

Josse, still angry and tense, was in no mood to appreciate the beauty of the great Wealden Forest in early October. He kicked Horace into a canter then, as the sweet autumn scents aroused the horse's interest, allowed him to have his head and break into a gallop.

For some time they rode, fast, along the track that wound around the skirts of the forest. Josse knew better than to turn off and enter in under the trees; the Forest Folk might be miles away but, on the other hand, they might not. And, as Josse knew very well, they did not welcome intruders.

Horace's pace had slowed to a comfortable canter and Josse, barely paying attention, was taken by surprise when the horse suddenly threw up his head and came to a shuddering stop.

Josse, keeping his seat with difficulty, shouted, 'Hoi, Horace! What's the matter?'

Horace snorted, shook his head until his mane flew and the metal of the harness jingled, then, as quickly as he had become frightened, calmed again. He stood quite still and, after a moment, jerked his head out of Josse's control and bent his neck to crop at some dry, dying grass by the track.

Josse slid off his back and secured the reins to the branch of a tree.

Then he began to look around.

There was, at first sight, nothing apparent that could have alarmed as sensible and experienced a horse as Horace. Josse stared along the track ahead, then behind; nothing, as far as the eye could see, which was up to the next bend. He stared out across the quiet land that sloped gently down and away from the forest ridge; one or two figures could be made out in the distance, presumably working in the fields, but they were far too far away to have acted as a disturbance.

Which left only the forest.

Despite his knowledge of it and its people, despite his respect for the place that amounted almost to awe, if not fear, Josse was not going to allow himself to be a coward.

He checked that Horace was securely tied up, checked

that his knife was in its scabbard, then straightened his tunic and arranged his cloak across his shoulders.

And, when he could come up with no more delaying tactics, he found a faint track that ran down the ditch and up the other side – made by a boar, perhaps, or by deer – and followed it. He scrambled over the top of the low bank, pushed aside the branches of a silver birch and made his way in beneath the trees.

The forest was very quiet.

It was autumn, aye, he thought, so you would expect to hear little in the way of animal activity.

But, as he had noticed before in the forest, the natural sounds of the world outside seemed not to penetrate in there. There was no breeze stirring the leaves, no distant cheery voice, no sound of human endeavour such as the regular thunk of an axe or the hee-haw of a saw.

Nothing.

He walked on, treading softly, his feet falling quietly on to the forest's deep carpet. A thousand years of dead leaves down there under my boots, he thought.

But, far from being a comfort, the thought increased his apprehension. So *old*, this place! It was ever here, always will be here, of the world yet apart, its people and its very spirit a law unto themselves . . .

Stop that, he ordered. Are you a little child, to scare yourself silly with superstitious tales? No, you're a grown man, with a job to do. Quite what that job was, and why whatever purpose he had was to be aided by creeping through the great forest, he did not stop to ask himself.

And, soon, he smelt smoke.

Striding on, refusing to allow fear to better him, he heard the small crackle of a campfire. He could see the smoke now, curling up gracefully into the soft, still forest air.

Caution finally winning out over bravado, he came to a halt behind a giant oak tree. Peering out from his shelter, he stared down into a glade. In its centre, where the smoke and the low flames would not reach overhanging branches, a little fire had been lit, the kindling and the small, neatly trimmed logs carefully retained within a circle of stones. A cairn of cut logs had been built, close enough to the hearth to be convenient but not so close that a stray spark might set light to it. Beside the fire was a bundle; it looked like a traveller's pack, and had been partly unfastened. Over by the first of the encircling trees a rough shelter had been constructed, made from cut and trimmed branches covered with a thick layer of bracken, dead and rusty looking. Its neat appearance made it look like the work of someone who had made such shelters many times before and knew exactly what he was doing.

There was nobody there.

Edging out from behind his tree, Josse crept on down into the glade. He stared around him as he went. No, he had been right; nobody there. Which was strange, when the flesh of his back crawled and trembled as if unfriendly eyes were boring into it. As if, indeed, it might at any moment receive the assault of an arrow.

Or the strange, curved blade of a Saracen knife.

18

He strode out into the middle of the glade.

Afraid though he was, it seemed a better option than skulking in the shadows, peering out nervously and waiting for someone to leap out and attack him. Besides, there was nobody there.

Was there?

He walked across to the shelter and glanced inside. There was a bedroll and what might have been a small supply of spare clothing, neatly folded. He wondered how this traveller had got there: on foot? On horseback?

Circling the glade, he looked for signs of a horse, or mule. Presently he came to a mound of horse droppings; they looked fairly fresh. It was beginning to look as if the visitor, whoever he was, had left his camp for the day, riding off on some pressing errand. Quite what that errand might be, Josse was not sure he wanted to know. Because, although it was but one possibility out of many, this man might be a killer. Might have murdered Prince John's spy and old Galbertius's servant, with swift, ruthless skill and no more compassion than if he had been slaughtering a pig to salt its flesh down for the winter.

Angry suddenly, Josse went to stand beside the campfire. He was on the point of shouting out, summoning whoever had made his camp here to show himself, when with no warning whatsoever there was a strong arm around his neck and the cold kiss of a blade at his throat.

A voice said, 'Keep silent. If you try to call for help, I shall kill you.'

Josse made himself relax. 'I will not call out,' he said. 'If you knew the forest as I do, you would let me yell all I want, because there is nobody to hear.'

'You are wrong,' the soft voice said. 'But no matter.'

As he spoke, he removed the stranglehold on Josse's neck and, with the blade still pressing in hard, was busy with his free hand tying Josse's wrists behind his back. Then he exerted strong pressure on Josse's shoulders and pushed him down to kneel on the forest floor.

With his prisoner thus disabled, finally the firm touch of the blade eased a little. Josse sensed the man move around behind him and, after a moment, he stood before him.

Josse stared up at his captor.

The man was swarthy-skinned, the flesh of his face an olive colour against the thick black beard. The hair of his head was also black, what could be seen of it; he wore a square of cloth over his head, held in place by more cloth wound into an elaborate turban. He was dressed in a heavy cloak of some deep-coloured material, fastened so as to hide whatever he wore beneath it. The eyes, dark, narrow, were heavily hooded and seemed to be elongated at the outer edges. Their expression was difficult to read; whatever the emotion they held, Josse was quite sure it was unfriendly. To say the least.

In his hand the man held a knife with a curved blade. Although slightly bigger than the one found lodged in the body of the dead spy, it was similar in shape and style.

'What do you want of me?' Josse asked. His voice, he was pleased to hear, sounded calm; his fear, he thought, did not show.

The man studied him for some moments. Then an expression of puzzlement crossed the dark face. His left hand – the hand not holding the knife – crept inside his cloak and, after some fumbling, seemed to close on an object concealed inside his garments. Wondering if he were about to draw out some weapon used for swift dispatch of victims, Josse closed his eyes and tried to pray.

It was interesting, he often thought afterwards, what sprang into a man's mind when he was sure he was about to die. In Josse's own case, the prayer was one of duty: dear Lord, of thy mercy and grace, help my brothers and my family and all at Acquin.

But that had not been what he had begged first. The swift instinctive prayer that had burst silently from him had been, please, Lord, protect Helewise.

But, this time, death had not come to claim him.

Feeling the blade busy at his wrists, cutting the cords that bound them, he opened his eyes. Just as the dark man, in front of him once more, fell to his knees and cried, 'Forgive me, I beg you, forgive me! You should have said who you were, called out your name as soon as you came into the glade!'

Josse struggled to his feet. Disorientated, the relics of dread still close, he said simply, 'Why?'

The man had pressed his face into the spongy leaf mould on the forest floor. Raising his head, he said, 'Because you are the man I have been seeking! You are Josse, son of Geoffroi d'Acquin, and so far have I travelled to find you that my home is now but a dim memory.'

Josse held out a hand and helped the man to his feet. 'What do you want with me?'

'I have brought you what is yours.'

'You bring—' But Josse hesitated to mention the Eye. Instead he said, 'I was warned that you sought me.'

'Warned?' The dark face creased into a frown. 'There was no need of warning, for I mean you no harm.' Then, suspicion clouding his eyes, the man said, 'Who issued this warning?'

Josse was about to reply when the stranger, nodding his head, interrupted. 'Do not trouble to tell me,' he said coldly. 'Save your breath, for I already know.' Then, passionately, he went on, 'He sees me, you know. He watches me, and I cannot escape his deep eyes. He knows that I come to you, he knows what it is I bear.'

'John Dee,' Josse breathed.

The dark man said, 'I perceive not his name. But he allies himself with one who is important in your land, who bears power and ever seeks more. But, powerful though he is, he is accompanied by one yet greater than he, one who is a magus of rare ability.' He paused. 'One who is spoken of with awe even among the great sorcerers of my own land.'

'Where is that land?' Josse asked, feeling that he already knew.

The man said, 'To you, my homeland is a part of the great region to the east of the Inland Sea, the area that you know as Outremer. But we call it Lebanon.'

The name was only vaguely familiar to Josse; he was ashamed of his ignorance, as if not to know of a man's homeland were some sort of insult. He did not wish to dwell on the thought; hastening on, he said, 'You did not know who I was at first, when you crept up on me. But then, quite suddenly, your attitude changed, as if you had been told who I was. What happened?'

Again the man slid his hand inside his cloak. 'I knew,' he replied. 'Is that not enough?'

It wasn't, not by a long way. But Josse felt that to pursue the matter would get him nowhere and might actually antagonise the stranger. He said quietly, 'I see.'

The man smiled, his regular teeth white in his dark face. 'I think not,' he murmured. Then, as if making up his mind, he said, 'I will tell you a tale, Sir Josse d'Acquin, Geoffroi's son, if you have ears to listen.'

'That I have,' Josse said; too quickly, for the man's smile widened at his eagerness.

'Come and settle by the fire.' The stranger took his arm. 'I will spread skins for us to sit on, to keep out the ground's chill.' He hurried to his shelter, returning with two neat rolls tied with cord. Unwinding the cords, he laid out what appeared to be sheepskins, the short fleeces cream and tightly curled, unlike any sheep's fleece that Josse knew of. 'Sit!' he said. 'Be comfortable!'

And Josse, settling down into a cross-legged position by the fire, did as he was told.

The dark stranger waited until he had stopped wriggling before sitting down himself. Then, his movements far more supple and graceful than Josse's, he sank down on the opposite side of the hearth and began to speak.

'Long ago, a Persian king bought a beautiful sapphire with an eye in its depths,' he said. His voice, Josse immediately noticed, had taken on the singsong tones of a professional storyteller, or perhaps merely of a man accustomed to entertaining fellow travellers by the fire. 'He was drawn to it above every other stone in the merchant's pack, so he trusted his intuition and bought it. He showed it to his magus, who told him that he had chosen wisely since the stone had power, and would bestow on its rightful owner many very useful gifts. So the king gave the stone to his jewellers, who shaped it and polished it until its shape was round and regular, pleasing to those who looked upon it. And, just as the magus had said, there in its depths, for those who had the patience to study it in silent patience, was its own eye, staring out at the beholder.

'Then the king gave the stone to his goldsmiths, who set it into a thick gold coin, its centre moulded into lips to hold the stone secure and safe. The magus told the goldsmiths that they must write an inscription on the gold coin. The style of writing and the language were those commonly employed in the land, but the words made no sense to the goldsmiths because they were in code, and the code was known only to the magus.

'The king treasured his stone above all others for, as the magus had predicted, it had many useful powers. It bestowed success and good fortune. It could stop bleeding, both from an external wound and that which mysteriously arises in a man's secret insides. And, like the magic of a mother's loving kiss on a sick child's forehead, it could take away fever. It could detect when poison had been dropped into a man's goblet of wine. And, most valuable of all, it warned of secret enemies.'

'Did the king have secret enemies?' Josse interrupted.

The stranger glanced at him. 'He did. As does every king, including your Malik Richard. Now, straight away' – he was clearly keen to continue his narrative – 'the king realised that all that he had been told was true, for it seemed that everything he attempted was a success. The land of Persia was strong and proud and, when the king felt that the time was right to challenge the might of the Babylonian Empire, his magus consulted the stars and dwelled privately on the omens, and then agreed with him. So King Cyrus – for that was his name, and he was ever known as Cyrus the Great – marched on Babylon, took it and founded an empire of his own, which was called the Acaemenid and was the greatest that the ancient world had ever seen.

'Now when King Cyrus's army took Babylon, they found dwelling there the sad remnants of an alien people who called themselves Judeans. The Babylonian king, Nebuchadrezzar, had attacked their city, Jerusalem, and brought the people to their knees. But the Judean king had unwisely listened to those who gave him bad advice, and allowed himself to be persuaded into a rebellion. Nebuchadrezzar sent his army back again and, this time, showed no mercy. Jerusalem was taken and destroyed utterly, and its people were led away into exile. Their king, whose name was Zedekiah, was captured with them, and both his eyes were put out.'

Josse gave an involuntary shudder of horror. The dark man, who seemed to sense it, shot him a swift look. 'I told you that Nebuchadrezzar showed no mercy,' he murmured. 'So a king deals with a rebellion. It is the way of the world, is it not?'

Josse did not answer.

'So it was,' the stranger resumed, 'that King Cyrus discovered the last descendants of the Judeans living in wretchedness in Babylon, far away from their homes. He took pity on them and allowed them to return to their own land, and he gave back to them many precious items of gold and silver which Nebuchadrezzar's men had stolen from the temple at Jerusalem. It was said that one such item was King Solomon's ring, set with a sapphire seal stone, but this ring was lost and nobody could say where it was. Now King Cyrus was troubled by this, and he consulted his magus and asked what he might do to make amends to the exiles returning home. "For it is my wish," he said, "to demonstrate to these people that Cyrus is not Nebuchadrezzar, and that he knows when to show mercy."'

'What did the magus suggest?'

'The magus said to King Cyrus, "You have in your possession, sire, a jewel that is the match of the sapphire in King Solomon's ring, if not its superior." And the King, although his heart misgave him, knew that the magus spoke of the great sapphire set in gold. But he trusted the magus and so, after much thought, accepted his advice. He sent for the leader of the Judeans and said, "I give you a treasure, a sapphire eye set in a coin of gold." In a sudden burst of inspiration, he held up the stone and declared, "Behold the Eye of Jerusalem, which I give to the people of that city in recompense for the eyes of King

Zedekiah, that Nebuchadrezzar put out." And the Judeans took it home with them, and put it in a place of safety in the temple that they rebuilt on the ruins of the one destroyed by the Babylonians.'

'It was a gift of rare generosity,' Josse said.

'It was. But the King was advised by his magus that he should not let the Eye entirely out of his sight, for it was ever possible that the people of Judah might one day use it against its former owner.'

'That would have been hard, when it was King Cyrus who had given it to them!'

'Indeed. But when necessity drives, a nation will take what steps it must to survive. The magus, who looked into the hearts of men and could understand them with a rare clarity, told King Cyrus what to do. "The Eye must be watched," he said, "in order that its whereabouts are ever known, as are the uses to which its powers are being put." He proposed to the King that two men be appointed Guardians of the Stone, and he suggested for chief Guardian a man he knew of and trusted. This man was an astronomer trained by the greatest of the Babylonian star-gazers, one Enil of Sidon; he had a young nephew, who was also his apprentice, who could fill the post of the second Guardian.'

'And the King agreed to this?'

'With alacrity. The Guardians were appointed and informed that, under Persian law, their post was to be in perpetuity, passed from father to son or, failing that, uncle to nephew or grandfather to grandson.'

'A woman was never to be a Guardian?'

The dark man looked almost affronted. 'Certainly not.

The great unseen forces of the supernatural are not for women.'

How little you know, Josse thought. But he said nothing.

'And so it came about,' the steady voice went on, 'that the Eye of Jerusalem was hidden away deep within the heart of the Temple of Solomon, safe, unused, almost forgotten, and the Guardians had little guarding to do. But they kept the tradition alive, each generation impressing on the next that theirs was a royal appointment and that it was to last forever.

'In time the Persian Empire fell, just as the Babylonians had fallen to King Cyrus. This time, it was a young general from Macedonia who led the invincible army, and this Alexander, like Cyrus before him, was also called the Great. He crossed the Hellespont and challenged Cyrus's descendant, King Darius, defeating him and going on to conquer Phoenicia, Palestine, Egypt, Babylon, Susa and Persepolis before marching on into India. Nobody can tell how far Alexander's great wings would have stretched, for he died and his empire was divided up between his generals.

'The land of Palestine fell to the general known as Seleucus, whose successor persecuted the Judeans. Once again, their temple was destroyed. But the Guardians, perceiving the threat in time to take action, removed the Eye by night and took it away to Damascus. And there it stayed, while in the outside world the power of the Greeks diminished and the Romans rose up to take their place, destroying the temple of Jerusalem yet again when the people of Judah rose up in revolt. The Guardians, now many generations removed from their originals, had kept the precious jewel in Damascus. Now no longer sure who they should be protecting from possible misuse of the Eye, they decided that the best thing they could do was to make sure that it went on being ignored.'

'Then how did Mehmed come to have it?' Josse demanded.

The dark man gave a faint sigh. 'Wait, and you shall hear. Soon after the death of their prophet, Jesus Christ, a Christian community had begun to flourish in Damascus. But then Mohammed and his followers, the great and holy founders of the Muslim era, moved from Mecca to Medina in the land known as Arabia, and the city of Damascus was thrust into prominence. It so happened that a young and ambitious Guardian had recently inherited the chief's post from his father, possibly too soon for the good of either the Eye or himself. He was driven to seek favour with the rapidly burgeoning power of the Muslims, and he offered the Eye to the rich and charismatic head of the Mehmeds. The Mehmeds were an influential family poised for power; the Guardian reasoned that a position in their household would be preferable to remaining in the background and, eventually, becoming lost in one of history's forgotten backwaters.'

'But he would go on guarding the Eye?'

'It is not thought he considered that, since his aim was, as I have said, to gain favour; although in fact he did continue to be the Eye's Guardian. However, as he was fetching the Eye from its hiding place and preparing to take it to the Mehmeds, he was overcome by a trance and he received what he believed to be a message. Obeying what he thought the Eye had ordered, he warned the Mehmeds that a day would come when they would have to give up their great treasure in exchange for something that they valued even more. Laughing, heady with the powers of the Eye as described by the Guardian, they took little note.'

'But then along came my father.'

'As you say, along came Geoffroi d'Acquin. Along came a Frankish knight of rare compassion, who saw a terrified child in mortal danger and who saved the boy's life at the risk of his own. And Mehmed – that is, the man who was head of the Mehmed family at the time – recognised that this was the event that had been predicted when the family first gained possession of the Eye.'

'It was a great gesture, nevertheless, to let the treasure go,' Josse commented.

The dark man smiled. 'Ah, you are as lacking in cynicism as your father,' he murmured. 'When the Mehmeds were told that they would one day have to yield up the Eye, they were also told that if they did not give it away when the moment came, its power would be lost to them. Oh yes, they would still possess a pretty and valuable jewel, but its unique abilities would no longer serve them; might, indeed, begin to work against them.' He chuckled. 'When he heard of Geoffroi's brave deed and how he had saved Azamar, old Mehmed spent many long hours trying to calm fevers and test for poisons deliberately put in wine goblets. And a hapless servant almost lost his arm while Mehmed waved the Eye over the deep cut he had just made in it, in a fruitless attempt to staunch the bleeding.' His eyes, still full of amusement, met Josse's. 'Mehmed did not give the Eye to your father until he was absolutely certain that it was of no more use to him.'

Feeling a strange sense of betrayal, as if the conclusion
to a favourite folk tale had just been changed for something
far less satisfactory, Josse said, 'The little boy survived into
adulthood, I am told.'

'Azamar? Yes, he grew up to be a fine man, who has
begotten many strong, healthy sons. He has been in his
time a mighty warrior and, now that he is gradually
becoming too old – and too precious – to wield a sword,
he is a valued advisor to those who carry on the fight. He
has the ear, they say, of Saladin.'

Has he, indeed? thought Josse. No wonder Prince John
had made that somewhat bitter remark about King Richard
and his knights not being entirely happy about Geoffroi's
having saved the boy's life.

But the dark man was speaking. '. . . has not forgotten
Geoffroi d'Acquin,' he said.

'Eh? Who hasn't?'

The stranger sighed. 'Azamar. Who else?'

Josse wiped his hands over his face. He was finding
it difficult to maintain his concentration, and he was
sure there were questions he ought to ask, mysteries
that could be solved, if he could only get his brain to
work properly.

One matter, however, stood out clear, even to a man as
weary as Josse.

'You killed the Prince's spy, and the young lad who was
servant to Galbertius Sidonius.' At this the stranger's head
shot up, and there was an expression of surprise on his
face. 'Oh, we worked out who was responsible for both
deaths,' Josse said fiercely. 'You would not deny your
guilt, would you?'

'No, no.' The man shook his head impatiently, as if he wished to brush the matter aside and proceed to something more interesting. 'The first man I caught up with on the road up out of the river valley. I guessed that he was on his way to steal the Eye, for I had tracked the bearer of the Eye to England and knew him to be nearby. I killed the thief before he could carry out his intention, and I stripped the body and hid it in the bracken.' He shook his head again, this time wonderingly. 'I did not know then that the Abbey and the shrine lay so near, or I should have concealed the body more efficiently, somewhere that it would never be found.'

'But it *was* found.'

'I know, I know. You must believe me when I say that I am not usually so careless.'

He only regrets that he did not hide the body well enough, Josse realised, with a tremor of alarm. He does not rue the fact that he murdered the man; not one jot.

'And the boy?' he asked, careful to keep his tone neutral.

'The boy stole the Eye from his dying master, who was bringing it to you, Josse d'Acquin.' The man sounded outraged. 'He did not get very far before his conscience began to bother him, but by then he was in mortal dread that the monks from the Abbey would hold him responsible for his master's death. He hid out in the fields and the hedges, seeking shelter in barns and outhouses when the weather grew chill. He had no food, and began to grow sick. He was making his slow way back here, I think to return the Eye and give himself up, when I killed him.'

'But he was innocent!' Josse protested. 'He had no hand

in Sidonius's death – the old man was gravely ill, and it was his cough that killed him!'

Again, the look of surprise crossed the stranger's face. Then he said, 'Innocent? The boy had stolen the Eye! I took it from him; it is quite safe, you must not concern yourself, and—'

'You murdered him!' Josse cried. 'Although the mark on the front of the throat was faint, it was noticed. What was it? A blow with the side of your hand?'

'Yes.' The man looked almost proud. 'Such skills the Guardians have ever been taught.'

'Aye, you're a Guardian.' Josse nodded. 'I guessed as much. You followed my father and the Lombard from Outremer to Acquin—'

'Not I,' the man put in. 'My father and his brother. They watched over the Eye while your father kept it, at Acquin, until my father died of a sickness that ravaged the region. Then, although I was quite young, I took his place. With my uncle I followed the man you call the Lombard back to his home. I was for killing him and returning the jewel to your father, but my uncle overrode me.' A scowl crossed the dark face. 'He said that the Lombard would repent of his theft, if we were but patient. He was right, but patience was not my way and I found the waiting cruelly hard.' He shrugged faintly. 'So we kept watch over the Eye there in the land of the Lombard until he came back north to Acquin, seeking Geoffroi, your father. We followed him, and then my uncle died. He was weak and old, and the long journey proved too much for him. The Lombard led me on from Acquin to England, eventually here to Hawkenlye.' He said the word slowly and carefully, as if unaccustomed to it. 'Although I did not know that he was heading here. I had imagined he would try to find you straight away. I lost him, briefly, which was when I killed the man who came hunting the Eye. But then I found him again. The rest, you know.'

Josse nodded slowly. 'Aye. And I guessed much of what went before. You followed Galbertius Sidonius for much of his life, you and your father before you, and—'

The man held up his hands as if in protest. 'This is what I cannot understand!' he said, puzzlement clear on his face. 'The man known as the Lombard, your father's friend who stole the Eye from him and then tried to bring it back, you refer to him as Galbertius Sidonius!'

'Aye, I do,' Josse agreed. 'He stayed with my family at Acquin, and my brother reported that his servant addressed him so.'

'No, you are wrong,' the stranger insisted. 'The lad may have spoken the name, but he cannot have used it when referring to his master.'

There was a pause then, with simple dignity, he said, '*I* am Galbertius Sidonius.'

19

Initially, Josse was certain he was lying, although he could not have said quite why. Leaping to his feet – the dark man got up too – he said, stupidly, 'You can't be.'

'I am,' the man said with a smile. 'I am descended from Enil of Sidon, the original chief Guardian. And I am the last of my line for, although I have bedded many women, not one have I impregnated. I leave no son to follow me.'

'There will be no more Guardians?'

The dark man shrugged. 'Unless there is a distant cousin of whom I am unaware, no. And, even if such a man exists, he is not here by my side, where he could be taught the role which destiny has decreed he must follow.' He sighed. 'But, in truth, what is the point? The Guardians existed to protect the Eye's first owner – indeed, the man at whose behest it came into being – from those to whom he gave it, lest they turn on him and use the jewel's powers against him. It was so simple then. But now? The Eye belongs to you, Josse d'Acquin. Whom should I protect, that you might threaten with the Eye's magic?'

'I will threaten nobody,' Josse said fervently.

'No?' Sidonius cocked an ironic eyebrow. 'Do not be so sure. Power once in a man's hands can have a corrupting influence, and only the very strong, the very wise or the very good are immune.'

'But—'

'Supposing I were to change my mind and try to take the Eye back?' Sidonius continued, ignoring the interruption. 'Suppose you believed I meant you harm?'

'I do not – I would not know how to use the Eye, either to protect myself or to attack you,' Josse said.

'You do not know *yet*,' Sidonius murmured. Then, cheerfully, he said, 'But have no fear. As I said, I mean you no harm. It would be difficult for me to hurt you, for not only are you the Eye's rightful owner, which in itself gives you a certain protection, but you also have . . .' He trailed to a halt, eyeing Josse speculatively. 'I do not know what it is,' he admitted. 'It is as if – as if someone else has put a guard around you, so that you are shielded from what small magic I can work and could turn against you.' Before Josse could even raise an arm to defend himself, the dark man had thrown up both hands and was pointing them straight at Josse's heart. There was a sound like the crackle of pine resin on a fire, and Josse thought he saw a flash of blue, there and gone before he had time properly to register it.

Sidonius, rubbing his hands together as if they pained him, said, 'There. You see? Someone is looking after you. Somebody quite strong.'

It must be Dee, Josse thought. And he seemed to be doing a good job.

Sidonius was again reaching inside his cloak. This time, he brought out what appeared to be a box made of silver. It hung on a chain which, like the box itself, was tarnished and worn. Sidonius touched the tiny fastening, and some hidden mechanism sprang into action. The lid of the box flew open. Sidonius lifted out what was within, then threw the silver box on the ground as if it were no longer of interest.

Compared with what he now held up, it wasn't.

And, before Josse's fascinated eyes, the Eye of Jerusalem swung gently in the light from the fire, its heavy gold surround glistening and the sapphire sending out sparks of brilliant blue, as if it were winking at him.

He held out his hand and Sidonius placed the Eye in it. Closing his fist, Josse felt the stone's weight. For a brief instant he seemed to see his father; Geoffroi was smiling, nodding, as if to say, there! It was worth the wait, wasn't it? Then Geoffroi faded, and there were just the two of them in the glade.

Sidonius gave a low bow, muttered something in a language Josse did not understand, and then bent to roll up the sheepskins. Watching him, Josse said, 'What are you doing?'

'I am packing up,' Sidonius replied. 'My task here is done. There is no need for me to stay.'

It crossed Josse's mind that there was actually quite a pressing need; this man had killed, twice, and should be brought to justice.

As if he had read the unspoken thought, Sidonius laughed softly and said, 'You would detain me, Josse d'Acquin? Ask me meekly to accompany you to that fool of a sheriff and give myself up for murder? Ah, but I was following orders. I am a Guardian of the Eye and, unlike my uncle, I carry out my duty instantly and without prevarication. I am commanded to kill those who remove the Eye of Jerusalem from its rightful owner.'

'Was that in King Cyrus's original instructions?' Josse demanded. 'You paint the picture of a just man, a man keen to redress the wrongs done by others. Do you really believe he would sanction the murder of innocents?'

'Innocents,' Sidonius repeated thoughtfully. Then: 'You may be right; I do not know.' He shrugged. 'I cannot in truth say what he would do. It was all so very long ago.'

He had tied the sheepskins to his satisfaction and now walked across to his bundle, picking it up as if it weighed no more than a dead leaf. Then he glanced inside his shelter, presumably checking to see if he had left anything behind. Once more coming to stand before Josse, he made a deeper, more formal bow.

'I take my leave of you, Josse d'Acquin,' he said. 'Use the Eye wisely. It can do great good, you know. Adieu.'

And, without a backward glance, he strode off into the trees. Josse made to follow him; he put out one foot and would have started to run, only he seemed to have been turned to stone. His limbs would not obey him.

So he stood there and watched as Galbertius Sidonius walked away.

He was soon lost from sight – had he some magic, Josse wondered, which, besides rendering a would-be pursuer immobile, made him blend with his surroundings? – and, after a while, there was the faint and distant whinny of a horse.

Sidonius was, presumably, mounting up and riding off through the secret paths of the forest. And Josse was perfectly sure he would never see the man again.

* * *

Whatever enchantment had rendered Josse so helpless was not long lasting. Quite soon after the echoes of Sidonius's passage had faded, Josse found that he could move again.

The Eye of Jerusalem was still in his hand. In the dying light of Sidonius's fire, he looked at it again. This time, without the tension of confrontation to distract him, he was able to study it in a calmer frame of mind. And, staring into its deep blue heart, he saw its eye staring back at him.

It watched him steadily, and he began to feel it was hypnotising him. 'What am I to do with you?' he asked aloud. He glanced down at the silver box that Sidonius had cast aside. 'Shall I put you back in your box, hide you away under my tunic and use you when I am threatened, sick or bleeding?' It was a tempting thought. 'Shall I keep you in my hand as I go about my daily round, gradually getting to know what you can do, how you are able to warn me of hidden dangers?'

What great heights I could reach, Josse thought, with such an ally ever with me.

Thoughtfully, he picked up the silver box and stuffed it inside his tunic. He kicked out what was left of Sidonius's fire, making sure the last glowing ember had been extinguished and smoothly raking over the charred remains with the side of his boot. The forest people were fussy about fires in their domain and it was wise, he knew, to take care when one had been lit. Then, still clutching the Eye in his hand – it fitted neatly inside his closed fist and could not be seen – he headed off towards Horace and the ride back to the Abbey.

*   *   *

He rode slowly, still thinking hard. He took Horace to the stables, where Sister Martha, with a friendly greeting, seemed only too happy to lead the horse away and see to him.

Not yet ready to speak to the Abbess, Josse cast around in his mind for a quiet place to go and sit by himself. The herb garden came to mind; he set off around the east end of the sisters' dormitory and made his way through Sister Tiphaine's neat beds to where a rough bench stood, under the shelter of the Abbey walls.

It was very peaceful. The gardens around him had the feel and the scent of autumn, and there was the faint smell of smoke on the air; presumably the herbalist had been burning garden rubbish. Herb cuttings must have been among the detritus, because he could smell something sharp and quite pleasant . . .

He closed his eyes. He had all but made up his mind; perhaps a brief period of silent meditation – of prayer – might bring him the wisdom to decide whether or not what he was planning was the best thing to do.

After quite a long time, he became aware that somebody was approaching, and had come to sit beside him.

'You have it,' John Dee said softly. 'Would you permit me a look?'

Josse opened his eyes. 'Aye,' he said. He opened his right hand, resting on his knee, and the Eye winked up at him.

Dee sat and gazed down at it.

'You may hold it, if you wish,' Josse said.

Dee looked doubtful. 'I am not sure . . .' But then, as if gathering his courage and hastening to act before he could waver, he darted out his right hand and took hold of the

Eye's chain, dropping the jewel into the open palm of his left hand.

He sat perfectly still for some time, staring at the Eye, unblinking, face impassive. Then he went to return it to Josse but, as Josse unthinkingly held out his left hand to take it – the nearer hand to Dee – the magician held the Eye back.

'It is time for your first lesson in the power of stones,' he said with a smile. 'You must always think before you take the Eye in one or the other hand. Are you right or left handed?'

'Right.'

'Then your right hand is your power-giving hand, your left the one that receives power.'

'Oh,' Josse said casually. Then, as he understood, 'Oh!'

Dee's smile widened. 'Yes. I, too, am right handed. And I took your Eye in my left hand because I wanted to take in some of its power. You do not mind?'

'I know virtually nothing of its power. As far as I'm concerned, you're welcome to take all you like.'

'A generous sentiment, but you should be careful over making such offers.' There was a pause, then Dee went on, 'Would you like me to tell you of the Eye's power?'

Josse sighed. 'I know it can stop bleeding and detect poisons, and warn of enemies approaching. But aye, I suppose you'd better tell me the rest.' Thinking that he had sounded ungracious, he added, 'If you will.'

Dee chuckled. 'For a man who has just been given the world,' he murmured, 'you appear very uninterested.'

'What do you mean?' Suddenly Josse was alert.

'Oh – nothing. Take no notice.' Dee seemed to be

uneasy. 'Now, you are right in what you say, as far as it goes, but those you have described are but the Eye's minor powers. In its heart it carries far greater forces, but they cannot be awakened except by one who possesses psychic powers.'

'Do you have these psychic powers? Can *you* awaken its forces?'

'I could,' Dee replied carefully, 'but I will not. The Eye is yours,' he said by way of explanation.

But it was hardly an explanation at all.

'What do these greater forces do?' Josse persisted. 'Would they bring me wealth? Power? Good fortune? Position?'

'All of those, and far more.' Dee's voice was low, sombre. 'Although, like an inexperienced rider on a fiery stallion, you would have great difficulty controlling them. Indeed, they would probably control you. Which is why' – his voice dropped to a whisper, and he spoke right into Josse's ear – 'it is vital that the Prince does not get hold of the Eye.'

'I thought you said the powers would only work for the Eye's rightful owner?'

'I did. So, imagine what harm he might do himself, trying to bend uncontrollable forces to his own will when their intent was already to work against him!'

Being a novice in the world of magic, Josse had no idea of what the extent of the potential damage might be. But, judging by Dee's horror-struck tone, it sounded as if it could be fairly devastating.

'I shall not let the Prince have the Eye,' he said firmly. 'You have my word, Magister.'

Dee looked at him for a long time. Then, slowly, he nodded. 'I believe you. Thank you, Josse d'Acquin.'

He went on staring at Josse. Just as the scrutiny was becoming really uncomfortable, he spoke again. 'The Eye now belongs to you and your descendants,' he said dreamily. His dark eyes seemed to look beyond Josse, out into the distance – or into the future – at something unseen by all except him. 'It will go to one who has the innate psychic skill to make the Eye come properly alive. Yes, for the first time in almost two thousand years, the stone will come into its full potential.'

After a moment – during which, it seemed to Josse, the echoes of vast invisible waves lessened and finally shrank to nothing – he said, 'But, Magister, I have no wife, and no child of my own. Will the Eye therefore go to one of my nephews? Is that allowed?'

'You have nieces?' The question seemed strange.

'Aye, several.'

'Ah.' Dee smiled, as if in satisfaction.

'Why do you ask?'

'Oh – it is only that I have the strong sense that this great sorcerer will be female.'

Josse felt afraid. The thought of one of Yves's girls, or of Acelin's sweet little Eleanor, having this great burden put upon them was, in that moment, quite intolerable. Which was, when he thought about it, precisely the endorsement of his earlier decision that he had been waiting for.

As if Dee were intently following Josse's silent reasoning, he laughed softly and said, 'Ah, Josse, how little you know of magical stones! You can do what you will – indeed, I think that, under the circumstances, you have decided wisely – but do not think that you can dust off your hands and finish the matter. The Eye, as you will discover, has its own ideas.'

'I can't lay this thing on the innocent shoulders of one of my nieces!'

'No, you can't,' Dee agreed.

'But I don't understand!' Josse protested. 'Magister, you speak in riddles!'

'Just as sorcerers always do.' Dee got to his feet, putting a hand to the small of his back. 'Ah, but I have sat here too long, and allowed the damp to get into my bones.'

Instantly Josse leapt up to help him. 'Lean on me, Magister, and I will help you to walk.' He hesitated, then said impulsively, 'I am going to seek out the Abbess. Will you come with me?'

'Thank you. I will.'

'You should ask Sister Tiphaine for some of her special remedy,' Josse urged. 'She has a firm hand, but the pain as she rubs in the ointment is worth it for the relief it brings.'

'Ah yes, Sister Tiphaine,' Dee said softly. 'I shall do as you suggest, Josse.' He stopped for a moment, staring into Josse's face. 'You are a good man. I have always said so.'

Embarrassed, Josse muttered his thanks and then concentrated on supporting the magician's weight as he led him away. As they proceeded out of the herb garden, he remembered something.

'Magister, I have been in the forest,' he said.

'Ah.'

'I – well, I'll save the full story to tell the Abbess first, if you don't mind. But I was informed that someone was using their power to protect me out there, and I imagine it was you, so I would like to thank you.'

'Ah,' Dee said again.

But, Josse noticed, he neither confirmed nor denied that he had lent his help.

Helewise put aside her books and gave her full attention to her visitors. She had been expecting them – at least, she had been expecting Josse – and she summoned one of the sisters to go and find Yves and invite him to come and join them.

'The Magister is suffering from a pain in his back,' Josse informed her.

'Then he must have my chair.' She got up and held out her hand to John Dee. With a graceful bow, he accepted her offer.

She went to stand beside Josse. 'Is all well?' she asked softly; he looked – *different*, somehow, and she was concerned for him.

'Aye,' he replied. Then he told her all that had happened since he left her.

When he had finished she said, 'So we were wrong all along, and Galbertius Sidonius was not the Lombard.'

'No,' Josse said.

Then – she could not prevent herself – she said, 'May I see the Eye?'

He opened his right hand and held it out to her.

She took it in her left hand. Immediately she felt as if some tiny creature were tickling her palm. It was not an unpleasant sensation but, nevertheless, she was wary. She handed the stone back to Josse.

Dee, watching, said, 'Did you feel the power, my lady?'

'I – er, I felt a sort of tingle,' she admitted.

'Ah.' Dee glanced at Josse.

There was a tap on the door, and Yves came in. He, too, was shown the Eye, and Josse told him of the meeting with the man who was Galbertius Sidonius.

'But he can't be,' Yves protested, just as Josse had done earlier.

'He is,' Josse insisted. 'You must have misheard the servant lad, Yves, because when he muttered about Galbertius Sidonius, he wasn't referring to his master.'

Yves was shaking his head, clearly disturbed at having what he had believed a certainty prove to be no such thing. 'You have my sincere apologies,' he kept saying, 'I have misled you all.'

Helewise felt very sorry for him. 'Perhaps,' she said gently, 'he and his master the Lombard had reason to know the name of Galbertius Sidonius. Perhaps they knew about the Guardians, knew that they were being pursued, and the lad, at least, was afraid. Would that tally with what you overheard?'

Yves, his brows drawn down into a scowl of fierce concentration, thought for a moment. Then: 'Aye. He was saying something about keeping out of Galbertius's way.' As enlightenment dawned, he exclaimed, 'Of course! He meant they *both* had to avoid the man, him and the Lombard! Oh, how foolish I have been!'

'No, no,' Josse protested, then, undermining his protest, 'Well, anyway, no harm done.'

Helewise gave Yves a smile. 'Do not upset yourself,' she said quietly, just to him. 'It makes no difference, in the end.'

But Yves, muttering under his breath, did not seem to be able to forgive himself so easily.

Josse was addressing John Dee, sitting regally in Helewise's tall chair. He said, 'Magister, why were you and the Prince looking for a man by the name of Galbertius Sidonius? Did you not realise that he was the Guardian, not the man who possessed the Eye?'

Dee gave a deep sigh. 'The name came to me,' he said. 'I knew that it was important – its revelation was accompanied by certain unmistakable signs. There was the question of the man's great age.'

'He is not all that old,' Josse said.

'I realise that. I think that what I was perceiving was the vast antiquity of the Guardian tradition.'

Helewise could not contain herself any longer. She said, more abruptly that she had intended, 'But surely you do not believe this fable, of a magical sapphire given by King Cyrus to the people of Judah! How can it possibly be true?'

As three pairs of eyes turned to her, two of them incredulous, one pair strangely knowing – almost, she thought, compassionate in their understanding – Josse said, 'Abbess Helewise! Of course we believe it!'

In the face of that sort of conviction it was, she decided, better to withdraw. Bowing briefly, she said, 'I see.'

Josse, still looking as if he had taken her remark as a personal affront, said rather stiffly, 'The Magister is in pain, as I said, my lady. With your leave, I will take him to Sister Tiphaine and ask her to supply and administer some of her special rub.'

'Of course.'

'I'll come with you,' Yves said hurriedly.

She returned their courteous bows as they filed out of the room, John Dee between them.

It seemed, she thought as she listened to their receding footsteps, that her remark had ruined their happy mood of fascinated enchantment.

But the tale cannot be true! she told herself. How could anybody know, after all this time, where that wretched sapphire came from, what its history was? If they chose to swallow the story without one single question, well, that was their choice.

She was quite determined *she* wasn't going to.

With a slightly injured sniff – oh, dear, Josse really had seemed cross with her – she returned to her books.

20

---•✦•---

Darkness was falling when Josse came back again.

Helewise had left her room to attend Vespers but, having no appetite, had decided not to partake of the last meal. She was sitting at her table, half-listening out for the summons to Compline and, afterwards, to bed, when she heard him approach along the cloister.

He would never, she thought, smiling, manage to surprise her there in her room.

She called out, 'Come in, Sir Josse,' just at the instant when his knuckles knocked on the door.

He did so. Then, without preamble, he said, 'Abbess Helewise, I am sorry if I was impolite earlier. I have thought about what you said and, of course, you are right. I have, I believe, allowed myself to be carried away by these tales of magic and sorcery, and what small amounts I possess of sense and logic have been quite absent.'

It sounded, she thought, like a prepared speech. Then he said, 'Phew! It's a relief to have said all that!' which seemed to confirm it.

She smiled, full of affection for him. 'There is no need of an apology. John Dee is a compelling man, I agree. And you have also had a long conversation with Galbertius Sidonius who, I imagine, is something of a living legend. What a life he must have had.'

'Aye. He seemed to be almost inhuman.' Josse frowned as he tried to explain. 'It was as if he was no longer any more than the job he was born to do. As if the decent parts of him had eroded away, leaving only the burning desire to carry out his purpose of guarding the Eye.'

'I suppose such single-mindedness must have come about gradually, down through the generations,' she mused. 'For all we know, growing in intensity with each step from father to son. If, that is,' she added hastily, 'we are to give any credence to the tale.'

'Aye.' He sighed, and, looking at him, she saw that he seemed desperately tired.

'Why not go to bed?' she suggested gently. 'You have had a demanding day.'

'Aye, I have that.' He rubbed his hands over his face. 'I want to speak to Saul and Augustus, too, so I ought to head off down into the Vale. I would tell the brothers all that has happened, Abbess Helewise, with your permission?'

'Of course.'

Josse grinned suddenly. 'I was just thinking about when I first asked the monks and the lay brothers if they recalled anything that might help us identify that first body, the one that the little lass discovered.'

'And?'

'Brother Micah spoke of a figure all in black creeping about the Vale. We didn't take him seriously, especially since he said he'd *heard* this saturnine figure, which, as Brother Erse pointed out, is impossible. But in fact he might have been right – Sidonius wore black, or at least very dark colours, so maybe Brother Micah did see him after all.'

'Indeed.' It was something she preferred not to dwell on; the thought of a professional killer stalking the innocent monks and pilgrims in the Vale was just too dreadful.

Josse came closer, leaning his weight on his hands, placed on her table. 'My lady, I have come to ask a great favour,' he said. 'I fully expect you to refuse, so don't worry if you have to.'

She gave a small smile and said, 'You'd better ask it, Sir Josse, and I'll see.'

'I want the Abbey to have the Eye of Jerusalem. Oh, I know you'll say it's mine and I must take the responsibility' – it had not entered her head to say any such thing – 'but let me explain my reasoning.'

'Please do.'

'This Sidonius fellow said that the Eye was now mine, mine and my family's, and that it would pass down to my descendants when I die. But, as you know, my lady, I am not married and I have no child. He also said that one day the Eye would fall into the hands of a woman of my blood who possessed strange powers, and she would be the first ever owner of the Eye to bring its full potential alive. Well, you see, the trouble is that I'm worried that he meant one of Yves's girls – Marie-Ida, Mathilde or even Madoline, who is but a year old, poor little lassie. Or he might have meant Acelin's daughter Eleanor. What a terrible weight I would put on them, if it were so. Neither they nor my brothers would thank me, would they?'

'Some might say that you were in fact giving this mystery woman a very special gift,' Helewise said quietly.

'Aye, but then there's this business of the girl having what Sidonius called psychic powers, whatever they may be,' Josse protested. 'Well, I can't be sure about my sisters-in-law – although they seem a pretty ordinary quartet to me – but I know for certain there's never been any of that magic stuff in *my* family!'

Helewise was silent. She was thinking very hard.

She knew – or at least she strongly suspected – something that Josse did not. And she knew that she must not tell him, because the secret was not hers to keep or give away. Always assuming that her suspicions were right.

He was waiting for her answer. 'Abbess Helewise? Will you take the Eye or not? It's a heathen thing, I know, but there must be some good in it. I'm told its magic will only work for its rightful owner, but if I give it away of my own free will, then the recipient surely becomes the rightful owner. Anyway, it would be for the best, I'm sure, to keep it here because Sidonius said the Eye was only safe in the hands of the very strong, the very wise and the very good, and you and your nuns here at Hawkenlye are all of those.'

Touched both by the generosity of his compliment and by his faith in her community, she raised her eyes to look at him.

'I will,' she said gravely. 'I shall speak to Sister Euphemia and Sister Tiphaine, both of whom will, I suspect, find better uses for the stone than I could. If it will work for them, that is. From what you tell me, I imagine that it could be a very handy thing in the infirmary, and Sister Tiphaine might find its poison-detecting ability useful when she is working on new remedies.'

She had seen the relief sweep through him from the moment she said 'I will'. His face was full of emotion: gratitude, certainly, but something more . . .

Preferring not to dwell on that, she said, 'However, Sir Josse, we at Hawkenlye Abbey will look upon our custodianship of the Eye purely as temporary; the stone will be on loan. We will keep it safely here as long as you wish it. But if ever the day comes that you and—' She almost said, you and your descendants, but managed to stop herself – 'that you wish to claim it back again, you will only have to ask. Is that all right?'

He was smiling broadly. 'More than all right, and I thank you with all my heart. And I won't want it back, my lady, I can assure you of that. I'll be delighted to see the back of it!'

She waited. He had it with him, presumably, so he would probably present it there and then.

Nothing happened.

She said, 'Sir Josse? Do you wish me to take over the Eye now?'

He watched her for a moment. Then he said, 'I have been selfish in making this request just at this moment, Abbess Helewise.'

'How so?'

'Because Prince John is here seeking it. And, although John Dee has given his word not to let his master know the truth, I fear that the Prince will not meekly ride away without further questions.'

Understanding, she said, 'And you would not have me lie, if he comes to me demanding to be told what I know of the Eye.'

'Exactly so. I'm thinking, my lady, that, were I to hide the stone somewhere myself, some place that you do not know, you could say to the Prince that you have no idea where the Eye is and be telling the truth.'

She smiled. 'I think that might be considered to be a falsehood by omission,' she observed.

'Aye, I was afraid you would say that.' He stared at her, the fatigue apparent in his face and his very stance. 'What am I to do?'

'First, you must allow me to be the judge of what lies I choose to state or to imply.' She had not intended to sound as if she were reprimanding him, but the droop of his mouth suggested that he took her remark in that way. 'Sir Josse?' she said kindly, and he raised his eyes to meet hers. 'I meant no reproof.'

'No, my lady.'

He did not seem to be comforted in the least. Very well; best, she decided, to proceed. 'I propose that you do just as you suggest, and hide the Eye. Should the Prince ask me about it – which I rather doubt that he will, since all along he has dared only to enquire about a man called Galbertius Sidonius, not what this man may or may not have carried with him – I shall respond as I see fit. The one thing that I shall not say' – she leaned forward, speaking earnestly— 'is that we now know who Sidonius is, that you have spoken to him and that he has given you what is rightfully yours.'

He said, with an air of wonderment, 'You would do that? Withhold the very information that he seeks, if he asks for it?'

'I would. I shall.' He still seemed perplexed. 'Sir Josse, it is, as you are aware, a sin to lie. To lie to a prince of royal blood may in addition be a crime – it might even be treason, I do not know. But even if so, it is better than the alternative.'

'Letting the Prince have the Eye,' he said dully.

'Quite so. And, as you told me, even John Dee indicated the folly of that.'

There was a silence during which she – and, she imagined, Josse too – considered just how Prince John's ambition, intelligence and ruthlessness might put a magic talisman to use.

'We would in truth be doing the Prince a favour, not letting him have the Eye,' Josse said eventually.

'We would? How so?'

Josse grinned. 'I won't give it to him freely, so, if he took it, he would not be the rightful owner. John Dee says the powers won't work for such a person. Could even work against him.'

'Ah, I see.'

Had she needed further justification of her decision – which she didn't – Josse had just supplied it.

There was a further, longer, silence. Then she said gently, 'I suggest you go and hide it now, Sir Josse.'

'Eh?'

'The Eye.'

'Ah. Oh, yes.'

It was a measure of his fatigue and his state of mind that he turned and left the room, quietly closing the door after him, without even bidding her good night.

She sat there in silence for some time after he had gone.

She had just remembered that, when he had left her

arlier in the day with John Dee, he and his brother had been going to take the old man to Sister Tiphaine, for treatment for his bad back.

Had the herbalist said anything? Oh, dear, supposing —

But with a deliberate act of will, Helewise cut off that line of thought. I am quite certain that she did not, she decided. For one thing, during our conversation just now Josse hardly looked like a man who had recently learned a life-altering piece of news. For another, Sister Tiphaine adamantly refuses to discuss the matter with me, so why presume that she would reveal the secret to Josse the moment she had a chance?

Wearily Helewise dropped her aching head down on to her arms, folded on her table. And all of that, she thought, presupposes that I am right.

Am I?

She thought back to her last talk with Sister Tiphaine. She had sought out the herbalist in her garden; it had been the day that Josse and Yves had set out to visit Prince John, and come back with the sheriff and his men bearing the dead body of the old man's servant lad.

She had told Sister Tiphaine what she suspected. Had asked – no, ordered – the herbalist to tell her the truth. Tiphaine had stared steadily at her out of those deep, mysterious eyes and said, 'I have nothing to tell, my lady Abbess.'

Which, as Helewise was well aware, was ambiguous and could equally well mean, there is nothing to tell, or – surely more likely! – I have something to tell you but I am not going to.

It was Helewise's duty, as Abbess of Hawkenlye, to

care for the souls of her nuns. And, if Sister Tiphaine were concealing something, something for which she was willing to lie, then it was up to Helewise to get her to admit it, confess it and seek absolution.

'But if it concerns Sir Josse!' Helewise had pressed, voice an urgent whisper.

And Sister Tiphaine, face a blank, had said, 'If *who* concerns Sir Josse?'

Now Josse had been in the herbalist's company. There must have been a moment when she could have taken him aside and told him . . .

But it seemed that she had not.

Which, Helewise reflected, slowly getting to her feet, probably meant that she had been wrong all along, that Sister Euphemia had been mistaken and that there was nothing to tell.

She had, she realised, come to the end of that particular road.

For now.

In the morning, the Prince came to see her. He apologised for having taken up so much of the Abbey's valuable time and announced that he and his party were about to depart for London.

'You still search for Galbertius Sidonius?' she asked innocently.

'We do,' Prince John agreed. 'I believe we have wasted our time in coming here to Hawkenlye; either that or your monks, my lady, are very adept at concealing things which they do not wish outsiders to know.' The intelligent blue eyes regarded her steadily; it was an unnerving experience.

ut she hung on to her courage and stared back. After a
moment, the Prince, with an almost imperceptible smile,
murmured, 'Ah, well.'

Then he said, 'Dee has been gazing into that black ball
f his, and he tells me there may be a sniff of the man up
a the city. The Templars, apparently, may have a lead.'

Bless you, John Dee, she thought. 'I wish you good luck,'
he said. 'May you meet with success.'

He stared at her with ironic eyes. 'Oh, my lady, how
hould I interpret that?' he murmured.

'However you wish,' she replied primly. He was clever,
he thought; too clever, really. It was proving difficult –
nore so than she had anticipated – to tread the delicate
ne between not telling or implying outright lies, and not
iving away things that she must keep to herself.

He was still watching her. Feeling that if he went on
taring quite so hard he would eventually see right into her
eart and what it contained, she rose to her feet and said
olitely, 'If you would reach London before dusk, it would
e best for you not to tally, sire. I will accompany you to
he gates, where I may wish your party God's speed.'

Short of actually demanding what it was that she was not
elling him – for which breach of manners he surely could
ave no excuse – there was nothing he could do but accept
er courteous dismissal. They walked together across the
loisters and over to the gates, where the Prince's men
nd the horses were waiting. Dee was already mounted;
e bowed to Helewise and murmured a greeting.

What a true friend you have been, she thought, meeting
is eyes and trying to transmit her gratitude. You are taking
our Prince away not a moment too soon.

As if he had heard, Dee bowed his head once more and
gave her a very sweet smile.

Josse and Yves came to join her, and they stood with
the nuns as the royal party set off. When they were almost
out of sight, Sister Martha gave a sigh and said, 'Ah well,
that's that.'

Helewise hoped fervently that she was right.

As she had known he would, Josse asked to see her
privately.

When they were alone in the safety of her room, he
reached inside his tunic and handed her a small silver
box. 'This is what it has been kept in,' he said, holding
it out, 'although you may of course prefer to make other
arrangements.'

'You hid it successfully last night, then.'

'Aye.' He smiled. 'I buried it carefully round behind the
latrines, where nobody in their right mind tarries long.'

'Ah. Quite. And the Prince . . . ?'

'Came down to the Vale early this morning. Said he
wanted a last look at the Shrine, to say his prayers there
and pray for the sick and the needy who come visiting.'

'I see.'

'No, I didn't believe him, either.' Josse laughed shortly.

'He questioned you again?'

'Aye. And the monks. To a man they gave the straight-
forward reply that they'd never heard of Galbertius Sidonius
and they spoke the truth. If Saul and Augustus – aye, and
Erse, too – suspected there was more to the question, they
had the sense not to say so.'

'And you, Sir Josse?'

'Oh, I lied through my teeth,' he admitted easily. 'Said I reckoned the fellow had never been here in the first place, and that I'd had no approaches by strangers bringing me long-lost family treasures. Promised I'd tell the Prince if anything came to light, too.'

'I think,' she said carefully after a moment's thought, 'that it might be wise to confess those lies to Father Gilbert, in due course. Bearing false witness is a sin, Sir Josse, even if done with the purest of intentions.'

'Aye,' he said, his face grave. 'Aye, my lady. I will seek out the Father.' With the ghost of a smile, he added, 'But happen I'll wait until Prince John has had time to get safely back to London.'

She bowed her agreement. It seemed the least she could do.

He was still holding the silver box. She held out her hand, and he placed the box in it. 'Do you want to have one last look?' she asked, about to see if she could work open the little fastening.

Josse came to stand beside her and said, 'You push that tiny lever and a spring makes the lid pop open. No!' – as she went to do so – 'please, Abbess, don't, not till I've gone.'

'Very well, but why?'

He grinned sheepishly. 'I might change my mind.'

Then, with uncharacteristic haste and the briefest of farewells, he hurried out through the door and was gone.

She sat quite still for some time. Then she sprang open the lid of the silver box and took out the Eye of Jerusalem.

Again, she felt the tremor in her hands, as if the stone were communicating with her. But stones are inert and do not behave like that, she told herself firmly. She put it back in its box and was about to fasten the box's silver chain around her neck when she noticed that it was broken.

Of course. Galbertius Sidonius had done that when he wrenched the Eye in its case from the neck of the Lombard's young servant. The box, the chain, even the jewel itself, carried death with them.

She knew then what she must do.

She waited until evening.

Then, after Compline, when the church was empty, she went forward to the simple altar and, praying as fervently as she knew how, fell on her knees and begged God's help.

I cannot turn this jewel away, she pleaded silently, because poor Josse has entrusted it to me, and he has good reasons for doing so. Also, we must see whether it can in fact help us in our work, because it may have been your intent, Lord, to bring it to us for that very purpose.

She thought hard, then resumed.

But the Eye carries the taint of violence, and I am not happy for it to be used until it has been purged. Therefore, dear Lord, I leave it with you, here in your holy house, and I pray that you cleanse it and make it fit for the healing work to which we would try to put it.

That was all she wanted to say. She prayed on, and the familiar, comforting words restored and calmed her, as they always did. Then, making absolutely sure she was alone, she crept round behind the altar and located the hidden ledge beneath it where a wooden support was concealed under the plain linen covering. She put the Eye in its box on to the shelf, then let the cloth fall back into place.

Perhaps the Eye should really have been placed *on* the altar. But then, she thought, the good Lord knows quite well where it is.

Feeling that her steps were suddenly lighter, she bowed before the cross, murmured one final prayer, and walked away.

In the morning, Josse came to find her and said that he and Yves were about to leave. Yves was eager to return home to Acquin, and Josse wanted him to put up at New Winnowlands at least for a night before he did so.

'I wish you both a good journey,' she said, 'Yves in particular, since he has the farther to go.'

'He'll be all right,' Josse said. 'I may even decide to go over to Acquin with him. It's time I paid my family another visit.'

'Will you stay in France for Christmas?' she asked.

He hesitated, then said, 'Perhaps. But there is another visit I now wish to make. Yves and I have been speaking at great length about my father, and about my mother, too. Summoning my mother's memory has made me realise that I should have made some effort to maintain contact with her kinfolk. After all, they are only at Lewes, which is not all that far from here.'

'Lewes,' she repeated. 'A pleasant town.'

'Is it? I can scarcely remember. Well, I dare say I shall be seeing it again for myself, before long.'

'Don't forget us here at Hawkenlye in all this travelling around,' she said. 'We are always pleased to see you.' Watching him, the comforting solidity of him, the honest face that expressed his total dependability, she thought tha[t] 'pleased' was perhaps understating the case.

'I won't forget,' he said quietly. Then, as if he were sud[-] denly finding this parting rather hard, he lunged forwar[d] took her hand and kissed it, instantly seeming ashamed [of] his courteous action. He said quickly, 'Thank you, Abbes[s] Helewise. From the bottom of my heart,' and hurried awa[y.]

She knew perfectly well the cause of his deep gratitud[e;] she hoped, in that moment, that it was justified and that sh[e] had taken the right decision.

She was not entirely sure . . .

She gave him a while to collect his belongings and orde[r] the horses. Then, wishing to say goodbye to him and t[o] Yves and to wish them God's speed, she went out t[o] the gates.

They were on the point of leaving. Yves, seeing he[r,] came over to her and thanked her for her hospitality[.] 'Keep us in your prayers, my lady,' he said. Then, lookin[g] intently at her, he added, 'I am glad to have met you at last[.] Now I—'

But whatever he had been about to say was brushed asid[e] by a call from Josse. 'Come on, Yves, don't be all day o[r] we'll be too late for Ella to cook up a decent dinner.'

Yves gave Helewise a last glance. Then he smiled at he[r] and, turning, mounted his horse.

Josse looked down at her but, other than a muttered 'Farewell, Abbess Helewise,' said no more.

There was, she reflected, little more to say.

She called out her goodbyes to them both, and stoo[d] waving until the two brothers were out of sight. Then[,] feeling suddenly downcast, she went back to her room.

Postscript

All Saints' Day 1192

Helewise had taken her time over deciding how to go about using the Eye of Jerusalem. The stone still gave out its strange emanations when she picked it up but, after its night under the altar, she no longer felt on it the dark shadow of brutal death.

But, as the end of October approached and the wet weather changed to bitter cold, the Abbey, the Vale and the infirmary steadily began to fill with people praying to be spared from sickness, praying for those already sick, and, naturally, with the sick themselves. It was just the time – if, indeed, the time were ever to come – to present Sister Euphemia and her nursing nuns with what might turn out to be a powerful ally.

The Eye lived up to its reputation. It lowered fevers. Or, of course, it might have been Sister Euphemia's endless efforts, her patience and skill. Sister Euphemia, that was, guided by and acting for God.

Helewise was still very aware that a Prince had been – probably still was – going to considerable pains to track down the stone. She therefore urged caution in its use and the infirmarer and her nuns, too busy for questions, merely nodded and got on with their work. Observing them, she was gratified – and hardly surprised – to see

that, overworked and tired as they were, still they obeye
her instructions faithfully; not even the merest glimpse o
the Eye was permitted to the patients.

But for the gifts it bestowed – *seemed* to bestow, sh
reminded herself, still determined to retain at least a degre
of scepticism – it might not have been there.

On the last day of October, All Saints' Eve, Helewise wer
to seek out Sister Tiphaine. The infirmarer was asking fo
the next brew of the herbalist's patent cough mixture an
Helewise, at that moment having nothing better to do, ha
offered to go and fetch it.

Sister Tiphaine was nowhere to be found.

Someone said they'd heard her remark that she ha
to go out to gather ingredients for her concoction. Th
somebody – it was Sister Anne, endlessly intereste
in the doings of others but never very astute – als
reported that Sister Tiphaine had said she might b
some time.

Two things struck Helewise.

One was that Sister Tiphaine should not have left th
Abbey without asking her Abbess's permission.

The other was that the herbalist would indeed be a lon
time, if she really had set out to gather fresh ingredients
Because it was October – almost November – and nothing
was growing.

February to the end of October, thought Helewise. Nin
months.

And she thought she knew exactly where Sister Tiphain
had gone.

What should she do? Follow the herbalist out into th

forest? But she had absolutely no idea where she had gone, if, indeed, she was in the forest at all.

And I still may be wrong in my suspicions, she thought, chewing at her thumbnail in her anxiety. Sister Tiphaine may know nothing whatsoever of the forest folk and those with whom they associate. She might be doing exactly what she said she was doing, collecting ingredients for the cough remedy. And what a fool I should look, if I go out searching for her, find her going peacefully about her duties and can find no excuse for having hunted her down except that she should not have left the Abbey without my permission.

Which, given the urgency with which Sister Euphemia requires that medicine, would be a little over-fussy of me.

I cannot solve this one, she decided. I have pressed Tiphaine as much as I can, and she stares blank eyed and declares she has nothing to say. I must leave this matter, I think, to her own conscience. If indeed she bears a secret and has been withholding something that I, her Abbess, have a right to be told, then it may weigh upon her so that, in time, she will confess it.

A thought struck her. Sister Tiphaine might well have done just that. And Father Gilbert, her confessor, would certainly not report it to the Abbess.

Helewise had come, she realised, to a stone wall.

She made her way to the church. In the peace of its cool interior, the light of the autumn day was already beginning to fade. She knelt in front of the altar and put the matter into God's hands.

Then she prayed, 'Of thy mercy, dear Lord, look after Sister Tiphaine. If she is abroad in the forest, guide her

footsteps so that she may go about her business – whatever
it is – watched over by Thee and, in her own good time,
return safely to us.

'And if what I suspect is right, please, Lord, look after
Joanna as well.'

Then she pressed her face into her palms and, in the
calm silence, thought, there! I have handed my burden
over to more capable hands.

As the relief washed through her, for the first time in
weeks she felt the serenity begin to come back.

In a hut out in the wild heart of the Great Forest, two
women sat either side of a fire burning in the small room's
central hearth.

One was ancient. Or so it seemed, judging by the long
fall of white hair. But her face was unlined, and her grey
eyes were clear and bright. And, when she moved, it was
with the supple grace of a young woman. Lora, venerated
elder of the forest people, had probably forgotten herself
just how old she was, but she had seen more seasons
turn than most folk; it was merely that she carried her
years lightly.

The other was younger. She had deep, mysterious eyes
that held secrets and were the windows to an intelligent
mind full of potions and remedies. She was the herbalist
of Hawkenlye Abbey.

'You should go back,' Lora said, breaking a silence that
had lasted for some time. 'You will be missed.'

'It is not important.'

'It is,' Lora insisted. 'Your absence will create questions.'

'I have already given my reason for being out.' Tiphaine pointed to a little basket made of woven willow that stood by the door. It held a collection of freshly dug roots.

'What use have you for those?' Lora queried.

'None. But nobody within knows that they have no medicinal qualities.'

Lora smiled. Then her face straightened and she said, 'You should not deceive the Abbess woman. I hear well of her.'

'Aye, she's fine,' Tiphaine agreed.

But she went on sitting where she was.

Presently there came another groan from the platform up to the right of where the two elders sat. Lora got up and climbed the short ladder that led to it. Above, lying in a tangle of bedding, violently twisting her naked, sweating body and flinging back the heavy fur rug that covered her, lay a young woman.

She was heavily pregnant, and in the process of giving birth.

Lora clambered on to the platform and settled beside her. Taking one of the outflung hands in both of her own, she said, 'Hold on, my lass. Clench on to me, and I will help you through the pain.'

Joanna de Courtenay, trying to cling on to her courage, gave up and let out a great cry. As the contraction rose to its peak, she clenched her hand on to Lora's. So fierce was the grip of her strong fingers that Lora winced.

After what seemed to both of them a minor eternity, Joanna relaxed and fell back against her pillows. Panting, she said through dry lips, 'They come closer together now.'

'Aye,' Lora said calmly. 'Not long now, lassie.'

Tiphaine's veiled and wimpled face appeared at the top of the ladder. She smiled at Joanna.

'You're still here, Sister,' Joanna said.

'Aye.'

Joanna glanced out through the little window to the right of the bed. 'It's getting dark. You should go back to Hawkenlye.'

'That's what I told her,' Lora agreed.

'Presently,' Tiphaine said. Crawling on to the platform, she said, 'I would see the child born. I have brought medicines which may come in useful.'

'Leave them with me,' Lora urged. 'Can I not administer them?'

Tiphaine grinned. 'Undoubtedly.'

'But you want to stay,' Lora finished for her. 'Well, if you get locked out and have to shin up over the wall, it's your own fault.'

'I know.'

'And I suppose you'll tell them you got *lost*.' There was heavy irony in the emphasis on the last word. 'You who know the Forest's secret paths and ways as well as the lines that cross your own palm.'

'Aye, that I will.'

Joanna, listening, gave a brief laugh and said, 'I'd better hurry up, then, and save your skin, Sister. I think—' But then another contraction came, longer, stronger, and more agonising than any so far. Joanna's smile faded to a grimace, then to a mask of pain, and, with one hand holding Tiphaine's and one holding Lora's, she flung back her head and screamed.

Then the contractions came so close together that they almost seemed to merge into one long pain. Tiphaine took Joanna's head in her lap, stroking the sweat-soaked forehead, massaging light fingers through the long dark hair, while Lora knelt between Joanna's spread legs and watched.

Suddenly Joanna cried, 'She's coming! I can feel something – it – I – *oh*!'

Lora took hold of her arms and pulled, while Tiphaine got round behind her, pushing her to a sitting position, then into a squat. Bracing herself, back to back with Joanna, she took the younger woman's weight, supporting her in her exhaustion. Lora released her grip on Joanna's wrists and, kneeling, bending low, cupped her hands beneath Joanna, fingers exploring, peering down to look.

She cried, 'The head's coming! Steady now, Joanna, slowly does it—'

Joanna gasped, moaned, then seemed to gather all her energy into another great push.

'*Steady*!' Lora cried. 'You'll tear yourself, pushing her out so fast!'

'I can't help it!' Joanna shouted back.

There was a brief pause, during which Joanna slumped back, spent, against Tiphaine. Then she cried, 'Oh, it's happening again – oh – *OH*!'

'Too fast! Too fast!' Lora muttered, but then there was a squelching sound, a cry from Joanna, and one by one the baby's shoulders emerged from out of its mother, swiftly followed by the rest of the tiny body.

Lora took hold of the infant in strong hands and held it up. The umbilicus pulsed, the child opened its mouth and screamed, almost as loudly as its mother had done, and its colour rapidly changed from newborn pallor to a healthy pink.

Joanna said, 'Is she – is it all right?'

'Aye, perfect, just perfect.' Lora was wrapping a clean cloth tightly around the infant, carefully wiping around its eyes, nose and mouth. 'And you were right the first time, my girl.'

With a grin, Lora tucked in the end of the swaddling clothes and handed Josse's daughter to her mother.

Not very long afterwards, the herbalist collected her basket and set out back to Hawkenlye. It was now almost fully dark, but she knew the way. If she hurried, she would be back in time for Compline.

She had had no need of the medicines she had brought with her. Lora knew how to find her if she was needed; if, for example, Joanna were to fall sick with the terrible, killing fever that sometimes took new mothers.

But Tiphaine doubted whether she would be summoned. Lora was as skilled in her own way as the herbalist, and would manage whatever she might be faced with. They preferred it that way, Tiphaine knew. She was only allowed what minimal involvement she had with them because Joanna liked to know how things went in the outside world.

Liked to be assured, in truth, that all was well with Josse.

She may not want him, Tiphaine reflected, striding out hard for the Abbey, but she needs to know he is all right.

Ah, well. It was Joanna's business.

She broke into a trot. Hawkenlye was in sight now, and it would be good to be home.

Back in the hut in the forest, Joanna was suckling her daughter. Lora had made her a drink, and was insisting that she finish it, every last drop. 'Your milk will be in, after a day or two, so it's best to get into good habits now and drink all you can take.'

Joanna, more grateful than she could say for Lora's presence – and for Tiphaine's – during the birth, now wished guiltily that Lora would go away and leave her alone.

She could manage. She had managed for the long months of her pregnancy, had got used to living on her own, depending on herself, coping. The little hut that was now her home was not really big enough for two.

For *three*, she corrected herself, staring down at the baby sleeping at her breast.

Margaret. My little Margaret.

She stroked a gentle finger across the baby's brows, which were knitting briefly in some infant dream. The child's skin was soft, downy, and the long, dark eyelashes curled and made shadows on the rounded, perfect cheeks.

Lora had earlier taken the baby outside. In a brief ceremony that Joanna knew about and accepted – even if she could not wholeheartedly approve it – the elder had briefly stripped the baby naked and laid her on the ground.

'Child of the Earth, feel the Earth beneath you.' Her quiet chanting tones had reached Joanna, inside the hut. 'Mother Earth, feel your child who lies on your great breast.'

Margaret had squawked her protest at the sudden chill of the night air on her bare skin, and Lora had bundled her up and brought her inside again.

But before she had given her back to Joanna, she had knelt down in the firelight and studied the child. Margaret, eyes wide open, had stared back at her.

'She will be one of the great ones,' Lora murmured. 'She will have the skill, Joanna. And, unless I am very much mistaken, she has the Sight.'

Joanna leaned over the edge of the platform. 'But why? She is not of the blood, is she?'

Lora smiled. 'Not at her conception, maybe. But you have spent the months that you have carried her learning new ways and new crafts, my lass. Do you not think that some of your acquired knowledge may have gone into her making, as she grew steadily in your belly?'

With wondering eyes, Joanna had stared down at her child.

Now, holding her once more, little body snug against her as the baby slept and dreamed, Joanna tried to work out how she felt. A daughter born safe and well was a joy, perhaps the most beautiful thing that had ever happened to her. Oh, there was Ninian, of course. There was always Ninian, even though he was now, and always would be, far away from her. Another son would have had to go the same way; living in a forest hut with his wiccan mother was no life for a boy, not once he grew towards manhood.

A daughter, now, was another matter. But a daughter who, only hours after her birth, was marked out as a great one . . . well, that was something else again.

After some time – Lora had gone to sleep, and Joanna

at last had the illusion, if not the reality, of being alone with Margaret – she came to the sensible conclusion that it was no use worrying about what might or might not be to come in the future. The baby was here, she was sound and, if she really was what Lora said she was, then there was nothing whatsoever Joanna could do about it.

'My job is to love you and keep you safe, my little Margaret,' she crooned softly. 'That, for now, is all.' Settling herself – it took some time to find a comfortable position for her bruised, sore body – she cradled the baby in the crook of her arm and, like the tiny child and the old woman lying down by the fire, soon fell deeply asleep.

Outside, the moon rose up in the sky and the small clearing was bathed in pale light. The forest was dark and silent, the stars above like the tiny flames of candles an unimaginable distance away.

All seemed still.

Yet the folk of the forest knew that another soul had been born to them and, in secret, unknown dells and caverns, there were quiet celebrations. It was Samhain, after all, one of the forest people's major festivals.

To have a Samhain child to welcome just made it even better.

Alys Clare
Fortune Like the Moon

His thoughts ground to a halt as his eyes focused on an object in the path. The smaller path, the one that led to the pool.
The path where Gunnora was found.
Not pausing to raise the alarm, he was off, running as fast as he could. Although, even then, some deep awareness within him was telling him it was too late for haste.

When a young nun from Hawkenlye Abbey is discovered in a nearby vale with her throat cut, the people of Tonbridge are quick to jump to conclusions. This brutal murder must be the work of some felon released by King Richard Plantagenet in an attempt to impress his new subjects with his charity. Richard sends his emissary, Josse d'Acquin, to investigate the gruesome death, with the unspoken order to absolve the king from all blame.

Josse, a brave and loyal ex-soldier, discovers an intelligent ally in Abbess Helewise of Hawkenlye: level-headed and pragmatic, she rarely misses a trick. Combining their talents, Josse and the Abbess peel back the orderly façade of life in rural Kent, to discover the menace lurking beneath.

'A rich medieval mystery' *Bolton Evening News*

NEW ENGLISH LIBRARY
Hodder & Stoughton

Alys Clare

The Tavern in the Morning

Market day, and the inn at Tonbridge has been busy since early morning. As night closes in, a man lies dying in the guest chamber, poisoned by a piece of pie made by Goody Anne herself.

Josse d'Acquin, a regular visitor to the tavern and an admirer of Mistress Anne's culinary skills, arrives to investigate. He discovers wolf's bane in the remnants of the pie. And learns that, among all the strangers through the tavern that day, one stood out – a charming, handsome nobleman, who asked for the same chicken and vegetable pie.

When he fails to persuade the Sheriff that the death is suspicious, Josse turns to his old friend, Abbess Helewise. Weakened from a severe bout of fever, she nonetheless provides a thread of common sense as Josse follows the trail of murder into the great Wealden Forest, and finds something there that will change his life forever . . .

'Proof that a writer of medieval crime fiction can deliver something fresh'
The Times

NEW ENGLISH LIBRARY
Hodder & Stoughton

Alys Clare
The Chatter of the Maidens

The serenity of Hawkenlye Abbey has been disturbed by the arrival of a new nun and her two young sisters. Recently orphaned, Alba has had to leave her convent at Ely to take her grieving sisters far away from the scene of their sorrow. However Abbess Helewise cannot reconcile the charity and selflessness of this gesture with what she sees and hears of Alba; Sister Alba is, everyone agrees, a mean-spirited and turbulent presence.

The Abbess's anxieties grow when her old friend Josse d'Acquin is brought to Hawkenlye, half-dead from blood poisoning. Then a body is discovered, and one of the sisters goes missing. In order to discover what really lies behind Alba's flight to Hawkenlye, Helewise sets off to visit the Fens. She uncovers not only a clever network of lies, but also something more horrific . . .

'A worthy heir to Ellis Peters'
Poison in the Pen